ONLY A BAD BOY CAN *Love* HER

The Finale

A NOVEL BY

PORSCHA STERLING

This PORSCHA STERLING, INC. book is being published by

Royalty Publishing House, LLC.

Cover Designer: Marion Designs

Format: Nina Simmons Designs, Inc.

Don't miss out on your chance to discuss the book LIVE with Porscha Sterling and the REAL Outlaw! Join Porscha's mailing list for announcements so you don't miss it!

ACKNOWLEDGMENTS

It's hard to say goodbye to the Bad Boys crew but I do believe this may actually be the finale. January and Legend took me through my full range of emotions. This was definitely one of the most toughest books for me to write.

That said, I have a lot of people who I would like to thank for helping me in completing the journey I needed to take in order to finish it. ♥

Al and Kingston, as always, you two come first. Thanks for being the best little boys I could have ever asked for. So loving, so forgiving and so happy… you make every day of my life worth living.

Huge thanks to **Tara** for putting up with me ignoring emails, dodging meetings and forgetting things that "I thought, I said, you said, we said—wait, who said that and when? Was it me who promised that? When did I say I'd do it? Okay, I'll get it to you yesterday." Yes—thanks for putting up with me asking/saying things like that, which make absolutely no sense, because I've been writing and my brain doesn't work anymore. I'm pretty sure that, as I'm writing this, there is something I've forgotten to do that I told you I'd do. *Sighs*

Nina—for also staying up late with me, pulling 12 hour shifts and helping me with my young kings when I needed to meet my deadlines. Thank you for listening to me talk through my plot ideas and struggles. Thanks for always being there.

To Gram, my Momty and my mom—thank you for stepping in to help with the boys. Especially during quarantine when all writers thought they were going to die sweet, slow deaths. Not because we were stuck in the house (of course not, we love to be home). But because we actually had to be stuck there with other people. I am definitely a person who needs to be free, uninhibited and in perfect solitude in order to write. Thank you both for helping me out so that I was able to balance mothering with the things I desperately needed in order to be me.

Special thanks goes to **@tharealoutlaw** for going above and beyond with promotion and inspiration for this novel that I'd decided I wasn't going to write many, many times but started back because you wouldn't let me give up on it. For being the most positive person I know who never seems to have a bad day and is always in the best mood, you are the sunshine among all of us blessed to call you a 'friend'. And, of course, infinite thanks for gracing the cover of yet **another** Bad Boys novel. Can't have a bad boys book without Outlaw.

To Michelle, I'm thinking of you and sending love always. My thoughts, prayers and love is always with you.

To the readers who support my passion. I love you all very much. Thank you for being around for another ride. I'm not sure how many more are coming, but I'll keep writing until it feels like I'm done. I hope you'll continue enjoying the stories.

I have the best family, friends, readers and supporters. Y'all are awesome 😌

SYNOPSIS

"LOVE IS A DRUG I NEVER WANTED TO TAKE. BUT NOW I HAVE AND IT'S too late. I'm addicted to you."

Legend is on a mission and it happens to be one he can't speak about. Always a man of little words, keeping things close to the heart has never been a problem. Or at least it never used to be until January began to occupy that space. Now he's fighting a battle between his mind and his heart and, unlike any battle he's ever fought before, this is a war that no matter how it ends, sacrifice will be required.

While Legend's battling his own demons, January's on a mission of her own. In some ways different from his, but almost nearly the same. With trust being a vulnerability that she's been the most reluctant to embrace, it's the exact thing that love requires. But how can she trust the man who broke her heart?

There are no shadows when you're surrounded by darkness, but when love makes way for the light to shine through, all the things you refused to face appear. Can January and Legend conquer their darkness to enjoy the light of each other? Or will fear of fully opening up to one another stop them from experiencing love's true bliss?

Download & listen to the playlist as you read.
Listen now on Spotify!

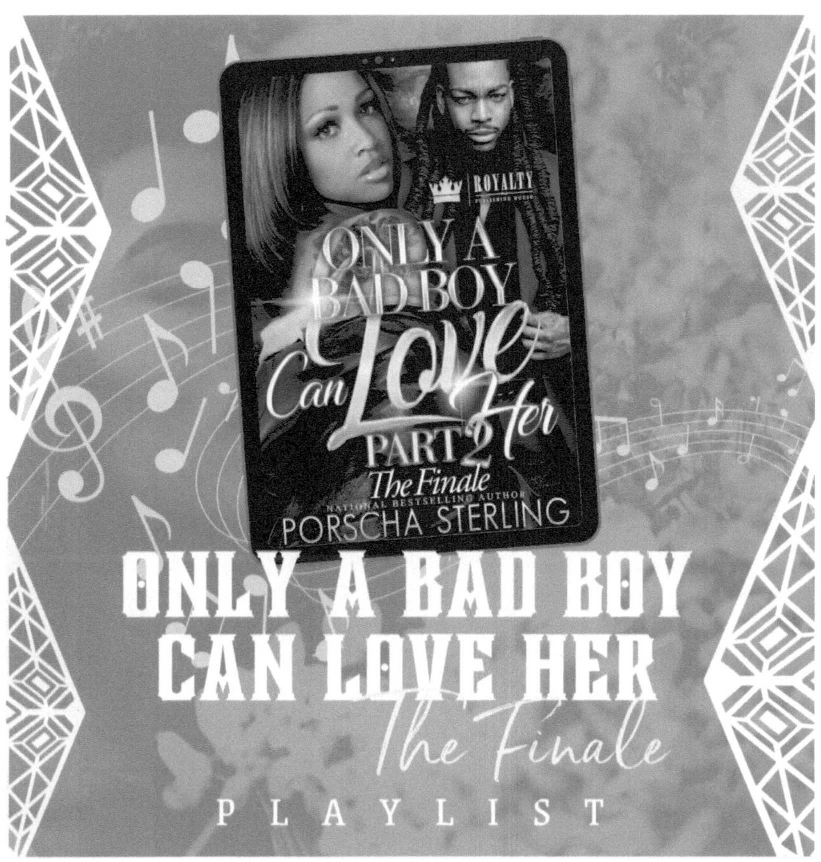

"Some say endings are more important than beginnings. But I say that it's the journey that makes all the difference."

PORSCHA STERLING

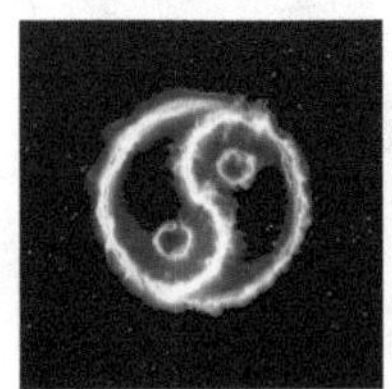

WELCOME TO HELL, WHERE YOU'RE WELCOME TO SELL.

"I CAN'T BELIEVE YOU GOT US BACK DOING THIS LOW-LEVEL SHIT again, bruh. We said a long time ago that once we made it up, we wouldn't fuck around with drugs no more."

There was a subtle clench to Legend's jaw but he didn't respond to Nico. Keeping his eyes ahead, he watched as the armed man standing in front of the car that he and Nico were in inspected the hood before stepping around to join another man standing near the back, inspecting the trunk. With wands in their hands, they ran the instruments over the whole outside and inside of the car, checking for weapons, wires, or anything that would get a young kingpin locked up for life. Though only in his twenties, one thing was for sure: Gunna didn't play.

"This nigga got this shit secure as hell. You'd think the Feds would be all over his ass. Ain't no way this young ass dude got enough legit shit going on to cover all the weight he moving," Nico said as one of the armed men waved them forward, indicating they were cleared to enter. Nodding his head, Nico drove slowly through the large iron gates that secured the entry to the massive complex of one of their old friends.

"Lil' Gunna done bossed up on us," Legend said, amazed by the sheer opulence of the grounds and everything around that paved the way to Gunna's estate.

Gunna was a young block boy when they all first met. Bad ass kid who didn't listen to shit unless his mama said it. He was a straight mama's boy and, to this day, she was the only one who could talk his finger off a trigger. The problem was, she never did. Gunna's mother, Guapa, was the Native American version of Griselda Blanco. She ran more dope through the country in her day than any legendary drug kingpin ever heard of. When she married Gunna's father, Blunt, she only became more ruthless.

Blunt was a Black kingpin who owned a territory that Guapa was trying to take over. Their battles were epic, leading to a war that the streets still spoke about. Blunt was the type to win at all costs, never backing down and never folding. But he was a few years older than Guapa and was smart enough to quickly realize that he'd met his match. One day, he called off his soldiers and asked her to meet with him. That one meeting was supposed to last thirty minutes and ended up lasting a lifetime.

Blunt said he fell in love with Guapa the second he laid eyes on her. The way he described it was as if it were something mythical... like love at first sight. Some shit that niggas in the streets would convince others didn't exist. Some shit that Blunt grew up never believing in. Until it happened to him.

The two joined together to create the most merciless, ruthless couple the entire west coast had ever known. But Guapa always said their greatest creation was their son. Gunna got his name from his father because he had a natural talent for gunplay, having an incredibly stable hand even at a young age. Now, at the age of twenty-three, Gunna was king of his own self-made empire after absorbing the best from both of his parents' worlds.

"You sure you wanna fuck with this crazy ass nigga, man?" Nico asked once Legend had brought his car to a stop in front of Gunna's front door—if it could even be called that. It looked more like the double doors leading to a castle. Custom-made; the front entrance was larger than life. A fort would be better a better way to describe it.

“I ain’t got no choice,” Legend said, rubbing his hands together. “It’s either link up with Gunna or I hand over January to the Rosarios.”

Nico shrugged. "Sounds good to me. They ain’t gone kill her; just hole her up at one of their big ass mansions until Outlaw gives in a little. Plus, you don’t like the broad, right? Ain’t that what you said? So you shouldn’t really give a damn.”

Cutting his eyes to his cousin, Legend wasn’t at all surprised to see the teasing smile on his face. Nico was full of jokes but he didn’t even bother responding. There was nothing to say. Nico was fully aware of how he felt about January. The fact that he’d even considered aligning with Gunna in order to keep her safe said it all. Though he had done a lot of unforgivable shit in his past, he’d always vowed not to go back to the drug game once he left it.

Working along with Outlaw taught him a lot, but the one lesson he took to heart was that there were enough evil motherfuckas in the world to make money off of. You didn’t need to build your empire off the backs or with the blood of the innocent. Outlaw’s upbringing, as well a Legend’s, was birthed in the hood. For that reason they’d always be tied to the hood and the people who lived in it. You don’t shit where you eat.

When drugs entered Black neighborhoods, they left a lot of victims in their wake. Most of them innocent: people burdened by life trying to escape their pain. Children who would end up orphaned or in the system due to their parents’ addiction. Wives left to hold down a home alone because their husbands were sprung off dope. Mothers who couldn’t trust their children anymore because of their addictions.

No matter how you tried to split it, the drug game was a sad business. And it thrived off of every hope and dream left unfulfilled. All the promises broken. All the love lost. Paranoia, fear, and disappointment. Fuck all the money, glitz, and glamour, niggas who dealt in drugs led the most depressing lives. They surrounded themselves with motherfuckas who would cross them for a dollar and bitches who would leave them for a come up with the next nigga if ever he was down bad and couldn't give her the lifestyle she craved.

Legend had formed his opinions about the drug game by living through it himself. And he knew firsthand, there wasn't shit lovely about sleeping with a pistol under your pillow just in case some nigga you trusted got some goons to run up on you for the jewelry you'd been flossing. It was a life of 'get it or get got' and he wasn't down for living that way anymore. Until January entered the picture. Now here he was…

The door began to open before Legend and Nico had even gotten close enough to ring the doorbell. It seemed to be operated with pulleys, gears, and motors.

Leave it to Gunna to opt for some out-of-the-world type shit, Legend thought with a smirk. He couldn't really hate. He liked it. Really wanted to make a mental note to get something like it for himself if ever the day came when he'd decide to settle down in a place for himself.

"Leave it to this flashy, over-the-top nigga to have some shit like this," Nico muttered, shaking his head.

"I heard that," a voice said from behind the partially ajar double doors. A few moments later, Gunna appeared, grinning hard as he looked back and forth into the faces of his old friends.

"Ain't surprised you did, my Navajo brother," Nico replied with a smile, greeting Gunna with his hand out for dap. "Them big ass ears you got on your head."

"Nah, man, that ain't how old homies do it. We family over here, bruh," Gunna said with his arm extended to give Nico a hug.

"If it ain't the Chief of the streets, himself. Good to see you, bruh," Legend said, also coming in for a greeting. "You doing your thing from what I been hearing."

"Always," Gunna replied, placing an unlit pipe between his lips.

"Nigga, you walkin' out here looking like Rico Suave the Pocahontas soldier," Nino joked, standing back with his arms folded. "All them muscles you done grew, you can't be still only eating carrots and shit."

Laughing, Gunna nodded his head. His long, thick, and curly hair, tugged into two long plaits, danced around his waist. "Motherfucka, ain't no meat goin' in this system," he replied. "The Earth Mother does a body good."

Turning around, he waved for them to follow him into the house, walking in between two armed guards standing at each side of the entrance. Not like he needed the extra security because, honestly speaking, there weren't many men who could beat Gunna when it came to gunplay or hand-to-hand combat. Not to say that Legend or Nico weren't challenging opponents, but Gunna wasn't the type to feel fear. He feared no man.

With a chiseled body, immaculately perfected night after night at the gym, Gunna's build was the envy of most men. He was a Navajo gangster. Just as Legend said, Gunna was Chief of the streets. He had a reputation that earned him respect wherever he went off pedigree alone. But in the times he had to draw his weapon, any respect not initially given was quickly gained. He was a straight shooter and he never missed.

Legend and Nico followed behind him into a large sitting room off to the side of an even larger foyer. Like everything else concerning the house, this room was over-the-top as well, decorated with a top-quality Swarovski crystal chandelier, exquisite, custom-made furniture, and a large Baby Grand piano sitting center. Grabbing onto a black and gold lion head cane that was propped up next to a suede chair, custom-made to look like a throne, Gunna sat down and motioned for Legend and Nico to do the same. Nico cut his eyes at Legend, and they exchanged quick glances before taking a seat in a matching black suede sectional across from Gunna. In the time they'd been out of the drug game, many things had changed. Gunna had become a motherfuckin' boss.

"So, let me guess, you need my help with protecting Outlaw's daughter until you can get her out the city, right?" Gunna asked, holding the cane in between his hands.

As usual, he got straight to the point, not willing to beat around the bush now that it was time to discuss business. He knew at the exact moment he heard that January Murray went missing that he would get a visit from the heir to the Dumas empire—either to assist with finding her or to help with hiding her. He had taken a gamble by suggesting the call would be for the latter and from the non-reactive expression on Legend's face, he could see that he hit the nail on the head.

"I might need help getting her a flight out to New York," Legend said, feeling tension in his neck.

The meeting was necessary. The assistance was needed, but he couldn't lie and say it didn't bother him to have to ask for another man's help. Especially when it came to January. He wasn't the type to ask the next nigga for shit, but the fact that this had to do with a woman he felt particularly protective of made it that much worse.

"Legend out here asking Gunna for favors," Gunna said, twisting the cane between his hands. "I never thought I'd see the day. This can't just be about Outlaw, because you ain't mentioned that nigga yet. Is she your girl? You love her?"

Legend's expression steeled and he didn't readily respond although the instant resistance was the only tell-tell sign needed. He did love her. He cared for January in a way that he didn't understand. His soul knew it even if his mouth wasn't ready to admit it just yet.

Though a gangster on all levels, Gunna was a sucker for real romance. As a walking byproduct of true love and the physical embodiment of how love conquers all, he had a soft spot for situations like this. He had already decided what he would do once the situation was presented before Legend had even contacted him to meet. Though he kept to himself, Gunna also kept an ear to the streets, and he knew about things far before the situations ever arrived before him.

Deciding to relieve Legend from the burden of having to admit to an emotion he was still trying to figure out for himself, Gunna didn't wait for an answer.

"I'll help you," Gunna said, nodding his head slightly. "Normally, you know I would've had to stay out this shit. It's in my benefit to remain neutral."

"I know," Legend spoke, nodding his head. "I understand it's a big favor that I'm asking. But I wouldn't if there was another way."

Out of the very short list of underground kings that Outlaw allowed to operate independent of the BBM, Gunna was one of them. Mainly, because he dealt in commodities that Outlaw didn't care for. In exchange for that privilege, Gunna normally stayed out of any disagreements that didn't directly affect him.

"But you know it'll cost you," Gunna added, stating a fact that was already known to everyone in the room.

It wasn't abnormal; it was the way of the streets. You scratch my back, I scratch yours. Legend honestly preferred it that way. He didn't like to feel like he owed a nigga anything. He was a man who always vowed to settle his debts.

AND THAT's where this story begins: with Legend settling his debts by going back to what Nico would forever refer to as 'low-level shit'.

"All we gotta do is pick the cars up and transport them across the border. Easy peasy," Legend replied, stroking his chin hair as they drove away from Gunna's compound.

He wasn't hype about the shit that Gunna was about to involve them in but, at this point, it wasn't looking like he had much of a choice. With his father wanting one thing and the Rosario clan wanting another, Legend really had no one else he could turn to in order to get January out of the state. Once again, he was in the same position he had been in years ago: suddenly alienated from everyone he had just been calling family. The only difference was that this time around, it was his own doing and he was prepared for it.

"You say 'all we gotta do' like it's child's play." Nico blew air through his nose, shaking his head. "This nigga wants us to move weight through Rosario territory, something that could get the average nigga killed if he gets caught. The difference is that we will get caught. Fernando got every motherfucka on his team suspicious about what the two of us are up to."

"That's gonna change," Legend replied with a slight shrug, as if it were nothing.

Nico turned and looked at him with bugged eyes.

"Hell yeah, it's gon' change," he started. "It's gon' change with a big one-two to the chest… When them niggas hit us with something heavy for transporting weight through their territory."

Legend didn't respond, not because Nico didn't have a valid point or because he wasn't concerned with these things, but because it seemed illogical to worry about something he knew he was already going to do. He was beyond raising the pros and cons. All that was left now was to plot the move and be careful.

"I'll hit you up tomorrow with a time," he said, pulling into their mutual meeting spot.

As he slid into a spot next to where Nico had parked his car, his thoughts went to January. She was still mad as hell at him. Still locked in her room, refusing to talk, ever since the night he'd taken her to his place.

He was going through all this bullshit, turning his back on people he'd known all his life, his own father included, just to protect a woman who was convinced he didn't give a damn about her. No matter what he told her, she wasn't trying to see things any differently either. January was with all the bullshit. All the drama. Whether he admitted it or not, Legend loved the hell out of her ass, he just wanted to get everything settled as quickly as possible so he could get her mean ass out his crib.

"Best wishes to you for everything happenin' on the home front," Nico said, extending his fist for Legend to bump it in a thug's goodbye, although his lips spewed bullshit. Nico knew that no amount of best wishes would come close to making January decide to end her cold war and wave a white flag.

"You know she in there actin' like she hates my ass."

"Why? Because you ain't tell her shit yet?"

"Yeah, but what the fuck am I gonna say? I've got the whole world, including my family, thinking I'm helping with your kidnapping and tricking your dad. But I'm really not because I'm trying to protect you? You think she gon' believe that shit?"

Nico grimaced and then let out a sigh. "Yeah, nigga. Good luck with that. Ya damn sure gon' need it. If she's anything like her father, you make her mad and she might blank out and stab your ass."

Noting the teasing, playful smirk on Nico's face, Legend extended his fist to his cousin to complete their ritual goodbye.

"You got jokes," he replied, unable to hide a smile of his own. As fucked up as it was how January was acting, the fact that she could even get under his skin to begin with was some funny shit. Even he had to admit it.

As soon as he and Nico parted ways, driving off in different directions, January once again took over his mind. If he were being honest with himself, he'd have to admit that she never really left.

Even when his mind should've been on other things, January was like a background computer program consistently present in his subconscious mind. Jury was still out on whether he enjoyed having her as a seemingly permanent presence in his life or not. Somehow, something in his soul told him that no matter what he did, where he went, or how far apart they were from each other for however many years, a part of January would always be lingering there, somewhere in the back of his mind.

"Here we go," he said under his breath as he pulled into his parking spot. Blowing out hot air, he sat in the car for a moment, stalling to collect as much mental energy as he could before walking inside.

Home was where the heart was and the woman a man loved was supposed to be his peace. But what was the result of a situation where the woman who had your heart, lived in your home and instead of peace, she brought nothing but unrest and chaos?

PERCEPTION OF LOVE.

"They say perception is everything. It is the basis of how we create our reality. Well... everything being perceived by me in my current moment said that I was living in some luxurious side of hell."

JANUARY

JANUARY AWOKE IN TOTAL CONFUSION. IT FELT LIKE A SOUL SHOCK of some sorts. Her mind felt fragmented and totally disconnected from her body. She couldn't place where she was or what had happened to make it so she'd ended up here.

Lifting her head, she craned her neck to look around, taking in the silk white window coverings, high ceilings, and exquisitely distressed furniture. Egyptian cotton sheets pooled at her hips as she sat still, unmoving while her brain began to download all of the events from the night before. Or was it a few nights before? She was losing track of time as she commit herself alone in her borrowed room, miring in her depression.

She rubbed her eyes as small flashes of bits of scenes in her mind's eye brought back the detailed visions of the events that had led her here...

Alone.

With Legend.

In one of what she assumed was his many homes.

Being alone with Legend in the lap of luxury might have been the stuff her dreams were made of a couple weeks before. Shit... even a couple days. But now? Hell nah. She didn't want anything to do with the man she now preferred to refer to as 'that nigga.' Calling him by his name seemed to be too much of an honor. He wasn't a Legend. He wasn't different from all the others. He was the same. Just another lying ass nigga. Maybe even worse. She felt like an utter and complete fool for ever trusting him in the first place.

Imagine that, she thought, snorting out her disdain in a harsh puff of air through her nose. *January Lukeisha Murray... daughter of Outlaw and a total fuckin' fool for love.*

She wasn't the type to fall for anyone... *ever*. She had only one boyfriend in her entire life and, while he was cool and all, she couldn't say what she had felt for him was anything like how she allowed herself to feel for Legend. And, unlike Legend, Kyle had been a safe choice to fall for as far as surface-level appearances could show.

Kyle McCoy was the type of boy any mother would love. Honor roll student, son of one of New York's finest Black couples, and star of the basketball team. There was no doubt that he would go pro when the time came. He was the apple of everyone's eye. All the girls loved him, and he might as well have been born with a sticker on him that said "mother approved" because every mom loved him—January's included. Which was saying quite a lot because Janelle really didn't like anybody; however, she couldn't stop herself from speaking about how cute January and Kyle were together. How they would make the perfect couple. Even went as far as to say they would give her some beautiful grandbabies.

The problem with Kyle was that *January* didn't like him. All those fuzzy feelings the romance novels talked about when boy meets girl? She had none of that. She couldn't picture herself kissing him, much less making babies with him. He was a nice guy. He just didn't seem like he was the guy for her.

But with Legend, it was just different. She'd never been in love before but somehow, she knew she loved him. And not in a normal way. It was a deep knowing in her soul that this was the man that she'd lived and loved through many lifetimes. Before they'd spoken a word to each other, there was a recognition she couldn't explain. A love that had been nurtured to fullness even though her mind couldn't remember when, how, or why.

The only issue was that it was becoming clear that the deep knowing, the complicated but true emotions she felt for him, wasn't part of a shared connection. How was it that she'd managed to fall in love with a man who didn't love her back? Fuck slipping into some feelings, she'd fallen headfirst into them and with the most emotionless of men at that. What the hell was she doing? What the hell had she been thinking?

"Obviously, nothing at all," she whispered into the dimly lit room.

Crossing her arms in front of her chest, she frowned and looked around, fully taking in her surroundings. The night before, she'd been too caught up in her emotions to see anything besides the bed. After waiting for an explanation or even a simple response from Legend and getting nothing but the dumbstruck expression on his face, she'd charged into the bedroom and slammed the door closed, making sure to lock it behind her. She didn't feel like he'd walk into her new prison without being invited but, then again, she didn't know him like that. Apparently, she didn't know him at all. Everything she thought she knew was appearing to be a lie.

Light taps on the door cut into her mental revival of all the things about Legend that she couldn't stand, and she groaned. Now, instead of only occupying space in her mind, he was back to annoy her in real life. He was back to remind her of her foolishness. Why couldn't he just leave her in peace?

"You're not going to answer me again? How long you wanna play this game, January? I know you're awake."

A pinched expression tugged January's face, and she crossed her arms in front of her, reveling in her agitation.

"Well, if you know so much why I gotta tell you anything?"

Legend sighed deeply and, somehow, it brought her a tiny bit of pleasure to know that she was making him just as annoyed as he was making her. Successful transfer of her energy. A satisfactory grin tugged at her lips, the first she'd been able to muster up in a while, and she sat back calmly on the bed.

"I got food out here for you. You need to come out here and eat," he said, pulling back enough to gather some patience. She was being difficult—nothing abnormal about that. But he also understood that matching her current attitude would only make things worse.

"No, thanks. I'm not hungry actually."

"What?" he snapped and then glanced at his watch. It was after noon. She was being ridiculous. Stopping, he took a moment to calm his tone.

"It's almost time for lunch. And I made this shit with my bare hands," he added as extra encouragement. Unfortunately, it only worked against him.

"Is that supposed to mean something to me? I'm supposed to think about you when you don't give a damn about me?"

His head flinched back slightly and his eyebrows squished together at that.

"The *fuck* are you talking about? I *cooked* for you. How the hell does that mean I don't give a damn about you?"

"You know what I mean!"

He had a point, but January wasn't willing to give in to that. In her mind, the food seemed more like Legend's version of a half-assed apology, and she had no intentions of accepting it in any way, shape, or form. What she wanted was the *truth*. The whole, raw truth and nothing but the truth. She didn't want a meal. He could keep that. What she wanted was for him to decide to be an honest man.

"Actually, no, I don't know what you mean," he replied honestly. He felt a throbbing feeling in the side of his neck. His patience was wearing thin. He'd only just gotten back from making an alliance to do some shit that put his life and his cousin's even more at risk just to keep January safe, and she refused to even come out of the room.

"Just go away, Legend. I'd rather starve."

"January... man, listen. I don't have time for this bullshit."

"I don't have time for your bullshit either."

Something about that snapped the final thread holding back his anger.

"The fuck are you *talkin'* about right now, love? You do realize I brought you here to keep you safe, right? *I* saved *your* life."

"No, *you* saved your *own*," she shot back, this time standing to her feet as she shouted at the door, as if she were looking right at him. "If you had failed in protecting me, we both know what would have happened to you. So don't act like you're doing me any favors."

There was a brief pause and January could almost visualize the screw-face Legend was giving her through the door right then. She was being impossible... but she really didn't care.

"January—what *the fuck* kinda twisted logic is that? Failed or not, the point is the only reason you're here is because I'm trying to keep you safe."

"You don't get credit for that."

"Man, come out here and eat."

"No!"

"Alright. Fuck it then. You can starve until your fuckin' stomach starts eatin' your ass."

Jaw tight, Legend did an about-face away from the door, feeling the on-set of a headache coming in. The tension from the short conversation had him wound so tight, it was remarkable that he didn't spontaneously combust. January had a way of working his nerves in a way that no woman had ever before. She knew exactly what to say, when to say it, and how to say it, in order to rattle him.

The worst part of it was, the reason it bothered him was that he cared so much. If it were any other woman, he wouldn't give a damn whether she ate or not. He wouldn't have cooked shit and wouldn't have given two fucks if she was hungry for the rest of her life. But it was sincerely pissing him off that January wouldn't eat, and he didn't know why.

Grabbing the dishes in his hand, he used a fork to scrape every bit of the food that he'd just made into the garbage disposal before turning it on. He hated to waste food. He was a gangster but a responsible one in a sense—at least most of the time. However, in doing this, he felt he could dispel some of his aggression.

Unfortunately, the shit didn't work.

What an overgrown toddler, January thought, jumping back into the bed with her arms still crossed in front of her. *He didn't get his way, so now he has to act out. Poor baby.*

Her stomach twisted and she sucked in a breath, sighing hard to repress a growl. She was hungry and desperately wanted something to eat. The fumes coming from the food through the door were enough to make her mouth water, but her stubbornness was supreme. She'd rather starve than to sit and eat with a liar.

And as Legend scraped the last bit of food into the disposal, he visualized with pleasure, the act of shoving the food down her throat, and was tempted to take action on this vision, but stopped himself. Forcing her to eat wouldn't be as satisfying as the moment when she would finally cave in and eat of her own choice. And the moment when that would happen would come soon. January was a pampered princess; she'd never missed a meal a day of her life. She couldn't refuse food forever. So, until then, he was willing to let her do what she wished. If she wanted to starve, he'd let her starve.

Doesn't get what she wants, so of course she throws a fit, he thought, tossing the empty plate into the sink. *Such a fuckin' baby.*

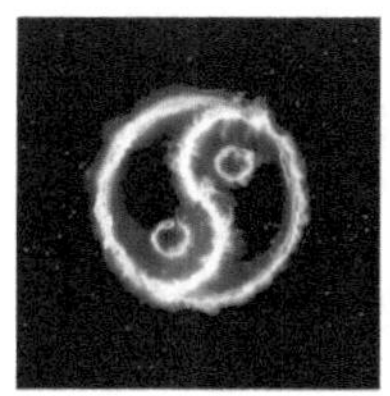

PSYCHOPATHIC NEAT FREAK.

Day turned to night and night had turned to day again. Each of the days before, Legend brought January food and she continued to refuse to eat. With her refusal, Legend had no other choice but to fight back his anger, cool his aggression, and walk away. They were both too stubborn to give in to the other and it left them at a stalemate.

January's stomach pains climaxed to an unbearable point, and she thought for sure that she'd gotten to the point when she would beg for food. But her stubborn nature overrode her hunger and before long, her body became used to the pain, making it nothing more than an annoying nagging at the back of her mind.

Never once had she drunk water that didn't come from a filter or a bottle but after a while of drinking from the spout in the bathroom, she couldn't even pick up on the aftertaste of faucet water. It was something that she'd consider unthinkable in her life before now, but her need to stonewall Legend was so great that it had her doing things she'd never done. Bottom line was, if she ever had to speak to him another day in her life, it would be too soon, so she was set on doing everything in her power to avoid him for as long as she could.

On the fifth day of her seclusion, she awoke the same way she did every morning, nearly jumping out of her skin when she realized that she was no longer in her dorm anymore. Blinking hard, January sat in place as her brain recalibrated and then reclined back into a full sulk.

"How long will I have to deal with this?"

She pressed her fingers against her temples, feeling the pressure building up inside of her head. She was sick of the mafia life. She didn't want anything more to do with it. She didn't like it—didn't glorify it the way the world did. There was nothing sexy about being constantly surrounded by the threat of violence. There was nothing alluring about living a life constantly involving some type of crime. She just wanted a regular life. Or at least the life she had only a week before.

How was it that things could be so right in one moment only to be so wrong in the next? Life wasn't supposed to work this way.

Neither should love…

Rolling her eyes, January fell back against the headboard of the bed and crossed her arms in front of her chest. This sucked. That was the only way she could explain it. It just fully and totally sucked. There was no other way to look at it.

In the back of her mind, she knew that this was necessary in some way in order to keep her safe, but the reality was the same: she was locked in a place she didn't want to be in, missing out on the life she really wanted to have. The life she was finally enjoying and settling into before whatever madness led to her being taken in the middle of the night by a man that it was becoming clear she barely knew.

Dipping the sheets from around her body, January stood up and went into the bathroom to wash up, hoping that the feel of the water against her skin would settle her emotions. However, as soon as the scalding hot water touched her body, it sent her mind into another whirlwind. This time about Legend. What was *his* deal? Who was he really?

Retreating deep into her thoughts, January couldn't help thinking about the time they'd spent together before whatever event happened that exposed his secret: that he was only around because he'd been paid to be. He'd been a much better actor than she'd thought. He'd fooled her well. But *some* of those moments had to be genuine, right?

He seemed like he really wanted her. January was usually good with people but this time she was wrong—very wrong, and she just didn't get it. There was no way she could imagine chemistry that had never been there. Could she? The attraction between them felt magnetic. Electric. Like a moth to a flame. Something like that couldn't be faked… could it?

Rubbing soap over her body, her thoughts made a sudden shift before she knew it and she found herself staring at an image of the most beautiful man she'd ever seen. Once again, Legend somehow found a way to creep into her mind's eye. Rock-hard abs, muscles sculpted to perfection, tattoos galore, and the most beautiful smile she'd ever seen on any man suddenly stood before her eyes.

He was one fucking sexy man. And she wanted him badly... even though she wanted *not* to want him just as badly. Maybe that was the real reason for her anger. She'd gone against all her core values and principles, surrendering fully to feelings she'd thought were mutual, only to find out they really weren't mutual at all. It was embarrassing. But beyond that, it was devastating.

January was toweling down after the shower, preparing to lotion up and put on the same exact clothes that she'd hand-washed and let air dry the night before, when she heard a knock on the door. She looked over at the digital clock on the dresser, glowing red with the numbers 10:00. Like clockwork, Legend was there, same as every morning.

"January, you need to come out and eat."

"I'll pass," she replied, the same as she did every morning before.

And, same as every other morning, he sighed deeply and then grumbled some inaudible words under his breath, fully illustrating how annoyed he was with her. January didn't give a shit. In her mind, that just made two people who were annoyed, because she couldn't stand his ass right now either.

Rubbing lotion over her legs, she waited for him to do the same as he did in the mornings before and stomp away angrily before tossing the food in the garbage disposal and loudly slinging the plates in the sink. But after a few minutes of nothing passed by, she realized that this morning would be different. Pausing from rubbing herself down, January lifted her eyes to stare at the door, as if she could see Legend standing on the other side.

"Who are you punishing right now, January?" he barked suddenly at her, speaking aggressively like a growl. "You're not eating. And I don't have to see you to know that you're walking around the room all day with that stank ass attitude and ugly ass look on your face. Who is really suffering right now? You or me?"

Damn. Well, that shit hit different.

For a fast moment, January considered his words and looked around in the room she'd been living in for the last five days as well as the clothes lying on the bed, the pajamas she'd been wearing when Legend first pulled her out of her bed in the middle of the night, that she was about to put on for the sixth day in a row. Yes, they were clean because she'd been washing them herself with soap and warm water every night, but she couldn't lie and say that she wasn't tired of pulling back on the same thong every damn morning. And it would be nice to not have to drink the same water she used to wash her ass. Or to sit down and eat a meal.

Meanwhile, Legend was doing whatever the hell he wanted to do because he hadn't confined himself to shit.

Basically, his lying ass had a point.

But, of course, January was too stubborn to admit it. Afterall, she was a double Capricorn… a goat in every single way. She would rather die than ask for help, admit that she was wrong, or be the first to give in. To *anything*. Therefore, with her chin high in the air, she acted like she couldn't feel or hear the loud, churning groans and pleas for sustenance in her belly and continued to lotion down her body as if she didn't have a care in the world.

"Fine," Legend said, finally. "Act like you don't hear me, but we both know that I'm right because I can hear your loud ass stomach growling through the fucking door."

As if on cue, January's stomach growled again.

Fucking traitor.

She wrapped her arms around her middle to try to dull the sound.

"Yeah, I heard that one, too," he said.

Damn it, she thought, grinding her teeth. *Sometimes the biggest betrayals come from your own body.*

"I won't be around playin' babysitter today. I've gotta go handle some shit and I might be gone all day. So, you can listen to your loud ass stomach all by yourself."

"Whatever," January scoffed under her breath between rolling her eyes.

Although she could see it for the ploy it was, her heart softened. This was Legend's way of ensuring that she ate while still being able to save face. He wasn't an idiot. He had to know that as soon as the coast was clear, she was going to raid the kitchen for any and everything that even looked like food.

January moved as fast as she could, pulling on her clothes and doing the rest of what she could of her morning regiment while keeping one ear out to listen for any and everything that Legend was doing. He seemed to be taking his sweet time, as if he knew that the only thing on God's green Earth that she wanted at the moment was for him to leave.

And then, finally, the moment arrived.

January was lying in the bed, trying her best to make herself go to sleep in order to make it easier to survive through the nerve-wrecking combination of anxiety mixed with hunger, when she heard synchronized beeps sounding off as Legend began to disarm the alarm system.

She sat up in the bed, eyes open just as wide as her ears, listening intently for the moment that he would leave. Finally, the unmistakable sound of the front door closing told her the coast was clear, and she jumped out of the bed. She couldn't wait to explore the rest of the place but at the forefront of her mind was getting some food on her stomach.

Just as she'd suspected, Legend knew exactly what her plan was as soon as she got the chance to leave the room. On the counter, was a long tray with enough food for her to eat for an entire day and maybe a few more. Multiple meals, different cuisines, she took liberty with all of it, eating as if she hadn't eaten in months rather than only a few days.

With a handful of grapes in her hand, January began to slowly walk around, finally taking a moment to look around the kitchen once she'd eaten enough to rid her hunger pains. Popping a grape into her mouth, she first turned her eyes to the coffee pot that looked like it hadn't been touched since it had been opened and placed on the counter. It seemed like it was there more for decoration than anything else.

And the more January looked around, the more she found that was untouched. Or at least *seemed* that way from how pristine clean it all was.

Like the stove, for instance. It didn't have any crust on the bottom of its insides. And yes, she did get on her hands and knees to check. Her curiosity ran that deep. It seemed to be brand new from the look of it. The glass flat-top didn't even have anything burned onto it. Or scratched into it. There was nothing about its appearance that indicated anyone had ever used it before, although she'd specifically heard Legend cooking. It didn't even have fingerprints on it, for crying out loud. Neither did the face of the refrigerator, either.

"So weird," she whispered.

January could tell that Legend liked things to be clean—well, his car, specifically. The second she'd sat down in it for the first time, one of the first things she noticed was that it was immaculately clean. There wasn't a speck of dirt anywhere to be found, but that wasn't all that strange to her. Guys were crazy about their cars, in general. And then once she saw how many expensive, exotic cars Legend had, it was easy to understand why. He was a car fanatic. She wouldn't expect his rides to be anything but clean.

But *this* shit right here? *This* was something else.

Slipping off her socks, January walked barefoot across the floor, sliding her feet across the marble tile floors, not feeling any bit of dirt on her soles. The face of the stainless-steel refrigerator didn't have a single fingerprint or any other markings on it for that matter. Neither did the microwave or the dishwasher. The bare granite countertops were wiped clean as well.

This nigga is a fucking psychopathic neat freak… was the first thought that came to her mind. But then she stopped, squinting her eyes as another thought came. She needed to do further research before she made that assumption.

Walking down the hall, she made a beeline towards where she assumed the other bedrooms were, hoping that Legend wasn't the type to keep his doors locked.

"Damn it," January whispered as soon as she reached out and tried the handle to what she'd assumed was the master bedroom.

It was locked. *Of course.* She should've known. Just to be sure, she checked every other door before realizing that they were all locked as well.

What the hell?

Now she really felt like she was in a prison. Obviously, the message was clear: Legend was doing what he had to in keeping her there, but she wasn't his house guest, she was someone he was being forced to deal with. She had no access to his personal life, he didn't want her rooting around in his things, he didn't want her finding out anything about him, because it wasn't like that with them. She was his mission and that was it.

Before she knew it, tears came to her eyes, fogging her vision. The fact that she'd gotten emotional about Legend once again was frustrating to her. There was nothing she hated more than getting emotional over a man, because it was simply something she didn't do. Years of having people, mainly men who she'd considered family, disappearing from her life for various reasons dealing with her family's lifestyle had taught her that people just didn't stay. There was no point in getting close to anyone or getting attached because their presence in her life was never stable or permanent.

After a while, January didn't even cry when someone she'd gotten close to was killed, was reported missing, or simply just disappeared from her life. At first, those things tore her apart. In her mind, it was the worst form of betrayal on their part.

BBM members were only killed, reported missing, or disappeared if they'd done something disloyal that led to that result. Very rarely was it because of any other reason. She'd been raised that it was unthinkable to betray the ones you loved, but it happened so often that she finally concluded that it was stupid to put her trust in anyone but her *blood* family.

Any and everyone else was cut off from her affection. If she were real with herself, that was the reason she never had any friends outside of her family. Prior to the accident, she'd had a few friends from her ballet class but once she could no longer dance anymore, they turned their backs on her too. Having nothing in common but dance led to the demise of those surface-level friendships.

It didn't matter much to her to lose them, though. January never let any of them get close enough to her to form a bond over anything else. She was guarded; she'd been so frustrated at her parents for the prison they'd subjected her to live in that she didn't even realize that she'd placed herself in a prison as well. She kept people at a safe distance, not revealing too much about herself, never appearing vulnerable or weak.

But then Legend entered the picture and that all changed.

She'd tried to treat him the same way, keep him at a distance just like she'd done everyone else; however, it didn't seem to work because he just *knew* too much. Not because she told him, and not because it was anything that could have been easily found either. Legend just *knew* her in ways that she couldn't explain. She didn't have to let down her walls because somehow, he'd already been looking at her from inside them. He read her like a book that hadn't even been written, could pick up on the uttering in her mind before she even had a chance to do it for herself. She didn't have to let him in because he'd already been inside of her before she knew it.

Somehow, being betrayed in this way was so much worse. It was the worst kind of vulnerable because she was being shown how incapable she was of protecting herself. She didn't want to love him, but she did anyways. She didn't want to need him, but now he was all she had. She wanted to mean everything to him, but it was becoming painfully clear that she meant nothing.

Wiping tears from her eyes, she turned around and walked away with her arms dangling to her side. Feeling so completely empty and lost inside, she didn't even realize that the few grapes she'd still had in her hand had fallen to the floor. Or maybe she did notice but didn't care.

Fuck Legend and his psycho-killer, hospital-clean house.

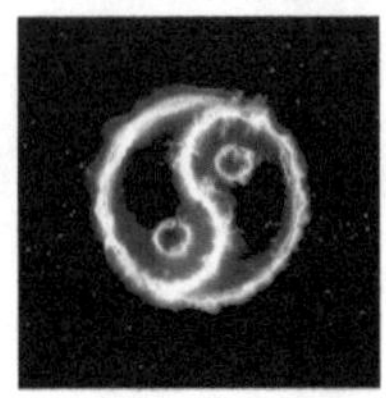

MY NIGGA, OSHO.

Exterior beauty, without the depth of a kind soul, is merely decoration.

"So, it's fuck my floors, huh? That's how you thank a nigga?"

Legend narrowed his eyes, peering at January on the iPad in his hand as she walked all droopy-shouldered back to her room, slamming the door shut hard as soon as she was inside.

Such a fuckin' princess.

Only January's ass would come out, eat up all the damn food he'd left her, and then have a fuckin' fit just because he'd locked the doors to his own damn bedroom. Legend couldn't understand her ass, really. You'd think she would be writing a nigga love letters on the counter with the whip cream he'd left her to go along with her fruit, but instead she was dropping grapes all over his fuckin' floor while running away, crying like a child.

Shutting off the video feed from his security cameras, Legend tossed it to the side and leaned forward to place his elbow on the counter in front of him, holding his chin with his hand.

"What? Shit ain't go how you planned it?" Nico asked, looking at Legend with a greasy ass grin on his face.

"How you figure that?" Legend grumbled, creasing his brow. "Shit *always* goes how I planned it."

"Not from that pouty ass look on yo' face." His grin spread wider, a miraculous feat, if Legend had ever seen one. Nothing made Nico's ass smile harder than seeing Legend's face twisted up over some shit he was dealing with concerning January.

"I'm glad you find this shit so fuckin' funny."

Nico shrugged and then turned around to pull all the ingredients he needed from the fridge to make their pre-workout shake.

"I don't find it funny," he stated, placing everything on the counter. "I find the shit *hilarious*. It's about time yo' arrogant ass met your match."

"And what about you?" Legend shot right back at him. Grabbing the freshly rolled blunt off the counter and pinching it between his lips, Legend looked at Nico and smirked. "What about you and the roommate? You ain't made yo' move yet?"

Legend saw the immediate shift in Nico's expression and instantly knew that something was up.

"I been reading some stuff from this nigga named Osho and he on point. He spit logic like that Muslim nigga named Akbar that used to live back in the hood. Remember Akbar? He was talking about how backwards the world is for us niggas. How we can stare at a beautiful flower and people will call us a mystic or poet but if we stare at a beautiful woman, they'll call the police. Ain't that some fucked up shit? This world we live in so backwards, man."

Legend almost choked laughing. Grabbing the blunt from between his lips, he sat it down on the counter again.

"Man, what the hell that got to do with what I asked you?"

Grabbing the blunt up, Nico gave Legend a pointed look before he lit it and took a quick pull.

"Everything," he said in a puff of smoke. "I like Brooke, but I can't fuck with her like that."

Legend blew air out through his nostrils, seeing right through to what Nico wasn't saying. Just the other day, he was sitting on campus with Legend, talking with stars in his eyes. And now he was telling Legend that he couldn't fuck with shorty anymore.

"So basically, shit got real is what you're telling me?" Legend asked, clasping his hands together as he leaned forward onto the counter.

"Nah, that ain't it," he replied, not meeting Legend's eyes as he fixed up a pre-workout smoothie.

It was the same damn smoothie that he'd made every day since before high school. But now that Legend had asked him a question about a chick, he was concentrating hard on it like the shit was rocket science. That alone told Legend everything he needed to know.

"It's just like Osho said," Nico continued with a shrug. "Shorty mental is fucked up. She done fucked with too many wrong niggas that when I come at her right, she don't even see it. I ain't got time to fuck with it."

"So that's why you still fuckin' with Drusilla over there?"

Legend smirked, nodding his head at the chick sitting behind them in Nico's living room. She was bad, sexy in all the ways she thought niggas wanted her to be, but when it came to the mental, she was dumb as hell. Simple as hell. Her brain couldn't take the challenge necessary to have layers to her personality.

Lifting his eyes, Nico looked up at her and Legend could see a hint of annoyance in his eyes. Legend didn't even know why Nico fucked with a girl he couldn't stand. Actually, he did know why Nico did it. His reasons were just dumb as hell.

"Man, she been watching that dumb ass 'Fix My Life' shit all fuckin' day on repeat and ain't caught a damn thing to make her think that maybe it's her fuckin' life she need to be thinking of fixing." Nico frowned shaking his head. "Maybe then she can move the fuck out and be somebody else problem." Legend laughed as Nico slammed his smoothie down on the counter in front of him, puffing hard on the blunt.

"Shit ain't funny man," he said. "I need to kick her ass out. Expeditiously."

"Why don't you?" Legend asked, just to fuck with Nico really. He was running from his own chaos. It was easier dealing with Nico's.

"I can't." Nico shrugged.

"I know. It's because you got heart. But I got you, bruh. Cause I don't give a shit," Legend said, standing up.

He turned around and looked at Dru doing the same shit she was doing every time he came over: sitting on the couch with a stupid ass expression on her face, letting the TV burn the last few bits of her brain cells away.

"Aye, shorty. Dru," Legend yelled out to her. He waited for what felt like forever for her to lazily pull her attention from the TV and turn her eyes to him.

"Yeah?" she said, letting her mouth hang open as she looked at him with sleepy-ass-looking eyes. Didn't matter what time of day it was. Dru always looked tired as fuck.

"You gotta get the fuck out." Legend used his thumb to point to the door. "Yo' lil siesta, or whatever the fuck they call it in your country, is over."

She frowned. “Huh?”

“Time to get the fuck out. As in *move* out. Pack yo’ shit. You gotta go.” Legend tried to keep a straight face as he waited for her to respond. If there was anything he liked better than fuckin’ with January, it was fuckin’ with Dru. She was such an easy target.

“Fuck you, Legend!” she finally said, once she got it. ‘You’re always fuckin’ messin’ with me.” She waved her middle finger at Legend before going right back to the TV, assuming her normal position. Wasting her fucking life until a rich nigga decided to come along wife her.

“You need me to help pack yo’ shit for you?” Legend asked, just for the sake of fucking with her. January had his mind heavy and he was on some demon shit. Trying to pass the pressure.

“Where yo’ bags at?”

Turning again, Dru looked at him with a glazed over, distant stare. One thing Legend couldn’t stand about her—one thing of the many fuckin’ things he couldn’t stand about her—was that she was slow as hell. And not slow as in she was dumb. She *was* dumb, but she also was just so fuckin’ *slow* in general. She moved slow. She talked slow. She even thought slow. Waiting for her to say something was painful as hell. You ask her a question and her eyes would roll up to her forehead and stall there as if she were trying to download some new software to her brain before she could respond.

She was a fuckin’ weirdo. But she was easy, simple as hell, sexy as hell, and didn’t give Nico any problems because she didn’t give a damn about shit. It was the only reason he kept her around.

“For real?” she asked finally, looking from Legend to Nico. “You serious? I gotta go?”

“Nah, you good,” Legend heard Nico say. That shit was all it took for her to turn around and go right back to watching her show. Just that simple, she had forgotten the entire altercation with Legend and was once again happy as hell, watching her show.

Turning around, Legend shook his head, chuckling to himself as he sat back down at the island and grabbed the smoothie Nico made.

"Fucking hilarious," he said, before taking the glass.

"Fuckin' peaceful as fuck," Nico replied with a shrug. "She's boring as hell but she don't give me no problems. She ain't giving me no drama. After being in the streets dealing with bullshit, the only thing I want waiting for me at the crib is peace."

Legend knew what he meant. It was real shit. It was part of the reason he'd stayed single and rarely involved women in his life. Honestly, Legend couldn't judge Nico because he'd been where he was before. When your mind was jumping all day, constantly reminding you that you had to watch your back, had to stay on your toes, couldn't trust any one, those few moments in between where nothing was going on meant everything. Having a chick who ain't give you no problems because she didn't expect shit from you but dick every now and then was easy. Of all the things a woman wanted from a man, dick was easy to give.

The problem with that was, it got to the point where Legend couldn't even do that shit anymore. He didn't know what changed, but he no longer had a desire for the surface-level shit. January was a handful and a headache. Scratch that—she was a whole fucking migraine. Full-scale trauma to the brain. She came into his life and brought him peace at the expense of fully wrecking his shit at the same time. But if he were honest with himself, Legend knew the only reason he wanted to avoid it was because she was forcing him to level up.

"Growth ain't comfortable," Legend said to Nico. "Don't shit happen if you're comfortable."

Remembering that the perfect example of everything he was saying was right behind them, Legend turned around and pointed his head at Dru. Sprawled out on the couch without a care in the world, she was the definition, the fucking epitome, of comfortable.

"Brooke ain't easy but she'll force you to level up. This empty-headed bitch easy because she ain't gon' press you to *do* shit, but she ain't gon' press you to *be* shit either. Every man wants a powerful woman… until he gets with her and realizes that he gotta step his shit up to keep her."

Nico fell silent, wrapped in his thoughts as he puffed on his blunt. Legend didn't say shit either. Although he was giving Nico advice, he was fully aware that he needed to point the finger right back at his damn self. He wasn't avoiding January, mainly because he didn't have a choice, but he was keeping her at a distance.

He refused to really fuck with her on a level that was real because he knew it meant he had to change. It meant he had to face his demons, deal with shit that was easier to leave alone. She brought out emotions that he'd rather keep dormant. She had him feeling shit that he was conditioned to believe was what made niggas weak. She was a queen, but Legend was comfortable being the devil. He wasn't ready for the challenge it took to be a king for her yet.

For some reason, Legend found himself thinking about Outlaw. If anyone understood this kinda shit, it was him. The one man he couldn't talk to. He'd given Legend a task but made it clear that, other than protecting January, wasn't no dealings between them. And Legend couldn't talk to his own father because he was on some bullshit; pissed because he couldn't use January to his advantage. But Legend couldn't force himself to betray the woman he loved just to settle some age-old beef that didn't concern him. Instead, he found himself settling some other age-old belief that did: the one that said thugs couldn't fall in love. Apparently, they could, because he had. Even if he couldn't admit that he did.

"Man, that's some deep shit you just said," Nico replied, blowing out smoke. "Tell me the truth. You been reading that nigga Osho, too?"

Chuckling, Legend shook his head. "Nah," he said. "Just been living life."

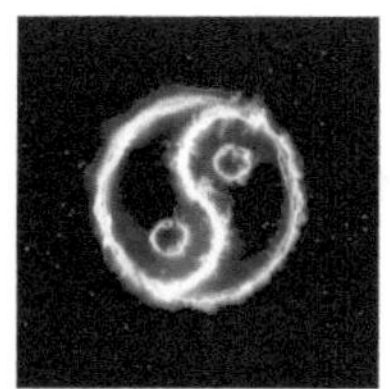

THE BLOCK IS HOT.

"JUST IN CASE I DIDN'T TELL YOU YET TODAY, THIS IS SOME FUCKED up shit you got us doing and I ain't ever gon' forgive you."

"Yeah, I love you too, bruh."

"Yeah, yeah, nigga. Just be happy you my cousin."

"Always."

Sitting in the old-school, drop-top Chevy that they'd received from Gunna in order to complete their current task, they applied silencers to each of their weapons. The anxious energy between them was high, the same way it was whenever the thrill that came along with the presence of danger was near. It was an adrenaline rush out of this world. Nico talked a lot of shit just to give Legend a hard time because, for once, it was Legend and not him putting them in the middle of a reckless situation for a change. If he didn't complain about it this time, he might never get the chance again.

But, truthfully speaking, he could barely hold back his anticipation. The weight of a gun in his hand gave him an all-time high. It sent a surge of power through him that he could never explain to anyone who had never felt it before.

Growing up how he did with dope dealers for role models, the one thing he was taught was that everybody had junky habits. The difference only came into play when it pertained to what you chose to be addicted to. Some people chose drugs, others chose love, some chose knowledge to get their ultimate high. For Nico, his thrill came through in the instances when he tempted fate.

There was something magical about the recklessness of placing yourself in the most dangerous of situations and finding a way out of that. When you were a young nigga in the hood with nothing to lose, the biggest gamble you can take is with your life. Longevity wasn't an option when it came to the streets, so any day you were able to survive against the odds was like a taste of the sweetest victory. And the greater the risk, the sweeter the taste.

"Drive slow," Legend said once they'd settled in the car.

"Yeah, nigga, duh," Nico replied, with a vicious snarl, grilling him hard. "You act like we ain't been on a million of these missions together. I know what to do."

"Yeah, that's what your mouth says, but the motherfuckin' speed demon look in your eyes begs to differ."

Unable to challenge that, Nico decided to keep his mouth shut. Legend knew him well and could pick up the subtle changes in him like no one else could. Nico was amped with adrenaline, empowered by the mission and the gun he'd just placed in his pants. He was cautious as always but also ready to shoot shit up. It was a deadly combination that usually ended with Nico alive and all his enemies dead. But they wanted to complete the job at hand with the least amount of bloodshed as possible.

"There is too much shit on the line with this. We can't afford to be reckless," Legend explained further.

"*Our* asses are on the line with *every* mission," Nico said, giving Legend a knowing look. "The only reason you're extra concerned right now is because ole girl is in the mix, too.

This time it was Legend's turn not to say a word, because Nico hit the nail right on the head.

"I'm important, too, Legend. *I'm* your cousin. We're blood. Motherfucka, you should care about me, too."

"Nigga… fuck you."

They shared their last laugh together before game time before Nico started the ignition and they fell into silence. Clearing their mind of all distractions, they meditated in perfect focus, concentrating solely on what needed to be done.

The hardest part of what they had to do was right at the beginning. Most niggas carrying weight across the border didn't come face-to-face with danger until that moment when they hit the border and had to deal with customs. For Legend and Nico, the situation was different. Dealing with customs was small shit compared to what they had to face the second they jumped into the ride that Gunna had waiting for them.

"Damn, this nigga done placed shooters on every fuckin' corner. Gunna didn't tell us the Rosarios had this shit on lock like this."

"I don't think he knew," Legend replied as Nico slowly drove right through Rosario territory.

"That motherfucka knows everything," Nico replied, sitting low in the seat. "Hard to imagine he wouldn't know about this shit."

Legend didn't say anything right away because Nico was right. As much as he wanted to defend Gunna, he had placed them in a fucked-up position. Of all the mechanics that he could use to chop up his cars in order to be able to safely traffic narcotics without being discovered by the police, Gunna used the exact same mechanic the Rosarios used, meaning Legend and Nico had to retrieve the car right from out of Rosario territory.

"Why he ain't have somebody else on the team pick it up from the mechanic and drop it somewhere outside of the city? Would've made our job that much easier."

"True shit, but we couldn't risk it," Legend explained, looking around observing everything as Nico continued to drive. "The less people who know what we are doing, the better. Gunna's team does business with the Rosarios. A lot of them have pledged their loyalty to Fernando's team."

"Makes perfect sense. Still fucked up though," Nico replied before they each fell back into silence.

Legend kept his head on swivel, watching closely for anything that moved… which happened to be a lot. The block was hot for it to be so late at night. It wasn't the best time of day to move weight, being that every dope boy and fiend in the city came out at night, but they didn't have much of a choice. The Rosarios' men would run down any car with dark tints so moving during the day would leave them fully exposed.

"And we have arrived," Nico said, pulling into the mechanic's lot.

The building looked a little run-down, a definite eye-sore, which was an obvious cover. There was no way that a mechanic who serviced both the Rosarios and Gunna's team wasn't rolling in cash. The fact that the building looked like this was most likely just to stop the police from deciding to look into it.

"Let's just do what we gotta do and get out of here. I don't like how this shit is looking."

Something felt off and his premonitions about things such as this were usually right. He could feel danger lurking almost like a second skin. It made him feel anxious in a way that thugs didn't like. There was a kind of paranoia that came with the position, but Legend was used to that feeling. This was different. This feeling only came on when something was about to go terribly wrong.

Nico pulled their car up next to the ride that they had been told to swap with and then cut off the engine. Moving fast, they jumped out and walked over to the other car, a renewed old-school Mustang, which was parked in one of the open shop garages. Without turning on a single light, they jumped in, disabling the inside car lights. They wanted to make sure that they were able to get in and out unnoticed.

"Alright. Now all that's left is for us to peel out of this bitch..." Nico said, reaching down to start the engine.

"Wait!" Legend said, jerking his hand up into the air.

In the corner of his eye, he'd thought he saw movement behind them, positioned somewhere in the darkness of the garage. The entire shop was supposed to be locked down and vacant per the intel they'd gotten about the job. Other than the two of them, there should have been no movement. After waiting for a few seconds, both of them with a hand on their pistols, Legend finally relaxed.

"Never mind. I thought I saw something but maybe it was just a dog or some shit. If it was a nigga, he would've bust some shots by—"

"Fuck! I just saw him!"

Before Legend could say another word, Nico jumped out of the whip, pistol in hand, locked and loaded, ready to bust on anything moving.

"Nico, wait!" Legend hissed out in a whisper, but Nico was moving too fast and furiously to hear him.

He was a hot head, had always been. When it came to any dangerous mission, Nico was the one you wanted or your team because he ran after any threat directly, attacking with maximum effort, full-throttle. The thing about it, Legend moved in more intuitive ways. He was very in-tune with the sensations he got when it came to certain things. He could read the surrounding energy. And something about this situation was telling him that it wasn't worth pursuing.

By the time Legend and Nico had jumped out the ride, the man they'd each noticed had ran out a side door in the garage that led to a backwards alley. Nico had the jump on Legend, moving at a fast-paced. He dove through the door, running at top-speed, pure adrenaline, gun in hand, finger on the trigger.

Zip! Zip!

The silenced shots ripped through the air as soon as Nico was able to get a clear shot. And, just as always, he hit his target right on. One in the leg, other in the chest. Instant kill shot.

"Nico, the fuck?!" Legend said, once he'd caught up.

The man who Nico had shot didn't look like a Rosario… at least not a member who was high up enough on the chain to make a real difference. In fact, he didn't even have a gun on him. He was definitely in the streets but he wasn't a hitta. That much could be told from the pliers, screwdriver and other materials he was holding in his hands.

"Look like he was trying to hot wire the car," Legend quickly summed up.

"Wrong car, wrong fuckin' time," Nico replied and nodded his head. "Fuck!" he cursed, kicking at the man's foot with his shoe. "I didn't want to kill him though."

"I know," was all Legend could say. "But you had to. He saw our faces. If he had told anyone about what he'd seen, the Rosarios would've killed the mechanic and would've cut their alliance with Gunna. Letting him go could've caused more bloodshed in the end."

"Could have doesn't mean it would've," Nico said with a shrug, knowing Legend was just trying to make him feel better about killing this man on one senseless shit. Senseless because it didn't have to happen.

Staring at the lifeless body lying below him stirred up an emotion Legend had never felt before. Sadness? Grief? It was so odd. Something he couldn't place. It had never quite happened this way before. He'd taken lives many times, but it had never affected him this way. And this wasn't even coming from a life he'd himself taken away. Nico had let go the shot that had laid this man to rest. So why was his conscience dealing with it?

"We gotta get out of here."

Taking a look around him down the dark alley they'd cut into, Legend tuned his ears in to any sound indicating that someone was around them. Hearing nothing, he held his gun to his side and began to take a step towards the direction they'd come when he stopped short, hearing a buzzing sound, a subtle vibration. Turning to Nico, they both locked eyes, an unspoken query traveling between them.

"The fuck is that? You got your phone?" Nico whispered.

Pursing his lips, Legend didn't respond. Nico knew damn well he didn't have his phone on him. That was a rookie move, and he was most definitely no rookie.

The buzzing continued and they both turned behind them towards the lifeless body they'd been about to leave.

"It's his. Should we take it?"

"We can at least check it. Just to make sure we wasn't wrong about who he is… or isn't. And to make sure we ain't raise no suspicions."

With a slight nod of his head, Nico walked over and stuck his hand in the man's pocket, pulling out his phone. Glancing at the screen, he took a deep breath as he looked at the image on it and then paused in his thoughts for a moment before shaking his head.

"Nah, it ain't nobody to be concerned about," he said, holding the phone up showing Legend the lit screen. "Looks like his wife."

One look at the screen and that was confirmed for Legend as the glowing image of a beautiful smiling woman holding a small child in her arms, with the words 'wifey' above her head stared back at him. An odd feeling passed over him as he tore his eyes away, feeling his chest grow increasingly tight with discomfort. In all the times he had been responsible for a life lost, he'd never taken a moment to consider the lives that were left behind. The people affected by the decisions their loved ones decided to make.

Whoever the woman was that was calling, she didn't even know it but from this night on, her life would never again be the same. And she would have to deal with the weight of that shit. The nigga who chose to walk the path that put her in this situation was gone. He'd taken the easy way out and now she was left carrying the burden and grief of his mistakes.

"That nigga had a whole fuckin' family. Why the fuck take the risk of messin' with some gang shit?" Nico said, once they'd gotten back to the car and had made it back onto the main street. "Taking risks don't mean a thing unless the shit goes right."

Legend nodded his head in agreement. "Better off just living to fight another day."

"Shit, I know I keep sayin' this but I still ain't mean to kill him though. Regardless to whether it was the best thing or not," Nico said. He sighed, running his hand over his face. "I was just moving too fuckin' fast. And you weren't there when he took his last breath. The *last* thing that nigga said was something about his wife. Then she calls. Like she knew something had happened. How fucked up is that?"

Unable to say anything, Legend continued to sit in his thoughts and allowed Nico to speak. Something about all of this hit him deep. He couldn't explain why, but he was trying to figure it out.

"The thing about it is, when it all went down, the only thing on his mind was her. All the robbing shit he was trying to pull, stealing the car, whatever money he would get from it, none of it mattered. His only concern was her," Nico continued with a sigh, shaking his head. "If all this shit we're doing goes bad one day, I wonder who the fuck would be on my mind when I'm about to take my last breath."

As soon as he said it, Legend knew that was what made all this so heavy for him. January depended on him this time. Shit *had* to go right or it affected someone he loved. That one thing made all the difference because it wasn't something that he'd ever had to deal with before. Sure, he had family who would mourn if anything happened to him, but it was a different effect.

Losing someone who you loved as if they were an extension of yourself—that was a different type of heartbreak. He knew it because that's how he felt. He couldn't imagine being able to go on if anything happened to her. It had been that way from the moment he'd first laid eyes on her. And even though they were at odds, the feeling was still the same.

He knew she was still pissed off at him, but he couldn't take the silly hunger games she was playing anymore. Life was too short, and shit had gotten incredibly real for him tonight. If anything happened to him, he didn't want to leave this Earth being at odds with the woman he loved more than his own life.

Whatever the way, whatever the method, he didn't care what he had to do. Somehow he had to make it right.

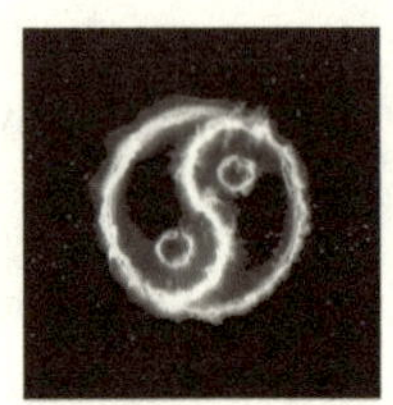

NOT US. NOT NOW. NOT EVER.

She was both hellfire and holy water. All depending on how you treated her.

I CAN'T EVEN BELIEVE I'M DEALING WITH THIS.

January was a motherfuckin' mafia princess. Her daddy was a king in every street, both nationally and internationally.

She was a star. She was the prize. She didn't have to deal with any nigga's bullshit. So what the hell was she in the bed, hiding up under the covers and crying for? Unfortunately, the answer to both questions was standing right at the foot of her bed.

"January, get up from under them covers before I snatch that shit up off you," Legend stated, standing solidly near her feet. Reaching out, he turned the tip of the drill in his hands at her feet, lightly pressing.

"Oww! Stop, Legend!"

"*Move* the covers!"

"No!"

Once again, Legend struck her with the drill, zapping her quickly, and she yelped out in annoyance at being bothered when she *really* didn't want to be. Especially not by him.

"*Stop* doing that," January snapped through her teeth, keeping the covers over her head.

"I'm not going to wait here forever," Legend replied, leaning back against the wall, propped up against the door that he'd just removed off the hinges.

He wasn't taking no for an answer any longer. He'd been patient. Even nice—something he specifically tried to never be. He had given her plenty of time to come to her senses, to realize that he was the only nigga on the planet right now who was risking everything and everyone who mattered to him to keep her safe. And the only thing he wanted in return was some appreciation for his efforts: nothing more, nothing less.

"Okay, fine," Legend said, pulling up from the wall, holding the drill up in his hand. "I guess you wanna do this the hard way."

Before he could take another step closer, January jumped up and snatched the covers off her body. Her eyes were puffy and wet. Crying wasn't a normal reaction for her, but she was exhausted and malnourished. Her psyche wasn't fortified enough to deal with the emotions Legend brought out.

"Why are you bothering me? Haven't you messed my life up enough already?"

"Me?" Legend pressed the tip of the drill at his chest, genuinely confused. "Out of all the niggas in the world you could blame, how the fuck I get the blame for your fucked up situation?"

"Because it's *your* ugly ass who won't leave me alone."

She didn't have a reasonable answer for him, so she had no other choice but to resort to being petty.

"Ugly?" Legend grunted, running his hand over his chin to hide his smirk. "Oh, you big mad, huh? With your delusional ass," he added under his breath. "Fuck all that shit. I been a lotta things, but I ain't never been ugly a day in my motherfuckin' life."

In spite of her rage and sorrow, January rolled her eyes.

"I can't take no more of this," she whispered, flopping backwards on the bed. As soon as her head hit the pillow, she lifted the covers right back up and over her head, successfully blocking Legend from her sight. If only she could block him from her mind.

"Hell nah, we ain't playin' this game no more," she heard him say. Bracing herself for another poke from the drill, she was fully determined to send a swift kick straight to his gut if he tried.

Seeing her defenses up, Legend slowly lowered to drop the drill to the floor before diving onto the bed, wrapping his arms around her to tighten the covers around her body. She panicked. Feeling trapped and unable to breathe, her fighter instincts immediately came into play.

"Get *off*!" January shrieked, trying her hardest to push him off of her. He reacted in a playful manner, strengthening his arms even more before finally releasing his hold. He barely had a chance to move before she ripped the covers off her head and hit him with a quick two piece to the chest and a slap on the shoulder.

"What the fuck, January? First, you get mad because I was forcing you out and now, you're mad because I'm helping you stay in."

"The problem with all of that is I don't want you *touching* me. At all. And not ever!"

Raising his hand, Legend squeezed the bridge of his nose, feeling his impatience begin to rise.

"This is fucked up, love. You're on some childish shit. I'm just tryin' to make you laugh. You need to stop this."

"No, what's childish is the fact that you're a grown ass man who felt the need to lie to me. And you *still* haven't come clean with the truth, yet."

She placed her hands on her hips, grounding her feet into the floor to steady her stance. "I'm not just some object that you can toss and move around from here to there without any kind of explanation. You have to give me some kind answer on something. This isn't fair."

Standing up, Legend turned to face her, his body as rigid as a war, which was highly appropriate being that his expression was pure stone.

"Life isn't fair. That's only something a child would think. You're a grown ass woman and this is real fuckin' life. When it comes to real life, shit ain't fair. Never will be."

"I'm not talking about life, Legend, I'm talking about you."

She watched his face for movement but, of course, there was none. He stared at her with piercing, black eyes, completely void of emotion. This was a talent he'd perfected over several years, she was sure. He was completely unreadable; not giving of anything. There was nothing about this that was healthy.

"You're right. When it comes to *real life*, shit isn't fair. Because life is always throwing something our way, so I get that," January replied, shrugging. "However, when it comes to two people who have a friendship, mutual attraction, bond, or whatever the hell it is that we have, we owe each other the truth. We owe each other fairness. You owe me some type of explanation for how you've been lying to me all this time and why. You owe me for making me feel the way I do about you and then pulling back like I'm nothing to you in the next minute. You owe me *something*."

And there it was. Her heart was now on the line, as much as she didn't want it to be, her truth was out there. All that was left now was for Legend to respond in a way that told her whether or not he was the person she thought he was.

Time seemed to slow to a snail's pace as she waited on edge for something in Legend to change in any way to indicate that he'd even heard a thing she'd said.

"No one is pulling away from anything," he said, finally deciding that January was deserving of a response. "I put my whole life on hold to protect you. Ain't shit in this for me."

She rolled my eyes. Who did he think he was fooling?

"You put your life on hold to protect me because you got the call from *Outlaw*," she said, adding extra emphasis, tone dripping with pure sarcasm. She didn't even curse like that, but he truly had her fucked up and she was ready to let him know it. Did he really think that she was naive enough to think that this didn't have anything to do with the fact that he was trying to get back in good with her father?

"This has nothing to do with me either," she added. "You've made it perfectly clear to me how much you don't care."

"Real deal… I'm sick of this shit," Legend said, shaking his head. Defenses down, patience gone. He was realizing that fighting fire with fire was no use. For the first time in his life, he figured he would give it a shot and see if he could win a war using love.

Before she could react, Legend was on her. Body to body, he rushed in fast, pressing against her hard, pushing her backwards until her back was flat against the wall. Shocked by the sudden movement, January gasped and he caught it, covering his mouth with hers. Her entire body went limp in his arms, fully surrendering into them. He lifted her up and her legs moved like they had a mind of their own, wrapping tightly around his waist.

Deepening the kiss, Legend pushed even closer into her, closing the space in between as they merged into one. Fireworks of passion went off inside of January, like sparks of electricity rippling through her. Her entire being responded to his body in a natural way, as if they'd been here before.

As if they'd done this before. Like they'd made love before.

"You are an interesting woman, January," he said suddenly, speaking against her lips as he kissed her.

His voice ripped her from her trance. "Hmmm?"

He pulled back slightly to fully look her in the eyes. "You're an interesting woman."

It was true. All this time he was trying to wait her out, starve her out, beat her fighting and all he needed to do to win over her love was to show her his.

"What do you mean?" she asked, frowning slightly.

"I mean, one second you're mad as hell, threatening me. And now this. But I have to admit, I've never met anyone quite like you."

She felt his breath pulsing against the tip of her nose and she almost couldn't speak.

"I've never met anyone like you, either," she whispered, speaking honestly.

He was so close she could smell him. Citrus, pine, and smoke. They filled her nostrils and inflated her lungs as she committed the scent to memory. Every bit of it fit him, too. Like a birthday kid to a cake. She could've sworn he was moving closer into her, too. Leaning over her, as if he wanted to hover to protect her body from the outside world.

Protect me all you want.

"January," he said huskily.

She swallowed hard. “Yes?”

“I need…something.”

“Yes?”

“I need—”

She closed her eyes. “What do you need, Legend?”

He growled softly. “You.”

The warmth of his breath against her neck had nothing on the feeling of his lips. Because when they touched down against her pulse point, her eyes turned toward the ceiling. They fluttered closed as she felt his hand cradle the back of her head. His teeth raked against her skin, pulling a moan from the back of her throat. She needed to back away from him. She needed to put some distance between them. But all she did was lean in closer.

Anything to feel his lips against her skin some more.

January gave her control over to him as his lips explored her neck, nibbling and suckling as his tongue explored her veins. He kissed along her jawline, traveling dangerously close to her lips. And when she finally puckered them, he was there. The heat of his kiss, waiting to connect with her own as his hand fisted her hair.

“Legend,” January whispered.

And with another growl, he captured her mouth with his own.

His kiss set her veins on fire. His tongue made her stomach jump. She’d never felt anything like this before, and while she knew it was bad, it made her want it even more.

It made her want *him* even more.

“Mmmm, Le—”

Before January could even moan his name like her entire body wanted her to, he pulled back. Her eyes ripped open and she stared at him as he shot up from her bed and moved over to the window.

Her skin began to crawl, and not in a good way. The fire rushing through her veins petered out into nothing but smoke that slowly dissipated into thin air. It was hard for her eyes to focus, and it felt even harder for her brain to focus. But, the second Legend's voice pierced through the air again, it ripped her out of her trance.

"We can't do this. Not us. Not now. Not ever."

And with that said, he turned around, not even waiting for her to respond, and walked right out the door.

January stood absolutely confused and frozen in place until she heard the familiar beeping of the alarm keypad at the front door.

He's leaving? She thought, frowning.

She didn't understand. What had happened? What did she do?

Fearing that she wouldn't get to ask him and would have to spend the night feeling tortured by her own mind, she ran out of her door towards the front of the apartment at the exact moment that the huge metal door slid closed. Seconds later, all the automatic locks fell into place with a series of clicks, beeps and buzzes, and all hope disappeared.

He was gone.

Once again, she was alone.

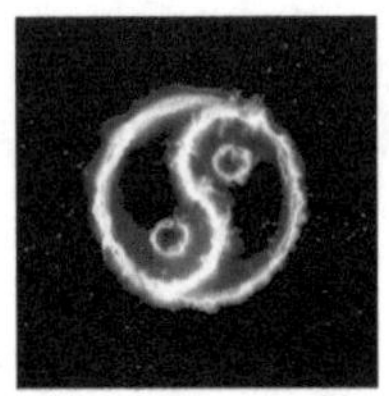

SLOW-COOKER.

"ONYX... ARE YOU SINGING AT THE CLUB TONIGHT?" BROOKE asked.

Standing at the entrance of Onyx's, she peeked through the open door and then frowned when she didn't see any sight of her.

"I'm in the bathroom. One sec!" She heard Onyx yell out about five seconds before she emerged from the bathroom with a hair curling rod hanging from her head.

"Yes, I am singing tonight... if I can get my hair together. I've been trying to do spiral curls but it looks a hot mess."

"Yes, it does," Brooke agreed cutting her eyes. "Girl, let me help you with that. It looks like you got a bird's nest on top of your head."

"Damn, bitch." Onyx frowned. "You ain't have to say all that."

As if it wasn't her intent, to be so damn disrespectful, when in reality she was the queen of petty, Brooke shrugged and they both laughed walking together to Onyx's bathroom.

"Well, the reason I was asking," Brooke began as she began to part Onyx's hair to wrap it around the wand. "Is because I think I may want to come with you tonight. I've been stuck in here, doing nothing but leaving just to go to class. Literally, just lying in my depression at Trevor doing his thing and not even thinking about me. I'm ready to go out and just vibe."

Onyx's nose wrinkled. "Wait… Trevor *still* isn't talking to you? Why the hell you still letting him stay in your apartment? And drive your car?"

Brooke responded with a sheepish shrug. "Brooke, somebody out here ready to love you enough to write pages and chapters to you about how he feels, but you're waiting around for the one motherfucka who won't even send you a text!"

Placing her hands in the air, Brooke gathered her thoughts so she could explain to Onyx what the reality of the situation was. Onyx had a point, but the reality of things wasn't what she thought.

"I'm not *waiting* for Trevor any longer. I've thought about kicking him out," Brooke said, nodding her head. "Especially now that Nico said I can't go back to the dorm for a while but, honestly, he's paying the rent *and* the car note. If I took that back, all I would be getting are two more bills. I don't need a car and with him paying the rent, I've been able to let my parents keep their money. It's working out in my favor, in a way."

Pausing to analyze it from Brooke's stance, Onyx nodded her head slowly.

"Yes, that makes sense. I never thought about it that way."

"Of course, *you* didn't," Brooke said, rolling her eyes. "You don't *have* any bills. Your folks pay everything for you and whatever extra you need is loaded up in your trust fund. But babygirl, I ain't got one of those." She smacked her lips saying that and gave Onyx a direct look. "So whatever bills Trevor wants to take on, he can have."

"Makes perfect sense to me," Onyx summed up before sharply changing the subject into a clear, opposite direction. "So what's going on between you and my brother? I need to know what I'm about to step in the middle of when the two of y'all see each other tonight."

As usual, Onyx hit the nail on the head. Brooke's current situation with Nico had everything to do with her wanting to go out tonight. Ever since they had sex, he'd been different. They'd had such an intense experience. Something that she'd never had with any other man. She could barely make herself be mad at Trevor for flaking on her anymore because, if he hadn't, she would have never met Nico next. Their connection was intense, it had been everything. And then afterwards, when she asked for some clarity on what they had going on, he opened his mouth and ruined it.

"Nico… what are we calling this?" she asked, still lying in the bed, wrapped up like a burrito in the covers. There was nothing better than the feeling that came from being dicked down right.

Nico did that! *She couldn't help but think, feeling the lovely ache between her legs.*

As she watched him put on clothes, she realized that she hated to see him go, though she understood why. It was enough that Onyx knew they were involved. She didn't need to know how *involved. It made sense that Nico would want to keep the fact they were having sex secret.*

Or at least—that was why he was leaving… right?

"I'd rather not call it anything," Nico replied, feeling uneasy about her question. "Let's not categorize it. Let's just let it be whatever it needs to be."

Brooke eyes fluttered as she blinked a few times in quick sequence. "Meaning… what?"

"I mean, let's not ask anything of each other. We can just be friends."

"Friends?" Brooke frowned, seeing clearly what he was saying. Niggas rarely were friends with chicks they fucked with. Him saying that he wanted to be her friend was just a nice way of saying that he wanted to have all the fuckin' privileges with none of the boyfriend responsibilities.

"So, basically," she continued. "What you're saying is all you can give me is dick? Doesn't that literally make you an 'ain't shit nigga' through your actions?"

With a sheepish expression on his face, Nico turned to look at her, not really knowing what to say. It wasn't all he wanted to give her, but all he could give her. He didn't feel equipped to give her much more. Honestly speaking, he'd never planned to feel for her the way that he did. If he had, he probably wouldn't have fucked with her in the first place. Brooke popping into his life had instantly fucked up the game.

"Both this and that can be true. I can be a good nigga who act like I ain't shit sometimes. Just depends on how you interpret it. It doesn't mean I don't care about you. It just means I'm still learning. I'm a slow cooker."

She frowned, jerking back her neck. "Nigga, what? Ain't nobody talking about no motherfuckin' food! I'm talking about my feelings and you're worried about your stomach. As usual, the only person Nico is concerned with is his damn self."

"Nah, shorty, listen," Nico said, sighing as he shook his head. "It just means I haven't grown into the man I need to be for you yet. I'm still figuring this shit out, but I won't let myself be there for you in that way until I can figure that side out and be the man I need to be."

Brooke stared at him blankly, not at all moved by his little speech. Who did he think she was? One thing for sure, she wasn't January. She wasn't new to the games that niggas played and she'd be damned to sit around being faithful and loving to a nigga who wasn't doing the same to her.

"I understand you're getting yourself together and that's cool. We all need to grow, learn and all that other shit. The thing is, I'm not going to sit around, be loyal, waiting for you while you play fuck boy games."

"Girl, I am a *grown ass woman,"* Brooke shouted, trying to ready herself into convincing Onyx about something that she already knew was a bunch of bullshit. "I know how to act in public and can't nothing a nigga does bother me anyways. Nico can't push my buttons like he thinks he can. Trust!" She lifted one finger in the air for extra emphasis. "Your brother is fine but he ain't that fine. I ain't bout to be one of those 'lose my mind over a nigga' kinda bitches."

"I CAN'T BELIEVE this nigga has the *audacity* to be in this club, where he knows I'm going to be, with another bitch on his lap!" Brooke fumed, cutting her eyes over at where Nico, Legend and some drunk and dizzy looking Becky were seated. Becky, who looked more like a Karen from how she was ordering the staff around, was seated on Nico's lap, a clear statement that she was claiming her as her own. And he wasn't making any attempt to make her move: a clear statement that he was okay with being claimed. And for a nigga who said he didn't want to be tied down and wanted to allow things to progress naturally, wasn't nothing free and natural about the shit that Brooke was witnessing.

"I knew you were on some bullshit earlier when you said y'all were fine," Onyx said and dropped her forehead into her hand. Lifting her eyes, she stared at her friend who was trying her best to look in any direction but the V.I.P. She was hiding it well, but she could see the hurt in Brooke's eyes very clearly.

"Brooke, trust me, don't get mad at this shit. Nico has thing with Dru that's backwards as hell. I can't stand the bitch and neither can Legend but Nico keeps her around because she's easy. That's all. She's not a challenge and she lets him do whatever the fuck she wants to do. She's a doormat in all ways." Brooke didn't seem convinced but Onyx was more than certain of what she was saying. She knew all about Dru and, yes, she was disappointed in Nico for still fucking with her because she'd thought Dru was a long lost and non-factor issue, but she still knew that she would never be the woman who earned her brother's heart. Nico was just lazy when it came to relationships. He worked hard at everything else, but he liked lazy love.

"They look pretty cozy though," Brooke said, still struggling to keep her attention from Nico and his new conquest. "I mean, she don't look like a doormat to me. She looks like the main while I'm sitting here like a side chick."

"Looks can be deceiving," Onyx replied, giving her a sideways look. "She's definitely a doormat. And a nigga might want to *walk* on a doormat but they for damn sure don't want to *wife* one. Don't get mad. He's just fucking up right now. Trust me on this."

That said, Onyx stood up to walk backstage and complete her set, making sure that she caught her brother's eye in the process. Lifting her hand, she flipped him her middle finger, discreetly so that only he could see it. What he was doing was fucked up. She had given him her blessing to come at her friend—something she never did—and now he was playing games. And with Dru of all people. Her beauty and superficial charm was literally all that Dru had to offer. She was one of the most empty-headed women that Onyx had ever met and she didn't understand how her brother could ever even have a conversation with her. It wasn't until she visited him once when Dru was staying with him and realized he *didn't* have conversation with her and that's how he managed it. All Dru did was exist and take up space. She was all beauty and no brains. The exact opposite of the women Nico had been raised to love, which is why Onyx knew whatever he had going on would never last. Dru wasn't his equal, she was his opposite.

"And now, I want to introduce to you all someone that I already know many of you know. The lovely songstress and main event of every Friday night, Onyx!"

The announcer said her name and Onyx sashayed her way to the mic with all the grace and sway in her hips that God had gifted to women. The lights dimmed and she peered out into the crowd, ready to sing her first song of the night: a ballad about falling into good love after suffering through a toxic situationship. It seemed like the perfect choice for the night, given the present circumstance. And when she saw a man approach her table, whispering a few words in Brooke's ear that made her smile, Onyx's lips spread into a grin as well as the man took her seat, pulling in his chair closer in to Brooke.

The piano accompaniment began, and she slowly cut her eyes over to V.I.P. to glance at her brother. It was a pure visual of poetic justice. Nico hadn't missed a beat. He'd displaced Dru from his lap and was leaning forward, his eyes laser-focused on the man who was stealing Brooke's attention.

Don't be mad now, baby bro, Onyx thought, opening her mouth to start her first song. *This is the situation you created. Now live in it.*

"WHO THE FUCK is this ballsy ass nigga sitting all up in Brooke's face?" Nico asked, sneering down at her table. "And look at her gullible ass. Just sitting there laughing it up. I'mma have to go down there an holla at dude."

"Nigga, what?" Legend asked, laughing. "Holla at dude for what? Because he's doing some shit that you don't wanna do? You literally just was talking about how you can't deal with her right now. How it's too much and she put a spell on you. Now what? You back catching feelings?"

"Nah," Nico said, folding his arms across his chest as he sat back in his chair. "I ain't never catching no motherfuckin' feelings. So you can cancel that."

"Yeah, I'll cancel it when you cancel that fuckin' attitude. Big grown ass motherfuckin' baby."

"Nigga, fuck you."

"You're angry because she won't wait... while you keep fucking around with Dru?"

A sheepish expression crossed Nico's face. He hadn't thought about it quite like that before. All he knew was that he wasn't ready. He wasn't ready to commit to one woman yet. He wasn't ready to be the man that Brooke needed. But he also wasn't ready for anyone else to be that man.

He was a mix of conundrums; a puzzle he couldn't put together himself. Because, deep down, he knew that she was the missing piece, but he wasn't ready to pull her into him yet. And until then, he needed to keep his distance from her. It was much easier to reject all your 'ain't shit' qualities when you didn't have to look in the mirror.

He couldn't ask her to wait but he couldn't bear the thought of her moving on. He knew he needed her in his life.

"I can't ask her to do something I can't do. I want her to stay with me through my bullshit, but I haven't been around to help her through hers." Lifting his arm, he used the side of his hand to nudge his nose. The discomfort he was feeling was shining through. "And, the fucked up thing about it is, the reason I can't help her through her shit is because every time I'm around her, she looks at me like she's really ready to be real with me. To let go. I can see that her emotions run deep. I'm not prepared for the responsibility that comes with that. And I know she don't deserve that."

"Because deep down you know you're no different from the last nigga she was fucking with," Legend said, finally knowing exactly how Nico felt. In a way, it was how he felt when it came to January. He wasn't ready to be fully involved because he didn't trust himself to be what she needed. But at the same time, he couldn't fully let go. He couldn't refuse the love that she was intent on giving him. For that reason, they were caught in a cycle of push and pull that neither one of them could escape.

The worst thing about that? Though Nico's feelings for Brooke were genuine, on the surface that's not how they appeared. On the surface, his actions made him inconsistent. On the surface, he looked like just another low-life nigga, fucking up the vibe of another good woman. Choosing a substitute who wasn't even half of the woman he was turning down. Choosing a junkie over a queen.

As if on cue, Dru walked back over, a freshly made dirty martini in her hands.

"Hey, daddy, can I sit?" She asked motioning to his lap.

"Yeah," Nico nodded, his expression darkening. "You can sit your ass right over there." He pointed to a chair on the opposite end of their section. "Or better yet, you can go home. I'll be there soon."

"But I just got a new drink," Dru started to whine, drooping her bottom lip in a sincere pout. "I don't want to waste it."

"Take the shit with you. Don't nobody care." Nico was getting even more frustrated at this point because the man with Brooke had made his move and no longer were they just talking. They were headed to the dance floor to slow dance. And now that Brooke was standing, he could fully see the way her shape filled out the silk red dress she was wearing.

Shit, she's applying major fuckin' pressure, he thought, practically eye-raping her with every step she made.

Running his hand over his face, he realized that, at some point, he had a choice to make. He wasn't ready to be the man Brooke wanted him to be. He wasn't ready to commit to anyone. But at the same time, he wasn't ready to let her go. He couldn't stomach seeing her with another man and it was taking everything in him not to step to her and break up whatever situation she had going on with this new nigga she was giving her attention to. At the same time, he knew he couldn't. It wasn't his place. He wasn't her man. And it was his fault because he'd made it that way. Still, it wasn't something he felt like he could fix just yet. He couldn't go to her unless he was ready to do shit right. For some reason, his feeling with her was that he needed to do this right or not do it at all.

"Fuck it, I'm going home," Nico said, standing in his agitation. "This shit is whack tonight."

"Damn sure is," Legend replied. "And I'm not talking 'bout the club either. You sucker for love ass nigga," he added, teasing his cousin with a smile.

"Man, nigga, fuck you," Nico grumbled, batting his hand at his cousin. It was easy doing the teasing until the shoe was on the other foot.

"Yeah, I would say the same, my nigga, but I'mma let Dru do the honors. Since that's the chick you going home with, I guess that means she be treating you right."

Cutting his eyes away from glaring at Brooke and the man who he was calling 'the ugly ass motherfucka' in his mind, he looked at Legend with a state just as piercing.

"I hate you, cuz. Don't call me no more when you need shit," he said.

Legend laughed and leaned back on the leather seat, placing his arms behind his head. "Yeah, yeah, nigga. I'll see your sensitive ass tomorrow for sparring practice."

"Aight, bruh," Nico replied, lifting two fingers in the air. "Peace."

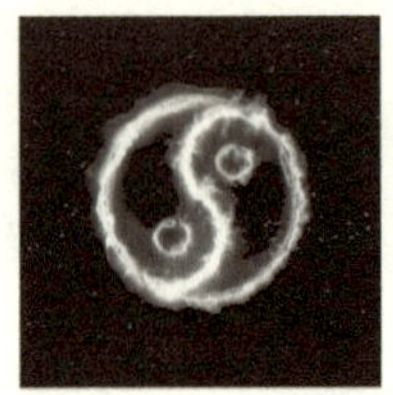

APOLOGY NOT ACCEPTED.

"WHERE YOU WANT ME TO PUT ALL THIS STUFF?"

Lifting his head, Legend didn't immediately say a word but pointed down the hall towards his bedroom.

"Outside on the balcony," he added once he was able to force the words out.

The battle inside of him was the reason for the delayed communication. On one hand, Legend was telling himself that it made things easier on him to keep January happy. On the other hand, he felt like it made him a soft ass nigga.

January was the type who loved being outside. She wasn't the kind of girl who needed much; just a little sunlight and nature was all it took to change up her mood. That fact about her made Legend curious about her and at the same time, confused as hell. Most chicks could be moved with little effort. But he couldn't come at January with little effort. She was raised by a nigga who did the most to make a point, so though she liked the little things, she wasn't impressed by simple shit.

"A'ight, boss," LeCrae said. He was part of the security team of men Outlaw had enlisted to be stationed outside of Legend's apartment building to keep watch. They weren't on record as official members of the *BBM*, which allowed them to work under the radar.

Sighing, Legend watched LeCrae, a man with the size and build of a linebacker, waist adorned with all types of high-powered weapons, knives, and other tools one would use to kill someone in many different, very imaginative ways, walk towards his room balancing two potted plants and roses in his arms. He, and the rest of the crew helping him, was the highly trained, special ops type. They'd been taught how to kill a man with things like a toothpick and popsicle sticks. Which made it crazy as hell that Legend had them shopping for sunflowers, daisies, and puff pillows.

"I think that's the last of it," LeCrae said about a half hour later. "We got O.T. out there arranging everything. Ain't no telling when that nigga will be done. He taking his time, talking 'bout he don't want no help because we messin' everything up. Real talk, I think that nigga enjoyin' that shit."

LeCrae began to laugh and Legend even let out a few chuckles himself before extending his hand out to LeCrae's. They bumped fist and LeCrae gave him a quick nod before turning around to leave.

"We'll be outside. Ready if you need anything."

"'Preciate you, homie," Legend told him as he watched him leave.

Brushing his hand over the top of his head, he turned to walk back down the hall, pausing for a moment to look towards January's room. He couldn't help but wonder what version of her was waiting for him on the other side of the door. He loved her more than he loved himself but he would be lying to say that she wasn't difficult to deal with.

January was stubborn *as hell.* Emotional *as hell.* Fucking annoying *as hell.* All she wanted was for him to show that he cared about her ass, but all she did was ignore all the obvious signs. She brought him chaos but he still found himself coming back to her as if he couldn't stay away. She was chaotic, in the most gorgeous way.

Regardless to what might come out to meet him on the other side of the door, Legend was there every day with food that he already knew she would refuse to eat until she was alone. He couldn't understand it. So many women in his life would've wished for him to treat them with half the respect and decency they deserved. But when he finally found a woman who made him want to do better for her, she simply didn't give a damn.

"I think I got everything like I want it," O.T. said as soon as Legend walked outside to the balcony area connected to his bedroom.

"Thanks, man, I appreciate it," Legend replied, pulling a few bills out of his pocket.

O.T. put his hands in the air. "You know I can't accept that, man. I'm just doing my job. And to be real, I should be thankin' you," he added with a smile.

"Oh?" Legend asked, cocking his head to the side. He hadn't considered when he asked the men to help him design a space for January that he'd get this response from any of them.

"Yeah, man," O.T. began. He rubbed his hands together and let out a sigh. "I got a thing with decorating shit. You should see my crib. Most people think my wife put it together but nah, that shit is *laid* and it's all 'cause of me." A broad smile rose up in his face as he looked somewhere in the distance behind Legend as if he were lost in his thoughts. "My mama always said that in another life, I must've been an interior decorator or some shit. Who know? The streets got me this time around though. So I don't get to do shit like this much but I appreciate the times when I do."

That said, O.T. came over and gripped Legend in a hug, thanking him again for the opportunity and left. Something about that conversation with O.T. had gripped Legend's mind and he was still thinking about it even as he'd left out the front door.

Walking to the outside balcony, he took a look at the final product and almost cursed to himself. O.T. *definitely* surpassed his expectations on how he'd completed everything. He'd enclosed the area in blinking fairy lights, had candles displayed everywhere, along with pillows, blankets and even a small decorative fireplace to set the mood. It was like a wonderland.

No way she can be mad at me after this shit, Legend thought, rubbing his hands together.

He knew after the other day that he had some making up to do and, for some reason, he just didn't think 'I'm sorry' would cut it. Not only that, he *wasn't* sorry. Deep down, he felt like he'd done the right thing because he was protecting her for himself. What made women bitter was when a nigga sold them a dream but delivered them a nightmare. In his present situation, he only thing he was capable of delivering was a nightmare. He didn't want to take January's love only to offer her that.

"January, you are strong and beautiful. Don't ever let any dumb ass nigga in the world make you think differently."

Yes, but what's the point of being beautiful and strong when you're still never good enough?

It wasn't what she'd said then, but it was what she felt now.

Wiping tears from her eyes, January lay in bed with her eyes to the ceiling thinking on the highlights of some conversations with her father from after the accident happened. In those moments, he'd stopped everything and made it his personal mission to bring her love and light every day. His only need was to make sure that she smiled, that she never felt alone, that she knew how important she was.

Thinking on it now, she felt like her father took the shooting personally. He knew that it happened because of the path he'd chosen for his life and how that affected his family. She never blamed him for it but he blamed himself.

"January? I have something to show you."

Her heart both lifted and ached at the sound of Legend's voice. Incredible how the heart literally showed her conflicted feelings. She didn't know how to feel. She was happy to be around him but wanted to run from him at the same time.

Life just sucks sometimes.

Rubbing her eyes, January rose from the bed and walked to the door slowly, knowing she looked like shit. She took a second to pause and glance in the mirror, considering whether she should fix herself up a little better, but then shrugged. What was the point of even trying? He didn't want her anyway.

As soon as January opened the door, Legend's voice caught in his throat. As always, she was beautiful as hell and his body reacted instantly to being in her aura. But his muscles tensed at the sight of her swollen, puffy eyes. She'd been crying. Somehow, he knew her sensitive ass had been in the room having a total fit, but seeing the evidence right before his eyes made his chest tight. He felt guilty about being so distant, staying away so long. He knew that it was getting to her but he didn't know any other way to protect him from himself than to not be around. Whether January believed him or not, he wanted her. But, unfortunately, she wasn't his to have.

"What do you want?" she asked, crossing her arms in front of her chest.

And just like that, his mood shifted. She was so *fucking* cute. Standing in front of him pouting like a baby about to throw a tantrum.

Pampered princess, he thought, forcing himself not to smile.

"Come with me. I want to show you somethin'," he said, softening his tone.

Legend watched as she eased her eyes back to him, taking a moment to look him up and down, as if sizing him up. He knew what she was thinking; he knew he had her mind fucked up, running from hot to cold.

"I'd rather not go with you." She turned her back to him, looking away.

Legend mused, pausing for a second to enjoy the view.

She is such a fuckin' baby.

She wanted him to react to her fire with fire. Deep down, he felt like she liked his aggression in a way. She tested him until he brought it out, seemingly losing control. She knew that if she could get to him in that way, it meant she'd won.

I'll give her that, he thought, shrugging to himself.

Steeling his expression, he tightened his tone and stared hard at her until she couldn't help but turn back to him.

"I didn't ask you what you'd rather not do," he said, peering down at her from under a partially wrinkled nose. "Now come on."

Turning around sharply, Legend didn't stop to see whether or not she was following behind him because he already knew she would. January had a lot of attitude, but she could tell when he was done playing around.

After huffing loudly, he heard her fall in step behind him, her reluctance showing clearly in every heavy stomp she laid. He led her across the hall towards his room and then hesitated for a second before opening the door. He couldn't even believe he was doing this, to be honest. But lately, it seemed like January had him doing a lot of things he wouldn't normally do. Pushing all the alarming thoughts from his mind, telling himself that he was soft as hell, Legend sucked in a deep breath and pushed the door open.

"Whoa..." he heard her let out behind him.

He gritted his teeth, not turning around to watch her take her time looking at every detail of his bedroom. He'd never allowed any woman in this room—not even this property. Of all his residences, this was the only one he truly called home. It was sacred in a way, and the fact that he was opening it up to January made him feel like he was standing in front of her naked. Exposing all the intimate details of his life.

"Your room is dope," January said. Legend turned to see her standing with her hands behind her back, nodding her head slowly while still looking around.

"This isn't what I brought you here to see."

With wide eyes, she brought her focus to him and he nudged his head to the side, pointing towards the balcony at the other end of his room. Her eyes widened even further, this time in complete disbelief at what she saw.

"Oh my god…" She crept slowly towards the balcony doors and then stopped short, looking back to him. "You did this... for me?" she asked.

Shrugging, Legend placed his hands into his pocket and shrugged.

"Well, all that pink shit damn sure ain't my style."

He followed her out the sliding glass doors to the outside space, giving her time to run around and 'ooh' and 'ahh' at it all.

"Thank you, Legend," January said, bowing her head. "I…" she paused, trying to find the right words to say. Her feelings were still so conflicted. "I appreciate the thought."

"So that mean we gon' stop fighting this war we been in?"

Wrong question. Legend peeped it as soon as he saw her expression shift.

"If this is your version of an apology, then apology not accepted," she said, folding her arms in front of her chest. "This is a nice thought but it doesn't *solve* anything Legend. It doesn't solve the fact that you know everything about me and I barely know anything about you. You left me the other night and… I still don't know why. You don't talk. I don't *know* you."

Feeling herself get emotional, January turned her back to him before he could see the tears gathering in her eyes. She couldn't do this any longer. Maybe it was better in her room. Being around him was too hard.

Stepping forward slowly, he walked up behind her and stopped right before merging into the curve of her ass. Legend felt the need to put her at ease. He didn't have the words to say to her—he was a man of action. Words weren't his expertise. And, in his opinion, niggas who talked too much were comfortable telling lies and couldn't be trusted. He couldn't see himself being the type to just spill his feelings for her like the men did in romance movies or books. But he hoped she could feel his love for her when she touched him and see it in his eyes.

"Look at me. You *do* know me."

She shuddered, feeling his breath on the back of her neck. And then, in the next moment, his body pressed against hers and her inhibitions fell to the wayside.

As he dipped his head into the crook of her neck, she felt his inhale as he took a breath. Tingles exploded in her belly and she let out a heavy exhale. Not because she needed to let out air; she needed to release the pressure. Legend had her on another level, thinking of wanting to do things she never thought she would want to do ever before. At least, not with anyone like him.

This isn't love. Love doesn't exist. This isn't love. Love doesn't exist, she chanted the lies in her mind, reminding herself of the one thing she'd told herself over a million times in her lifetime. Definitely at least a thousand times since Legend had trapped her here.

Love didn't exist. At least for *her*, it didn't. It was something she'd always felt and had apparently forgotten somewhere along the way between seeing him again and getting a quick reality check once she realized she'd been getting played.

January felt his grip on her wrist weaken, and she knew it was time to make her move. He thought he had her right where he wanted her—back in his clutches, available for his every beck and call, willing to be his whatever in exchange for whatever. Only so he could leave her high and dry again when he realized that she wasn't who he really wanted.

No way.

"Get off of me," she snapped, as she snatched away. Whirling around to face him, she delivered one final order straight to his face. "And don't ever touch me again unless I give you permission to."

Before he had a chance to react, she was out of his reach, out the door, and out of his room. The only thing left was to get out of his life so she could fully and completely get him out of hers.

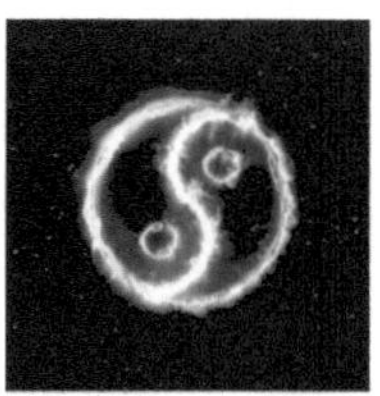

BLAST FROM THE PAST.

"Let me apologize in advance… I been smokin', so I'm movin' a little slow."

Laughing a little, Legend continued putting on his boxing gloves as Nico stood on the other side of the gym doing the same. Normally, he didn't spar in the middle of the day, but he had a need to blow off some aggression.

"You good, fam. I really just want to get a quick work out in before some moves I gotta make later. We ain't gotta be here long."

Nico seemed to be good with that, nodding as he finished strapping his gloves before securing his mouthguard. They had been boxing since the age of three, meeting each other in the ring and going at it as if they weren't even family. Their fathers were brothers, and one lesson that was pounded into their skulls from the day that they were born was that family was above everything.

Legend's uncle Murk was always by his father's side when they ran the streets, shooting any and every nigga who even bothered to think that he could try them. Nico grew up to be the same for Legend. Truthfully, Legend didn't need a shooter because he could hold his own. But Nico was always around and wouldn't have it any other way. They were raised to be soldiers; there was only one time in Legend's life when he was involved in some street shit and didn't have Nico by his side. The years he was working for Outlaw.

Legend's father and Outlaw never got along. And anybody who knew enough about the two of them could easily see why. Both were bosses, neither one took orders from anyone other than themselves, and both had an ambitious goal that included having every major city answering to them and them alone.

Head-to-head, they were absolute equals in every way, having so many similarities that the shit was crazy when you really thought about it. Both were the youngest of a crew of brothers who owned their cities when it came to street shit: Miami for the Dumas brothers and New York City for Outlaw and the Murray crew. Though the youngest, each one was the unofficial leader, the hot head of the crew, but also the most respected, most infamously adored, and the ones known as the 'loose cannons.' If they didn't have the same goals and could put their egos aside enough to work together, they could probably be best friends.

Unfortunately, neither one of them was having that. They were too alike.

Because Outlaw was married to a Federal judge with a father-in-law who was the governor of Georgia, he and the Murray brothers had a clear advantage over the Dumas when it came to claiming territory. Once he had a hand in the political arena and was able to take command of the lawmakers and the police force in every major city through his family connections, it was curtains for the war brewing between the Outlaw and the Legend. Legend's father had no choice but to admit that he'd lost, and Outlaw had won.

But, of course, Legend, Sr. wasn't about to do that. He was never one to lay down without a fight. Hell… he wasn't one to lay down *period.*

Even though it was obvious that Outlaw was the victor, and the Dumas were severely outnumbered when it came to holding on to their territories, Legend, Sr. refused to give up Miami. For him, that was *his* city, and the only way he would give it over was over his dead body.

Blood wars went on between the Murrays and the Dumas all during what became known as *Blood Summer*, three months of murders and bloody messages sent from one team to the other, as attempts to force each team to give in. So much chaos ensued that it became bad publicly for Outlaw, who was trying to flip his public image as Janelle was more and more in the public eye.

Therefore, a truce was made: The Dumas Brothers could keep control over Miami and Outlaw wouldn't threaten their control of the city for as long as Legend, Sr. lived, and Legend, Sr. wouldn't attempt to spread his control into any other cities.

The second the truce was formed, all the violence stopped. Outlaw's team retreated from the city and life went back to normal. However, though Legend, Sr. agreed at the moment, as time went on, Legend, Jr. watched his father become increasingly angry over the fact that Outlaw was living the life that he'd dreamed of for himself. His hatred for Outlaw really came from his deep-seated jealousy.

By the time Legend was thirteen, Outlaw had formed the *Black Bag Mafia* organization and was running shit all around the world. He didn't deal with drugs, the Murrays never really did, but with the formation of the *BBM*, a powerful organization consisting of the most powerful Black families around the world, they didn't have to.

They worked behind the scenes like the Black illuminati, making laws, under the table deals, and sharing top-secret information making them untouchable while also all-powerful. They were like gods. However, their overall message was to make life better. Just like how the Murrays used to rob major corporations back in the day in order to share the wealth with the Black community and better the neighborhoods in which they lived, they did the same thing now but on a broader scale.

Through force and fear, they made sure that equality for all was a right. Life changed drastically for Black people everywhere and, in turn, it changed drastically for the entire world. The days of injustice where Black men and women would get shot for no reason by the police, who would receive no consequences for their actions were over. The *BBM* took care of all of that and more.

For this reason, Legend's personal views were more in line with the mission of the Murrays. Though he was born a Dumas, he secretly had a dream of being part of the *Black Bag Mafia* from the second it was formed. He felt like there was more to life than living for violence and selling drugs. His father used to have dreams of helping the community, but every day Legend saw his jealousy and hatred for Outlaw turn his father into someone different and more malicious.

Legend, Sr. had a greed for power, and it seemed like he would go at it using any means necessary. He didn't give a fuck about the community anymore; he was only in it for self. He'd rather spend his money on material things to prove that he was just as good as Outlaw rather than to understand the reason Outlaw had those things was because of how much he enriched the lives of others.

By the time Legend was thirteen, he convinced his parents to let him stay with his grandmother in New York City, and he secretly joined the *Black Bag Mafia* by first becoming a street runner and then working his way up. By eighteen, he had sailed up through the ranks, becoming part of Outlaw's personal team of hittas and became something like his protégé. With Outlaw not having a son, it was an unspoken notion that he was training Legend up to take over and run the *BBM* for him when he was of age.

However, all that went down the drain the day that January was shot.

. . .

"I STILL CAN'T BELIEVE you doin' this college shit even with all the other bullshit we got going on now," Nico said, wiping the sweat from his face with a towel.

The two had just finished up doing some light work and were sitting on the bench relaxing for a minute before hitting the showers.

"I'm just tryin' to give my mama somethin' to be proud about," Legend shot back, shrugging.

Nico turned to him, his mouth twisted as he shook his head. "Aunty knows the deal. She knows what the hell she married into. You can't tell me the only reason you decided to take up college this year was for her benefit. So, what's really up, nigga?"

Legend laughed a little as he stood, tossing his own dirty towel into one of the bins to his side. Nico was his cousin and pretty much his only real friend in the world, but beyond that, he could read Legend like a book. He always knew when Legend was holding back on something, even though he didn't do that often. The last time he held back from telling Nico anything was when he had gone to New York City and was working with Outlaw.

"I already told you what it was: It wouldn't be a bad thing to take a couple classes and figure out what else we're good at. I don't plan on doing this street shit forever and I know you don't."

"How you figure?" Nico joked, calling me out on my bullshit. "Me and you are made for this shit. Ain't too much else available for niggas like us to do."

Standing up, Nico walked up beside Legend and they both began taking strides towards the lockers to shower up and get ready for the night. The night was like daytime for men like them; it was when they really went to work. When the sun went down, it was time for them to clock in.

"That's bullshit. You only think that because we ain't never considered nothing else. I'm a Magician, nigga. I can do any motherfuckin' thing I want to." He grinned while playfully beating his chest. Nico laughed.

"Real shit though," Legend said, speaking in all seriousness. "I don't see myself doin' the same shit over and over for the rest of my life. At some point, it's time to change."

To that, Nico responded by looking at his cousin like he had grown a third eyeball on the top of his head. He wasn't sure if he was ready to consider pulling out of the game yet. In Nico's mind, he hadn't even come close to making a name for himself. He was still on some small shit and taking classes was unnecessarily detouring him from where he really needed to go.

Legend couldn't blame him. Like his father, Nico loved the thrill of the fast and dangerous life. Nico lived for it. But things were different for him. Legend didn't like doing shit just for the sake of doing it. He felt the need for a bigger purpose when it came to what he chose to do. He wasn't reckless for the sake of being reckless.

His mom always said that he was an old soul: one of the ones who had been here many times before, and that was the reason that he never really did the teenage shit that other kids did. He didn't give a fuck about prom, flexing on niggas just to get the attention of some broad he didn't give a damn about, buying shit just to please the next motherfucka… none of that mattered to him.

Legend's mind was always on building up his own shit, stacking money and buying shit—not for anyone else—but because he wanted to get it. Now that he had accomplished all that. He'd built wealth, lost it all and built it again, but now that he had all the material shit back, it was bittersweet because he knew it wasn't lasting. He could lose it all again in the blink of an eye. And it was at that moment that he realized money, power and respect didn't make him feel any different when he was in his home alone. He was ready for something new.

With a sigh, he turned the knob for the shower and as the hot water thundered against his body, Legend closed his eyes and was greeted by the sight of January's face in his mind's eye. The vision of her soft, milk-chocolate skin, gentle, expressive eyes, and intoxicating curves gave him the exact reaction he didn't need in that moment. Not from her, anyways. Still, he couldn't fight away the fact that his attraction to her was strong. She wasn't even around and was able to tug at his mind in a way that he couldn't explain. His entire reason for making Nico come out to spar with him was to get her off his mind, and yet, here she was again, deep in his thoughts.

"This is some bullshit," Legend thought, running his hands over his eyes, pressing hard as if that would push away the sight of her from his mind.

He rushed through a shower, dried off, and changed into his attire for the night, but the thoughts of her in his mind remained. Obviously, he was going to need something more than a few rounds in the gym to get her off his mind.

"Aye, you sure you don't wanna roll with me tonight? I ain't stayin' out late. Just long enough to clear my head. Let off some steam, ya know." Nico shrugged, placing his duffle bag on his shoulder.

It was as if he'd read Legend's mind. He could use something to clear his mind.

"I might join you for a lil' bit," he said as they stepped out of the building.

There was a chill outside. A light breeze brushed past Legend's nose and in his next inhale, he was fully convinced that he smelled January's perfume in the air. He stopped short so suddenly that Nico smashed into him from behind.

"The fuck?"

His hand went to his side, grabbing at the pistol he had stashed there. It was habit. They were shooters and it was a natural reaction to any type of alarm.

"Nah, you good," Legend told him, his eyes still scanning the parking lot. Besides them and a couple of guys coming in for practice, there was no one there.

Nigga, what the fuck kinda bullshit you on? Legend thought, trying to bring himself back to his senses.

He was buggin'. January was so heavy on his mind, she had his ass hallucinating and shit. He had to do something to balance this shit out.

"You sure you good?" Nico questioned, his hand still gripping the piece at his side, ready for whatever if it called for it.

"Yeah. I'm good." Squaring his jaw, Legend pulled the strap of the duffle bag higher up on his shoulders. "I just thought I forgot something."

"Next time, you gotta say that shit," he replied, laughing a little. "I thought somebody was tryin' to creep us. I was 'bouta light it up like fireworks in this bitch."

There was humor in his tone, but he wasn't joking. Legend glanced his way and happened to pick up on the disappointment in his face. He knew the exact reason for it. The worst thing in the world for a shooter was to snatch up his weapon and not end up having to use it.

"You always ready to light it up like fireworks in this bitch," Legend replied. "Ain't nothing new."

There was a sense of thrill that came with being involved in a shootout. It was like experiencing the highest of highs, and they chased that level of excitement like it was a drug. For them, being able to bust shots was like a junkie injecting heroin straight into the vein. In fact, they *were* addicts, but people had no idea. Murder and mayhem just happened to be their drug of choice.

Legend was fucked up in the head that way. Nico was, too. It was an indisputable fact that they'd learned to live with and accept over time. Legend's insanity was easy to live with because it was so easy to blend in. Not because he tried to hide it, but because people were slow as hell. They didn't bother to look below the surface to really analyze anything.

And *that* was the exact kinda shit that made it so fuckin' easy for people like him. They lived in the information age, but the majority of the motherfuckas in the world still managed to be more brain dead than ever before. The average person spent half their time filling their minds with bullshit to the point that they couldn't decipher the truth if it slapped them in the face.

Take Legend, for example. He was brutally honest. Not because he had some moral code that he chose to follow. It was because he didn't care about anyone enough to put energy behind coming up with a lie. What was the point of it? Lying was what you did when you cared what people thought. And he most definitely didn't give a fuck what anyone thought about him.

If asked, Legend told people exactly who he was. He was a hitta. A monster. The devil's spawn. He didn't bat an eye when he was given the order to lay someone down for all eternity. There was an empty voice in his chest where his heart should've been. Not a block of ice —it was literally like a black hole. He'd learned how to turn off his emotional switch by the time he was thirteen years old, and by the time he hit sixteen, the ability to cut it back on had been taken away for good.

He zombied his way through life without a care in the world. He didn't even care if he died. Outlaw always told him that, by some odd twist, his lack of care for his own survival was the exact reason why he survived. It was a quality he saw in Legend that he'd been apologetic about. He'd groomed Legend to be a soldier, but he'd never meant for him to lose my soul. After Legend, Outlaw changed up the rules, making it a violation for anyone under the age of eighteen to be brought into BBM. He could see how being brought into the mafia lifestyle at such a young age had permanently changed something inside Legend. He didn't want to have any more lost souls on his conscience.

"Damn," Legend muttered, pulling up to the lounge that he was meeting Nico at.

The first person he saw as soon as he looked towards the front entrance was someone he had vowed not to deal with anymore. Someone he hadn't seen in a while and probably the last woman on Earth he could have asked to see right then.

He cut off the engine at the exact moment that his cell began to ring.

"What's up?" he answered, still staring at the person who represented one of the darkest moments in his past.

"You see her?" Nico's voice came in through Legend's speakers. He glanced to his right, just as Nico pulled in beside him. Nico's eyes darted from Legend's to the front of the club pointedly, and Legend nodded his head.

"Yeah, I saw her as soon as I pulled up."

"She ain't never been here before," he said, shrugging. "Not on any night that I have."

Legend didn't respond to that. Jessica was someone from his not-too-distant past. She wasn't an ex—he didn't have any exes because he'd never had a girlfriend before. There was no place in his life for that. Women wanted a man to feel some kind of way about them: love, hate, jealousy...*something*. The only thing he could give them was indifference.

For that reason, the women Legend bothered to deal with never stayed. Once they realized that no matter how much they showed him love and dedication, it wouldn't grow a heart from their magical love dust, they gave up fuckin' with him. He couldn't blame them. He'd given up on fuckin' with himself, too.

"You wanna leave? You know how she gets."

Legend snickered at that. "Nah, fam, you know I don't run from shit."

They ended the call with Legend agreeing to meet Nico inside and once he left, Legend was again left with his thoughts.

Jessica still looked the same as she had the last time he'd seen her. The only difference being that this time she was conscious and there wasn't blood leaking from her body.

Stepping out the whip, Legend closed the door behind himself and then tucked his hands into the pocket of his hoodie as he walked to the entrance of the club where she was standing, talking with a couple of friends. They were all giggling, laughing hard, most likely over some bullshit.

Watching her, he could see the exact moment he entered her awareness. Her body jerked suddenly, and her eyes began searching throughout the dark for something she wasn't aware yet that she was looking for. The second her sight leveled with his, her muscles tightened and the smile on her face disappeared. Her eyes widened at the same moment that her bottom lip began to tremble. He wasn't shocked in the least. Worry and fear were the emotions that he expected from her, especially considering their past.

"Legend!" she gasped, eyes still stretched to the max.

"Don't say my fuckin' name."

His voice never once rose above what was normal, but he knew she heard what he'd said.

The closer Legend got to her, the more she shrunk into herself as if she were trying to disappear into her own skin. Most people never got the chance to see who he really was—not while being able to live long enough to speak about it. Most people never got access to the real him. They only saw who he appeared to be on the surface and made assumptions about the type of man he could be. And no matter how much he told them the truth, they clung to the lies in their head, saying things like "Stop playing!" or "You must be kidding!" That was the kind of world they lived in. One where people admired the cover but never bothered to open the book. If they ever took the time to, they'd see he was all fucked up inside. Beyond repair.

Jessica was the only one who ever did. Which was why he allowed her to stick around longer than most chicks he'd dealt with before. It became clear that doing so was a dumb ass decision when she got too attached. She was so desperate to make a point to herself that she felt love between them that wasn't really there. Once she realized that she'd fooled herself and he didn't give a damn about her, it was too late. Their last encounter ended with her almost dead and him nearly locked up for life for murder.

Without even turning in her direction, Legend walked right past her, towards the club's front doors. The club's bouncer was standing at the door. Seeing Legend, he gave a quick nod before stepping to the side to let him in. He didn't come here often but he was known by anyone who worked there whenever he did, so they never checked for I.D. And they knew there was no point in patting him down because he always stayed strapped.

"Good seeing you, champ," the bouncer said as Legend passed by.

He replied with a simple nod. "Good to be seen."

Typical reply for an asshole like him. Most people would just return the polite gesture nut Legend never did; he chose to be honest instead, and people never seemed to mind.

Despite the fact that he'd ignored her, purposely walking by without even bothering to look in her eyes, Legend could hear the clacking of Jessica's high heels behind him, approaching fast. It didn't take a genius to know it was her; no other chick around would have the nerve to come up to him. The permanent 'get the fuck away' expression he wore on his face stopped them in place before they ever built up the courage to try. In the few cases when any girl had, he didn't hesitate to embarrass her in front of any nearby witnesses. L.A. was a big city, but news still traveled fast, so this no longer happened often.

"Champ, she with you?" Bongo asked from behind Legend.

"Nah, but let her do what she do," he told Bongo without breaking his stride.

Nico, who was already in V.I.P., noticed the moment Legend entered the doors, and he also picked up the woman Legend had on his tail. Cutting his eyes from Legend's face to somewhere behind, Nico gave the signal that Legend was being followed. Legend nodded his head, letting Nico know that he was fully aware. Nico gave Legend a warning look before turning back to some model-looking chick he was chilling with, leaving Legend to make his own mistakes. A mistake was exactly what Jessica was.

After almost fuckin' up his life from dealing with her before, Legend swore never to deal with her on any level again. There was too much risk involved when women got too attached, and Jessica was one crazy bitch. Like fuckin' medical-grade level insane. But he was looking for something to get January off his mind, and the fact that he'd run into Jessica after all this time seemed kismet.

Taking a turn towards the back of the club, Legend popped into one of the private rooms the owner allowed him and Nico to use at their discretion. Once he'd entered, he stepped to the side, waiting. And, just as he'd expected, only a few seconds later, Jessica was knocking on the door. He hadn't closed it, but she knew better than to enter any room he was in without permission.

"Um...Can I come in?"

"Yeah," was all he said because he was too busy taking off his belt.

By the time she'd fully stepped in the room, he had finished with that and was unbuckling his pants. There was no point in faking polite for shits and giggles, both of them knew the deal.

"Close the door behind you," he ordered.

Without delay, she did just as he said.

"Legend, I—"

"Didn't I tell you not to say my fuckin' name?"

Legend paused, frowning for a minute, wondering why the hell he was even doing this shit. She hadn't even done much and was already getting on his fuckin' nerves.

"I tried to contact you after everything but didn't think you wanted me to." She paused, swallowing so hard he could see the ripple going down her throat. If everything went how he planned, in less than a few minutes he'd have his hand there, squeezing hard as he hit it from the back.

"I missed you, but I wasn't sure if you felt the same. The last time I saw you, it seemed like you really didn't care if I died."

"I didn't," he told her, being totally honest. "Still don't."

She winced at his honesty.

"Don't say that," she whispered, ducking her eyes, staring at her feet.

"It's the truth," he said, shrugging.

"It's *not* the truth."

"Trust me, baby girl, I don't give a fuck enough to lie."

She shook her head. "You can't sit there and say you didn't love me. I hurt you... that's why you're saying that."

Motherfuckas always asked for the truth but only believed what they wanted to hear.

"You can't hurt me," Legend said, chuckling as he ran his hand over his mouth, wondering why he was even wasting his time like this. "It's not possible. No need to let that weigh on your conscience."

Pulling his dick from my pants, Legend looked from it up at her, making it obvious and clear as to what was the only thing on his mind. Sex and head had always been the only things that were part of their arrangement. It was all she could ever offer because it was all he'd ever wanted when it came to her. She wanted to give him love and affection and tried to force it on him even after he told her repeatedly to save that shit for the next nigga because he didn't want it. She never did because she never believed him.

"We doin' this or not? Already wasted enough time doin' all this fuckin' talkin'."

She hesitated and he knew what was on her mind. She didn't want to say no, but she also didn't want to lose out on the chance to play a role in his life, no matter how small it was. He waited for a moment to see if she would change her mind. He didn't give a fuck either way.

"Yes... we can," she said, placing her hands under her dress to tug on her panties.

"No need to do all that, shorty. I ain't in the mood for no pussy."

She looked disheartened, genuinely disappointed about that. He didn't get chicks like her; the worse they were treated, the more they convinced themselves they wanted it. She could have plenty of niggas wrapped around her finger, but she wanted the one who didn't give a shit.

"Oh...okay," she said, walking towards him. Lowering slowly, she dropped to her knees and started to put in work.

Legend was playing with fire and he knew it, but he was desperate for something to get January out of his head. The problem was that he'd have to deal with whatever came after. Somewhere deep inside Jessica's twisted mind, the fact that he was willing to touch her at all, even if only with his dick, was a show of love. No matter what he said, did, or how much he showed with actions and words that he sincerely did not care, the insanity spiraling in her head was what she went with.

Their insanity was what had kept them together before. Neither one of them was capable of a normal, loving relationship. The difference being that Legend was fully aware of that fact and she wasn't yet. Like attracted like, and they were both broken inside. There may still be hope for her, but it was over for him. There wasn't a girl in the world that he wouldn't ruin.

Which was the exact reason he had to put some distance between himself and January. He'd already fucked her up before. He didn't want to fuck her up for good.

"You like that, daddy?"

Legend's mind slammed back to the present, thanks to the sound of Jessica's voice. He'd been so deep in his thoughts that he'd forgotten she was down there, sucking, humming, and swallowing with all her might, trying to bring life to his half-limp dick. Her use of the word 'daddy' deflated it the rest of the way. All he could think of at that point was January and her accusations that day at the bookstore. Which obviously made the next thought after that about Outlaw, and from there, this shit was a wrap. It was over before we'd even started.

Jessica wasn't a replacement for January. Not even a decent downgrade.

"Time to fall back," he said, pressing two fingers towards the top of Jessica's head to nudge her away. "This ain't workin'."

"N-no, just let me keep trying," she begged, sounding fucking pathetic.

He switched on the lights and took a step back. She was staring up at him like a deer in headlights. He could see sheer terror in her eyes.

"Just let me try to—"

"Nah, it ain't you," Legend said and took another step back out of her reach when she leaned forward, trying to grab his legs. The bitch was crazy as hell. How the *fuck* did he forget?

"I know it's not *me*," she said, smiling a little as she playfully rolled her eyes. "We always have fun together because we love each other.

But I can tell you have something on your mind blocking you. I don't know what it is, but I know it's not me."

How the hell did she put all that together?

"When I said it's not you, I meant that it wasn't you I wanted with me. I ain't attracted to you like that, Jess. Not now and not ever again."

A frown creased her face as she sat with that dose of honesty while Legend fastened his pants. Then, as if a switch had been flipped in her head, she looked up at him and smiled again.

"Well, can I just see you later?"

The desperation in her eyes was a pitiful sight to see. He'd played on it in the past, using it to his advantage because it made all the things that he wanted from her come easy. But things were different now.

With nothing left to say, he ignored Jessica's question and left the room to find Nico and let him know that he was leaving. There was no point in staying. He'd come here to avoid one woman and found another that he needed to avoid.

Outlaw always said that there always came a day when a man had to reckon for his wrongs. He said that for men like him and Legend, who had a lot of shit to reckon for, days like that could break them all the way down. In some cases, for good.

Whether it did that or not, one thing was promised. Whatever happened when it was time to atone for their sins would forever change their life. Outlaw had never told Legend how this happened in his case, but he could easily see the changes that had come from it.

For some reason, everything he'd buried in the past was being resurrected in the present moments, which only meant one thing: Legend was quickly approaching his own judgment day.

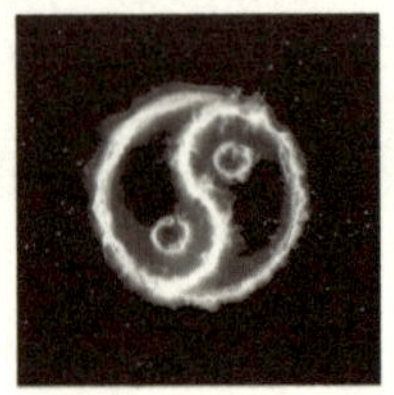

IN DENIAL.

"THERE MUST BE SOMETHING IN THE WATER—NO, SOMETHING IN THE air that makes these niggas so fuckin' inconsistent. And don't try to argue with me, because I'm fully convinced."

Pursing her lips, January couldn't help but shrug. "Trust, I'm *not* going to argue with you."

"I know." Brooke sniffed, rolling her eyes. "Because you can't. You know I'm right. They come in all aggressive, pretending they only want you and no one else, but as soon as you trip, slip, and fall into some feelings, they pull back and all the demons come out." Raising up her hand, Brooke began counting off with her fingers. "First, you find out they have commitment issues. They don't want you to be theirs but don't want you with anyone else because they have abandonment issues. They want you to be at their beck and call, always respond when they call or you'll trigger their fear. They'll say they love you but can't show you shit to prove it because they are emotionally unavailable and detached. Child, I'm just over Nico's shit." She ended her rant by falling backwards onto the bed, her long braids fanning out around her.

"Nico?" January thought, blinking hard. "I thought the two of you weren't really seeing each other. And don't you need to decide what to do about Trevor?"

"Do it look like I'mma fuck with a broke nigga? I mean, I have before. But we were broke *together*. A bitch ain't broke no more. Financial aid hit and I got bands, now. Plus, Trevor has basically decided what I'm going to do about him for his damn self. He's just not around. The only reason he even sends me a text every now and then is because he's in my apartment. He's not a boyfriend, I'm his landlord."

"True," January said, agreeing. "But you did say you needed time and space before jumping into something with Nico."

Sitting up on her elbows, Brooke looked at January and nodded.

"Yes, that's right. That's what I *said*, but that was just it—before. The more I thought about it, I was only saying it because Nico was being so fuckin' inconsistent and I figured I didn't have any other choice. Now I *know* myself. I've been practicing self-love so I *love* myself, too. And I want a nigga who can love and appreciate me the same way. I'm just at a different phase of my life."

"Well, you can't just expect things to change just because you want them to," January told her with a look that was perfectly condemning for the selfish brat she was trying to be. "You started something one way and he was with that. Now you're feeling different, which is cool, but he ain't feelin' that yet."

Brooke's face balled into a frown. "Well, I don't like it."

"Well, doesn't that make *you* inconsistent?"

"Bitch, no! It's different."

January couldn't help but laugh. Brooke was the type of person who wanted everyone to bend easily even though she refused to give an inch.

"January, trust me. It's not me, it's *him*."

"How so?" January asked for the sake of asking. She knew whatever was about to come out of Brooke's mouth would be nothing but excuses. Leaning forward, she positioned the phone in front of her face and cradled her chin in her hands.

"Because this isn't even about commitment. I'm good on that. From jump, he's been fine with just sex and *now* the nigga don't even wanna give me that. He's in and out and all over the place. Then the other day. he even hung up on me when I said that I was about to do a new moon ritual and was burning sage but wanted to know if he could come over tonight for dinner because I was cooking. Like hung right up in my face. He's just *weird as fuck.* I can't get with that."

Laughing, January couldn't help but know exactly what this was about. Brooke had just started diving into the world of spirituality, but January had been in it for a minute.

"You know men act crazy about anything chicks do that makes them think they're on that witch or voodoo shit. Just because they don't understand it. He probably thought you was going to put some blood in his food. You gotta ease into stuff like that."

"Yeah, but how about his ass got over that quick and was right over here a few hours ago after I said I was tired and we could skip the food. But then he didn't even want sex. He came over talking about watching Netflix but with *no fuckin' chill* afterwards! Like what the hell kinda sense does that. He came over here and I was all dressed in my best half-naked lingerie, and that nigga didn't even try to have sex with me!"

"Yeah, but Brooke didn't you *just* say you weren't emotionally ready for all that right now? We talked about that the other day. You put that out in the Universe and… now it seems that you're getting the support you need on sticking to it."

"Bitch, that was then, and this is now. I'm horny."

"No, that was yesterday. One day ago."

"And your point is?"

"My point is that I don't know what Nico's reasoning is for doing whatever it was that he did, but it ended up being what you said you needed. Well... when you weren't horny and had the capacity to think with a clear mind. Sometimes what you want isn't what you need."

"January, look at me!" Brooke lowered the phone to put her body on the screen. "My ass is out and my titties can be clearly seen through all this lacy shit. Do it look like I'm worried about what I need right now? All I am worried about right now is want, want, want. I want dick. And I want him to give it to me!"

January sighed. *What the hell am I going to do with her? She's my best friend and even I have no idea. So what in the world can anyone expect Nico to do?*

"Brooke, you've got a long road to healing ahead of you, but I promise not to give up on you."

"Give up on *me*? I should be saying the same thing about you!" she shot back.

January frowned and sat up. She had just decided to start polishing her toenails but changed her mind to focus in on what Brooke was trying to say.

"Come again? What do you mean? I'm all good over here."

Brooke scoffed. "Yeah right. You wanna act like me and Nico the only one with issues when you and Legend walking around here acting like you don't wanna fuck each other."

"We are *not*—"

Before January could finish her sentence, she nearly fell out in a fit of coughs, sputtering and hacking so much that she had to cover the nail polish and place it to the side.

"That's what you get." Brooke rolled her eyes indignantly. "The Universe made you choke on your lies."

"I was not choking on my lies," January said, cutting her eyes at Brooke after she finished gulping down nearly a gallon of water.

"Mmhm." Brooke's lips twisted to the side. "What were you choking on then?"

January opened her mouth to answer and then stopped short when she realized that she really didn't have one because she'd choked on... well, thin air. She couldn't even say she'd choked on her own saliva.

And then, as if she needed the sudden reminder right then, a quick image of the other night shot through her mind. Legend's lips on hers, his hands running along her thighs before he flipped her around, pressing against her from behind, teasing the skin on her neck with his teeth as he squeezed her ass.

She got hot. Her cheeks flushed and she had to press her hands against them and swallow hard to force away the fluttering feeling in her stomach.

"Yeah, you're right," January said, giving in. "I was choking on my lies."

She sulked, dropping her forehead into her palm as Brooke laughed hard as hell, finding absolute pleasure in her reluctant admission of the truth.

"Hey, don't feel bad," Brooke said with a shrug. "The first step is admitting that you have a problem." Brooke pause to sigh and shake her head. "But my philosophy when it comes to situations like this where there is a lot of pent up sexual energy is… 'why choke on the lies when you could be gagging on some—"

"Don't even say it," January interrupted placing her hand in the air.

The both began to laugh, despite the fact that Brooke's logic was all over the place, and January went back to polishing her toenails.

"The issue is that I don't want to have that problem. I just don't *want* to like him."

"Hell, why not?" Brooke asked, frowning at her through the camera. "I hear all that you're saying about the promises you made yourself and blah, blah, blah—" She rolled her eyes dramatically. "—But Legend is not a bad guy. All the crazy shit to the side, think about it."

Lifting her hand in the air, Brooke began to count off on her fingers. "He's smart, got his own money—lots of it, might I add. He's responsible, dependable, he ain't in these streets giving out community dick, he's blunt as hell so definitely not the type to have you out here looking dumb as hell, making promises he can't keep while he throws parties in your apartment every night, taking pictures and making videos to post on Instagram of him laughing and dancing with random ass hoes!"

January's eyes widened at Brooke's sudden catapult into a vent that they both knew had nothing at all to do with Legend. Taking a deep breath, Brooke crossed her legs into a poise of meditation and pinched her thumbs and index finger together, closing her eyes as she took several additional breaths.

"Whoo-sahhh... Goos-fraaa-bahhhhh," she said, finalizing up quickly before opening her eyes. "Girl, my bad. I lost myself, thinking about Trevor's dumb ass."

January laughed. "Obviously."

"But anyway," she continued. "My sudden outburst aside, the main point of this message is to tell you that you're full of shit—"

"Why thanks."

"—Legend is the kind of man that every lonely bitch with standards is waiting on, and here you are being undecided, like that sickening Chris Brown song. I'm so tired of hearing that shit. Love it, but tired of it."

January snorted out a laugh. Brooke was on one. "I'm not undecided because there is nothing to decide on," she corrected her. "Legend has not offered me anything for me to decide on. And, even if he did, the reality of all of this is that he is a liar. The only reason he was ever around me was because he was a spy for my dad."

Brooke stared at her with a lazy, "I-wish-I-could-slap-a-bitch-but-she-too-far-away" expression on her face.

"Even if that *was* true, what does it matter how y'all met? If yo' daddy was the one signing his checks, why the hell you think he gon' be loyal to you? Bitch, he ain't know you like that!"

January winced but she couldn't say shit because Brooke was kinda right.

"What your ass should be concerned with is how well that nigga kept that shit a secret! His loyalty didn't waver in the least. And that ain't the norm with most motherfuckas out here, especially when it comes to pussy." She pursed her lips and shook her head. "Most niggas out here will fold for less. You so busy being mad at Legend for being loyal that you're totally missing out on the fact that, news-flash, *his ass is loyal!* You should be happy about that shit. Loyalty is a trait you can't buy. A nigga either got it or he don't. And most of 'em out here don't."

Dropping her eyes, January took a deep breath and considered what Brooke was saying. Hell, she wasn't lying. January had had more than a few run-ins with people who were disloyal. Her father always said that disloyalty was an unforgivable action. There was a lot a man could do that could possibly be pardoned but faltering on loyalty wasn't something that could be excused. The fact that he'd placed so much trust in Legend spoke volumes about his character.

Deep down, January knew he wasn't a bad guy. She knew he wasn't a liar. Still, she couldn't understand why thinking about the circum-stances behind them meeting made her feel so betrayed.

"Logically speaking, everything you're saying makes sense," she told Brooke, shrugging. "I just—I don't know. Whenever I think about it, I just feel so mad. I feel like he betrayed me. He made me think he was someone that he wasn't."

"January..." Brooke began and then paused. January looked up at the camera and could easily see the discomfort in her face.

"What is it?"

Glancing to the side, Brooke licked her lips before letting out a breath.

"Don't take offense to what I'm about to say, but you can't blame Legend for your parents' mistakes— *your parents* lied. *Your parents* withheld the truth from you. Legend may kinda act like your dad, even kinda look like him a bit, but Legend *isn't* your father. And, even with them, from what you told me, what your father kept from you was only to protect you. You're real smart… but sometimes you got a fucked up way of viewing things."

"I know Legend isn't my dad," January replied quickly. "I wouldn't take out my issues with my father on Legend."

Brooke's expression shifted as she looked at January matter of factly. "But you kinda are," she said. "He didn't betray you. He didn't owe you shit and never pretended like he did. And, yet, you feel betrayed."

Falling silent, January retreated into her thoughts, willing herself to temporarily shove her feelings to the side. Brooke was right, even though January hated to admit it. Legend hadn't done anything. He'd never promised her his loyalty. And, according to him, when she asked him about working with his father initially, he hadn't lied. He wasn't working for him at the time. Maybe she *was* blaming him for shit he didn't do.

"Girl, I gotta call you back," she heard Brooke say. "I need to apologize to Nico."

January's eyes bulged. "What?"

Running her hand over her face, Brooke shook her head somberly.

"Trust me, I don't want to, but talking to you made me realize that I was doing the same shit. He's a decent guy and he don't owe me shit either. I've been tripping on him for no damn reason."

January laughed hard as Brooke finally came to the realization that she'd been trying to get her to see and accept forever ago.

"So you get it now, but it didn't mean a thing when I was telling you that you were your own worst enemy? And didn't you say Onyx told you that, too?"

With a suck of her teeth, Brooke shook her head.

"First of all, no, it *don't* mean anything just because y'all both said it." Her expression deadpanned. "For one, Onyx is his twin. And even though I love the girl, I don't really expect her to say shit against her brother. Those two are loyal to a fault. It's just ridiculous how much she makes excuses for him. And *you…*"

She paused, and January braced herself for whatever Brooke was about to say next. For some reason, she felt like it was going to be something that she didn't really want to hear.

"Well, I ain't trying to say that what you think don't matter, but what you think really don't matter. You're in denial your damn self."

Lying in the bed, staring at the ceiling, January allowed herself to get so lost in her thoughts that she didn't even realize it when the front door opened then shut. Her mind was so wrapped around Legend, she didn't know that he'd returned and was standing right at her open door staring at her.

Fucking beautiful sight, he couldn't help but think.

In that moment, it was clear to him that January was all he'd ever wanted. This wasn't a new revelation; it was just the first time he was allowing himself to fully accept the truth of the statement. She'd come into his life and completely wrecked shit in every way. He'd turned against his father on a renegade mission and even involved his cousin in his bullshit. For January's sake, he was aligning himself with a man who still wanted him dead. The shit was clearly insane. And he couldn't even fuck with other girls to reduce the stress of the situation. It was as if January had his mind and body on lock. What he didn't know was that she felt the same way.

This shit is crazy, they both thought simultaneously, totally frustrated with the reality of their shared situation.

Suddenly felling intrusive for watching her, Legend started to move away at the same moment that January noticed him standing there.

"Legend," she called out, stopping him. "I didn't know you were home. How long have you been there?"

He looked up into her face, feeling the need to defend himself until he took a moment to settle into the softness of her eyes. There was only warmth there; and then she lifted her hand to beckon him in, instantly making him relax. Shifting her body, she made space for him on the bed so that he could sit down. When she patted a space across from her, indicating that he should sit down, Legend's tilted his head to the side, rubbing his chin.

The hell is she up to? he thought, trying to access the moment..

"Why are you being so nice?" he questions as he finally took a seat. "You tricking me into relaxing in here so you can kill me?"

January giggled, although Legend seemed totally serious in asking that question. And as he looked at her quixotically under lifted brows, he couldn't say that he *wasn't* serious.

The fuck kinda new shit she on right now? he thought, scratching his head. Suddenly, his thoughts went to Jessica and he began to immediately feel some kind of way about considering doing something with her, even if it was just shooting his seed down her throat. There was no commitment between him and January that required him to be faithful about anything, but somehow, he still felt like her trust had been betrayed. He fidgeted in his discomfort. This wasn't a feeling he was used to feeling.

"Calm down," January said.

Reaching out, she placed her hand on his leg to pull his attention to her face. She'd simply wanted him to see that she was genuine, but what she wasn't prepared for was the fire that was awakened within her when his eyes met hers. Her chest tightened and she let out a long breath, exhaling out the fear she felt about relaxing into the passion she had inside. The feeling was intoxicating.

"Hard to stay calm with your hand so close to my dick," Legend said with a slight chuckle. It was supposed to be a joke, but when January looked down and saw the bulge in his sweatpants, she felt the full seriousness of the situation. But, instead of moving her hand away, she shifted it forward, sliding it further up his thigh until she was cupping her palm around the thickness of his hard dick.

Legend watched her with intensity, noticing the curiosity in her eyes but also the desire that lived there as well. He had a feeling she was telling him something; it was as if he could read her vibe on the wind. But it wasn't until her eyes connected fully with his that he knew what he'd felt she was saying was right.

"You sure?" he asked, giving her the chance to change her mind. He stared at her with all focus but no pressure. He needed her to tell the truth because he wouldn't be asking again.

"I'm very sure," she replied with all certainty.

That was all the assurance Legend needed.

"Wait here," he said as he stood to his feet. And before January had a chance to respond, he left the room.

I can't believe I'm about to do this.

Nervous excitement pulsing through her, January sat on the edge of the bed feeling as if she would die from anticipation. She felt light-headed, anxious even. She couldn't believe what she was about to do but knew she wanted to do it.

If any man on Earth was worthy enough to be the one for her first time, it was Legend. Regardless to what may happen between them later or what happened before, the fact of the matter was that she loved him like she never loved any other before. In fact, she felt like she would never love anyone the way she loved him ever again.

There was a supernatural nature to it that gave her a deep inner knowing that this love was one of a kind. It wouldn't happen again.

"Ready?"

She lifted her head to see Legend standing at the entrance of her door, shirtless, wearing nothing but a pair of grey shorts made of the same material as sweatpants. They left nothing to the imagination and her eyes were having a great time exploring every bit of the sight. He reached his hand out towards her, snapping her out of her mental reverie. Standing up, she walked over to meet him and placed her hand in his, following his lead.

As Legend walked to his room with January behind him, he fought to quiet his mind, silencing all the thoughts in his head that spoke against what he already knew he was about to do. Part of him felt like he wasn't worthy of this moment. He was a street nigga, a hitta, someone who had done a lot of grimy stuff in his life. What had he done to earn the honor of being with January? What kind of bad karma would come to him for undeservingly having her?

Before he knew it, a memory of a conversation they'd had before everything went crazy came to mind. It was from the night when he'd taken her to his personal gun range. He'd been so patient with her, taking his time, showing her everything she needed to know, over and over again until she was comfortable. When she hit her first target, nearly in the center, she'd looked at him with awe. He looked at her in the exact same way. Never had he ever seen anyone be able to hit a target with accuracy so fast.

"You did it," he said with a smile. Reaching out, he pinched her chin lightly, then laughed when she ducked and batted his hand away.

"Only because you're such a great teacher," she told him.

Legend chuckled and shook his head. "I ain't shit."

For him, it was just a statement, but January saw more to it than that. She could read through his words to understand what his soul felt. And this time, she didn't like what she saw there. So much pain. So much sadness. So much worthlessness.

"You're worth more than you think, Legend," she said, not a hint of a smile on her face. "You're a king. You were never meant to be 'regular.'"

January's words spoke life into him in ways that she would never know. She opened his heart; saw through the window to his soul. She didn't complete him, she showed him that he was already complete.

Pulling her into his room, he released her hand and pressed the entrance door shut, enveloping them in complete darkness, outside of the lanterns and lit candles he'd placed all around the room.

"You set the mood," January remarked with a smile as she looked around.

"It ain't shit." Legend shrugged off her words, feeling uneased by the compliment.

"No, it's everything," she replied. Then she turned to him, pressing her eyes into his and loving the depth she felt there. "You're everything."

Something about the way she said it set his soul on fire. Which, in turn, only increased his need for her. But he was trying to keep his cool. He wanted to take things slow. He *needed* to. Legend had addictions, many of them, none of them were good. All of them led to people getting hurt. It had never made a difference in his formal life before, but things were different now.

He didn't want to continue taking out his frustrations by finding pleasure in hurting the woman he was with. He didn't want to hurt January. He had to take it slow.

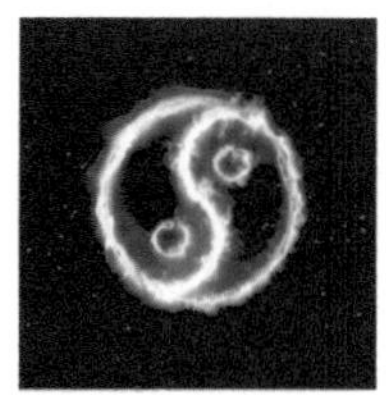

CAUGHT IN ILLUSIONS.

"You look nervous," January said, picking up on the vibe through the unsettled expression on his face.

"Looks can be deceiving."

"What about touch?" She asked.

Stepping in close to him, nearly nose to nose, January grabbed his hand and pushed it up under the thin material of her silk blouse, settling right on top of her soft, round melon breast.

Closing his eyes, Legend groaned, trying to control the awakening of his sexual nature. He wanted to take things slower. Much slower. He wanted to be the one in control. But it was starting to be clear that somehow in his hesitancy, January had absorbed his usual take charge nature. She let him have his way in every other instance, but now they were in the bedroom and she was taking charge in a way that he hadn't been expecting. And somehow that was turning him on.

"Do you like how I feel?" January asked, closing her eyes to fully enjoy the sensation. Of Legend's hand on her bare breast.

"Yes," he replied before taking the tip of her pebbled nipple between two fingers and giving it a pinch. "I do."

A soft moan escaped through January's lips and before she knew it, she'd stepped even closer to him, rubbing against the hardness of his dick, needing to pull him into her. She'd never done any of this. It would all be her first time. But in some way, it didn't feel like it would be. It felt like her body remembered being with him in an intimate way. She was simply following along with the different things her body was saying it wanted.

"January, you have to… wait. We gotta take this shit slow."

It was a warning. She could tell by his tone. But what was he warning her against? She was fully intent on having sex with him so she knew full well where all of this could lead and that was her goal.

Maybe he doesn't know that yet. Maybe he thinks I'm still unsure, she thought..

Well, in the words of Kevin Hart, you're gonna learn today.

Instead of slowing down, she took it up a notch. Throwing her arms around his neck, she pulled him to her and pressed her lips to his. She deepened the kiss as much as she could, giving him full tongue while grinding against him. Legend matched her intensity, gripping her ass and sucking on her lips. He was a gentle beast, but a beast nonetheless and she was beginning to feel it.

"I told you to fuckin' slow it down," he said through his teeth as he nibbled lightly on her lips. "You keep doing this and it'll get you in a few positions you won't be able to get out of." The nibbles turned to sucking and January was instantly brough to the brink of losing her mind.

"I can't," she panted, feeling as though she were melting from between her legs. "I want it too bad."

"Fine," Legend said, suddenly pulling back. "You don't want to take things slow?"

Confused about whether she should answer but still caught up in the throes of her passion, January couldn't speak, so she simply nodded her head.

"Come with me," he said, as if she had a choice to do differently.

"Where are we going?" she asked, frowning.

As usual, he made no attempt to answer, letting her question hang unanswered in the space between them. With his hand gripping hers, he took off walking through his larger-than-life L-shaped closet. January scanned it liberally, marveling at how organized he was. He held rows of clothes, all arranged by style, color, length, and type. Same with his shoes, rows of sneakers, loafers, and slippers all arranged according to style and color.

Pausing, he slid off the Gucci slippers on his feet and placed them neatly in an empty space. She almost rolled her eyes watching as he arranged them with precision, perfectly distanced between the shoes next to them. He was obsessive about it, that much was obvious. Now she understood the cleanliness of his space. Legend was the perfect fit for the profile of a psycho-serial killer.

Pushing apart a row of clothing, he revealed a door that she hadn't noticed before. Pressing into a space on it with his thumb illuminated a pad with serial numbers. Legend keyed in a code of numbers and the door clicked, unlocking.

Turning back to January, he reached out his hand for hers, not saying anything. She swallowed hard, took a deep breath and then laced her fingers with his, once again, following behind him. They entered a long hall that led to a single large room, glowing with a soft red ambiance. The room was about twice the size of his bedroom, but it was almost completely bare except for a larger than life, to die-for, circular bed that sat in the center. On the ceiling was a circular mirror, perfectly arranged over the bed. January's lips parted in surprise, fully understanding Legend's level of kink. And she liked it.

What gave her pause were the *other* things in the room.

On the wall, Legend had multiple contraptions, objects, and things, many of which she'd never seen before. All black, all leather, all holding the assumption that they were to be used to inflict some level of pain.

Legend's into BDSM, January thought, pursing her lips. *Why am I not surprised?*

"Drawn to anything in particular?" he asked, stepping back.

Drawn to? She wasn't sure. Curious? A definite yes.

Walking around the room, she took a moment to look at the objects hanging from hooks on the wall. Nipple clamps, batons, hand cuffs, ankle cuffs, whips, leashes, anal probes and so many other things that she'd never seen before. Sitting in the center of the room was a leather chair that had a big hole cut out in the seat area. Her eyes widened. She could only imagine what that seat was used for. A swing set hung from the ceiling. But not any swing set that she'd ever seen before. This room was like Legend's personal arcade for sex games. It partly excited her but, on another end, she didn't know what to think about it.

"You bring women in here to…"

She didn't finish the statement, but Legend could already see along what lines she was thinking.

"Don't make this about anyone but me and you," he replied, trying to silence her thoughts.

It was too late. As soon as he brought her in here, it had become about everyone *but* the two of them. All of this was new to her. She'd never done any of it. This was all stuff he'd done with someone else. Many other someone else's. And now she felt pressure that she hadn't felt earlier. It was obvious that he was used to much more than a simple sexual encounter. But that was all she knew to give—she'd never eve had sex before. Could she *really* satisfy him?

Walking to the wall, Legend grabbed the flogger, noting that it was time to swap the mood. He was losing her. She was getting caught up in other emotions and it was pulling her away from him. He had to grab her attention.

Snapping it against the floor, the whip-cracking sound made January's neck snap up. Her rounded eyes showed alarm and she teetered a bit from leg-to-leg in an innocent way that reminded Legend of a few things he loved about her.

"What's that?"

"Don't ask," he replied. "Just take off your clothes."

"But—"

Before she could say another word or think of another woman, he cracked the flogger again, making the sound even louder. He had lost control of the situation and he was trying to get it back, by use of more control. What he didn't understand was that January was different. He didn't need to get her back using control, all she needed was love. His love would have made her open up fully to it, but he was distancing her from it.

When they were in the room, love was what he was giving her, and she fully blossomed in it. It allowed her to want to give herself to him. She was aggressive even, throwing herself onto him. But in that moment, it was Legend who felt the discomfort. He wasn't used to pleasure without pain. It made him feel like something was missing. The more pleasure she provided to him, the more it increased his need for pain to level it off. It was a sickening addiction, but he didn't know what to do about it. But if wanted to really be with January, it was something he was going to have to learn.

Legend watched January from under hooded eyes. Never looking away. The intensity in his gaze only heightened her anxiety about the situation.

What the hell am I doing? she thought placing her hands on either side of her head as if it could expel some of the pressure. He'd told her to stop. He warned her that the teasing would get her in a position she wouldn't be able to get out of.

A ***few*** positions, is what he'd said actually.

But of course, hard-headed as she was, January didn't listen. And now look where she was... alone with him inside of what looked every bit like a sex dungeon, and she was about to have a fucking fit.

"Take it off."

Legend ordered her with a tone that oozed pure sexual wanting. It sent vibrations straight between her legs, awakening the most sensitive part of her. The part that Legend seemed to have complete control over. Whether he knew it or not, her body belonged to him. And from the look in his eyes, he did.

"Take it off," he repeated, this time with a growl that set her sex aflame.

January felt like she was going to burst open but still couldn't bring herself to move. She'd never been completely naked in front of a man. Lifting the flogger, he brought it down so quickly and suddenly, cracking it against the tile floor with so much force that she flinched. Something about the sound of it reminded her of a gunshot and her mouth went dry every time he snapped it. Closing her eyes, she took a deep breath and forced herself back into the moment.

"I'm not going to ask you again," Legend ordered after a few seconds. "Do it. Now."

"Aren't you gonna say 'please'?" January joked to ease the tension. Or at least to give her a bit of time to make a decision on whether she was going to stay put or run the fuck up out of there.

Legend looked up at her with a stare that could've melted bricks. Then, as if he'd just noticed she was joking, he let out a soft chuckle. However, his expression didn't change in the least, and the chuckle was more like the steely snicker that came right before Hannibal Lecter killed and ate his victims. It was like a curtain had lifted and she was gaining access to his dark nature; a side of him she hadn't seen before.

January's thoughts went silent, and she glanced up at him as he walked back over to her with his hand out and open, waiting for hers. Slowly, she placed hers in his, unable to ignore the icy-cold gaze in his black eyes. Something had changed in him but although she could feel it, she couldn't quite place what it was or when the change had occurred. But it was felt, and it set off a very different emotion inside of her. Something along the lines of curiosity mixed in with a bit of fear.

What the hell kind of stuff have you been through? She thought.

She got a little excited by the thought of some simple bondage, just like the next chick did. But this wasn't *simple.* The tools Legend had in here wasn't for a little pit-pat, and he didn't wield that whip like he was trying to give a love tap. These tools were here to beat somebody's ass. *Beat somebody's motherfuckin' ass*, in the voice of Samuel Jackson, to be specific.

Legend's eyes were trained to pick up the slightest change of emotions but the one that he could read the best was fear. And he saw it all in January's eyes. Normally, when it came to anyone, the fact that they feared him brought him excitement. It was a thrill, a rush of power to know that he was feared. He'd always felt that to fear him was to respect him. With January, he was thinking of it differently. If she feared him, it meant there was still doubt. There was still no trust. And she was different from the other girls he'd been with. He never gave a fuck about whether they trusted him or not. Long as he got what he wanted and they couldn't press charges, shit was all good. But with January, he couldn't take her in this way if she didn't trust him. He couldn't do her like that. She was different.

Fuck, he said, coming back to his senses. *I knew I should've taken things slow.*

"We can't do this," he said, expelling a heavy breath. "Not like this."

"What?" January asked, frowning. Immediately, she began to feel insecure. Was it something she did? Something she'd said? Was it something she *didn't* do? Why the sudden change?

"Is it because I'm not...experienced?" She asked, pulling together her words carefully.

Now Legend had to frown. "What?" He shook his head. "No. *Hell*, no, that's not it. You're perfect." Shrugging his shoulders he sighed once more, feeling another pain in his chest. "You just don't completely trust me yet. And I need you to trust me."

Rolling her eyes, January threw her arms across her chest.

Here we go again, she thought.

"I *do* trust you," she said and was greeted by a doubt-filled look in Legend's eyes. "Or at least I would if you would just tell me—"

"I need you to trust me enough to not have to know everything," he said with an elevated tone. "I need you to trust me enough to know that what I'm doing is for the best... of both of us. I need you to know that whether or not you think we are on good or bad times, whether things are fucked up or not, that I'm always making decisions that are in your best interest."

Coming in close, with the flogger still in his hands, Legend cracked it once against the floor. The sound of the whip cracking made January nearly jump ten feet in the air.

Snickering a little at that, Legend moved all the way into her and out his other hand underneath her face to lift her chin so that she was looking him directly in the eyes. She saw nothing in them but love. The purest kind.

"And I need you to trust me to the point that if I have you face down, ass up, strapped down in that bed, you can surrender to me completely. To the point where even if you can't move, if you're blind-folded so you can't see, and the only fuckin' thing you can do is hear and breathe, that you'd be open to whatever I decide comes next. *Anything* I decide."

January was moved beyond words. The concept was deep but in hearing it put that way, it told her a lot about Legend and what was important to him. It was beyond control and it was beyond inflicting pain. He wanted to know that whoever he was with was someone who trusted him fully and completely.

It made perfect sense. He did a lot of shit in his life that could get him caught up in many different ways. If a person doesn't trust you, you can't trust them. Scared people are the worst kind to make money with. They will get you caught up on some bullshit every time. She knew these things just from listening to her father.

"I do trust you, I just…"

She couldn't even complete that sentence because it wasn't true. She had just been going on about how he'd lied to her to Brooke. Could she say that she really let that go? The fact was, being with Legend meant that she would never know everything about how he moved. It was done that way to protect her. It was how things had to be. And she had to be okay with that. She had to stop insisting he tell her everything.

"I understand what you're saying," she replied, bowing her head. "I get it."

Although the kept his expression straight, hearing her say that made his heart smile.

"Let's just take it slow. Let things happen when it's time. And I won't bring out the hand and ankle cuffs yet," he said with a smile. Then he lifted the flogger in the air. "But I might keep this."

January laughed and nodded her head. "I'm cool with it."

Grabbing her hand, he pulled it to his lips and kissed the top. Then using it like a lasso, he whipped her into him and hugged her tightly before planting another kiss on her forehead.

'Let's just take it slow', one of the many voices in his head taunted him. *You soft dick ass nigga.*

CASTING SPELLS.

"MAN, I CAN'T FUCK WITH BROOKE NO MORE."

"Why not?"

"I know you ain't gon' believe this shit… and you better not fuckin' laugh. But… I think she put a spell on me."

"Nigga, what?!"

Staring Nico dead in his eyes, Legend waited for him to get to the punchline of what had to be some whack ass joke. There was no way Nico could possibly be serious.

"I'm fuckin' serious, cuz," Nico said, as if knowing exactly what Legend was thinking.

Pausing, he sighed heavily before pulling off his sparring gear. He hadn't been planning on telling Legend shit, though the thought had been on his mind for a minute. But his thoughts had been so scattered that he was fucking up terribly and knew he had to give Legend an explanation for it. Ever since his encounter with Brooke, thoughts of her clouded his mind in ways no other woman on Earth ever had.

The fuck is going on with me?

It was the question he was asking himself almost daily. He couldn't explain it. And he was too embarrassed to speak about it with anyone else. What *would* the homies say? It wouldn't be nothing good. In fact, he could almost hear them now, laughing and joking about how young Nico done finally got himself pussified.

This is some bullshit.

"Nigga, what the *fuck* are you talking about?" Legend asked taking a moment to sit down in a seat and gulp down some water. "Brooke ain't on that kinda bullshit. If anyone gotta worry about casting spells and shit, it's me. January stay on that witchy bullshit. Every time I walk in the fuckin' house she burning sage and shit, giving me the evil eye. Got a nigga feeling like I'm the fuckin' evil spirit she trying to get rid of when *she* the only devil in the room I see. I can't even leave food out because then I don't want to eat it later. She got me thinking she might fart in my bowl or something out of spite. And then, she randomly flip that shit on me at other times and she's nice as fuck. Brooke's easy. January's on some psycho bullshit for real."

"Damn, nigga," Nico said, taking a seat. "That's some fucked up shit."

"Ain't as fucked up as what you talkin' 'bout," Legend replied with a shrug. "January been acting crazy as hell but I ain't been thinking she been casting spells on a nigga. Just a little crazy. But spells? Nah, that's some other kind of shit."

Unable to hold back any longer, Legend started to laugh, wondering what in the world kinda craziness Nico was on. Truthfully, he was still waiting for the rest of the joke. Or at least some explanation that made sense. It wasn't until after several seconds that he realized that Nico's face hadn't folded in the least into anything even close to a smile.

"Wait… are you serious?" He asked, frowning as he stared hard at his cousin. "You really think Brooke put a spell on you?"

"Nigga, I'm serious as a heart attack. I know you been noticing since we been in here sparring that my moves ain't been as sharp and I been moving slow, doing crazy shit."

Scratching at his jaw, Legend had to nod his head. "Yeah, I ain't wanna say shit but you been fuckin' up for a minute. Definitely been off your game. I might have to get somebody else to help me train for—"

"Damn! All you gotta say is 'yes, I noticed a change'," Nico snapped. "You ain't gotta add all that extra bullshit."

"My bad." Legend raised his hands in the air, chuckling to himself.

Maybe she did put a spell on this nigga, he started to think, holding in a laugh.

He'd never known Nico to be so sensitive over anything. Definitely never knew him to start fucking up in the ring. Although he was the only one out of the two of them who formally took on opponents and accepted matches, Nico had been his sparring partner for a while now, helping him prepare for whoever he would meet in the ring. However, something had changed and Nico wasn't performing as he normally did. Legend thought that Nico was on some bullshit, partying, smoking and drinking instead of being as focused as he used to be. Apparently, that wasn't it.

"Maybe she didn't jump in circles, chant, and toss charcoal in my face, but she for damn sure put a love spell on me," Nico said, somberly. "I ain't been the same since the last time I saw her. The night after shit went wrong with at the mechanic's. I don't know what the fuck goin' on if it ain't a spell. This shit ain't never happened before."

What Nico didn't understand was that everything was energy. It may not have seemed like it on the surface but in everything in life, there was an equal give and take, whether he knew it or not. He'd chosen to take a woman's love, open up her heart, knowing full well that he didn't want to be the man that she needed him to be, he willfully decided to rob her of her peace.

Nico willfully decided to take love that wasn't his to take, knowing that he wasn't planning to stick around in any solid way. His father had warned him to never awaken a woman's love unless you were ready to make good on it. Instead of listening, Nico had always dismissed Murk's words as the bullshit warnings old men told their sons after they had already fucked everything they wanted to in their youth, but now he understood. He'd awakened a lot of women's love in his days, knowing he wasn't planning on giving them shit in return. And now it seemed he was catching his karma with Brooke.

"I went to her trying to find some peace and ended up leaving just as fucked up as I was before. Like, I can't get her off my mind. It's fuckin' up my vibe."

"Damn, my dude. That shit sounds intense."

Legend still wanted to be on some bullshit and tease Nico for what he was saying but he couldn't. Mainly because he completely understood. The same thing that he was describing that was going on in his head was exactly what Legend felt he was going through with January.

"What you gon' do about it?" Legend asked the question more out of curiosity and needing to pick out advice for himself than anything else.

"I don't know. I think I'm going to just stay away from her. Avoid her as much as I can. Maybe fuck somebody else to shake off the effects."

Unable to avoid the thought, Legend immediately went back to his run-in with Jessica. His own attempt to run up in something else to avoid the tension and obsessive thoughts he felt. The attempt that ended in tragic failure. He wanted to tell Nico that the shit wasn't going to work. For whatever reason, his interaction with January didn't follow the same rules that his flings with other women normally did. He couldn't discard her in the same way. That single fact angered him so much inside but, at the same time, it left him feeling love for her that made it so he couldn't stay away. It was an unexplainable situation so he resorted to not even trying to explain it to anyone. Not even Nico. But now it seemed like Nico was dealing with the same thing.

"I don't know how I'm going to do it," Nico admitted. "Because, real shit, I can't get her out my head. But I just want my normal shit back. I want my world the way it was before she popped up in it."

"So you're going to be an asshole and hope that she stays away."

Smiling, Nico nodded his head. "Yeah, but why you gotta say it like that? Sounds like some toxic shit."

Laughing Legend stood to his feet. "It *is* some toxic shit. I don't think it's going to work but… shit, that's on you."

Standing to his feet, Nico shrugged, not paying much attention to Legend's warning. Mainly because he didn't have the experience that Legend did with being a thief. A true product of his father, Nico was a dope boy to the core. He prided himself on never being what folks in the hood called a 'stick-up kid' back in the day. He never robbed anyone, never took anything that wasn't his to take. He made dirty money but in his mind, he made it the most karmically-clean way: selling to grown ass motherfuckas who made their own decisions to kill themselves. And for that he had no empathy.

In fact, part of him looked down on Legend when he left their family unit to go work for Outlaw. Outlaw and his brothers were known takers, known robbers. They waved their legacy of being the 'Robin Hoods of the Hood' around like a flag, something to be proud of. But Nico was disgusted. He judged them for that they did but didn't realize he was looking at himself in a mirror because, in reality, Nico was a taker too.

He didn't realize that with knowledge comes responsibility. And each time he took a life, either with his gun or through selling poison to others for financial gain, he gave up a piece of himself in sacrifice. For every action, there is a separate and equal reaction. It was a universal law. He'd taken a life that night he went to see Brooke and it had robbed him of his peace. And in looking for peace, he again robbed her of her love, knowing he intended on never returning back to her the love she deserved.

Unfortunately, for a Black man, a Black woman is the closest thing to God and doing her wrong resulting in a different type of consequence. One that was haunting him like a ghost on his shoulder whispering tormenting thoughts in his ear. Spirits he couldn't see trailing around with him, like a burden on his back, punishing him in ways she never could. Karma was the greatest love spell and he had a feeling in the deepest part of his mind that his would continue to haunt him until he gave up the fight, stop resisting what he knew he had to do, and went back to Brooke to make things right.

Nico: *Aye... Can I come over and lay with you?*
Brooke: *No.*
Nico: *Why not?*
Brooke: *Because there is something about a lack of commitment that makes my vagina dry.*

"MAN, Brooke, why you always on some bullshit?" Nico asked, pushing open the door to her bedroom, as if he'd properly asked to enter. Which, of course, he didn't.

"Nico! What the fuck are you doing here? And who told you that you can come in my room?"

"Who the fuck you think?" he asked, frowning deeply. "*I* did! What the fuck I look like asking you or any other motherfucka for permission when it comes to some shit I own?"

Blinking hard, Brooke looked at him, totally confused. "*You* own? This isn't your apartment. It's Onyx's."

"And I own the building, love. Don't get shit twisted."

Sitting on the bed, Nico began to take off his shoes, as if he were at home. As if he had not one care in the world about anything, especially not caring about the fact that she'd specifically told him that he wasn't welcome.

"Nico, what the fuck are you doing?" She yelled, looking for his face to his shoes and then back to his face again. "Imma need you to put your lil ugly ass shoes back on your feet and get to stepping. You ain't gotta go home but you gotta get the hell up outta here."

Nico sighed, running his hand over his face. "Fuck man, don't tell me you done became one of them chicks that spend all day in front of the TV, too. That shit kills your brain."

"No, what kills the brain is dealing with inconsistent ass, wannabe big pimping ass, undeserving of love ass, only able to give a dick-lationship—" She used air-quotes for emphasis. "—ass niggas!"

Finishing up her rant, she put her hands on her waist and stared Nico directly in his eyes, daring him to say something she didn't like. For the first time since she'd met him, he appeared stricken… like he sincerely didn't have a thing to say.

"Well, damn," he let out, simultaneously doing what Brooke called the 'ain't shit nigga scratch' where the man in question hangs his head sideways and scratch at the top of it.

"Ugh!" She groaned, rolling her eyes.

Nico was giving her all the red alarms. He was showing *all* the signs that he was just like every man who had come before. Mainly, Trevor. The worst of them all.

What the fuck is it about me that makes a man see me and say "Oh, she looks like a pretty bitch with a good heart. Let me see how much I can get from her? Let me see how much I can take, take, take and take."?

She couldn't understand it. As much as she tried to get the guys she chose to be with, here she was dealing with even more bullshit. This one just happened to be fine ass hell, actually sexy as *fuck* to be precise, wearing designer clothes and driving foreign rides. But the inside was all the same. He saw her as an easy target—a woman whose love came easy so he didn't have to put up much of a fight for it, but it also came fully so that she wouldn't hold anything back.

Right bitch, wrong timing. She wasn't playing those kind of games this time.

"Nico, you got to go," she said, wringing her hands together to keep herself from putting them around his neck. "It's bad enough that you came over here randomly without my permission after having sex with me and then ignoring my calls and texts for a *week*. I'm not trying to do the same shit that I did with Trevor all over again. I've got one lame ass in my life. I don't need two."

Well, fuck, Nico thought. *This is not how I saw this going.*

At the same time, he couldn't blame anyone but himself. He had to clean up what he messed up and this wasn't the right way to do it. He knew he was dead ass wrong for ignoring her calls. But shit, the pussy had him spooked. For him it was a valid reason. But there was no way in *hell* he was gonna tell *her* that. It would be like handing over the remote control to his life to a woman. She would have all the clout if she knew that he felt like he couldn't truly ever let go. So while the only thing Brooke needed to put her trust back in his hands was an explanation, Nico's pride made him choose not to give her that.

"Alright," he said, placing back on his shoes. "If you want me to go, I'll go." He shrugged.

Standing as far away from him as she could, Brooke leaned against the wall of the room. She didn't want him to go but she bit down on her bottom lip to stop herself from saying it. She only wanted an explanation. She wanted him to tell her that he cared. She wanted to be with him outside of the four walls of this room where he seemed to be perfectly fine with fucking her like she was his dirty little secret.

Can I lay with you? He'd asked.

She sucked the skin of her teeth as she thought of it. Lay with her. It seemed like that was all niggas she met wanted to do.

"Bye, Brooke," Nico said as he started to walk away. Once he got right outside her door, he started feeling differently. He wanted to stay. He wanted to apologize. Shit, he didn't really know what he wanted, he just knew he wanted *something* and it had to be from her.

Turning around, he poked his head back through the door and searched for her. She was still in the same place where he'd left her.

"Aye, Brooke," he began. "Can I get a hug?"

Lifting the corner of her lip into a half-smile, Brooke pulled away from the wall and walked slowly to the door.

"Actually, I got something better for you," she said.

The second Nico look as if he was about to come in for a hug, she leaned back and slammed the door shut right in his face.

Whap!

"Oh shit, what the fuck?! Brooke, you hit me in the nose!" His voice seemed muffled like he was holding his hand around his mouth and nose.

"And I hope I broke that motherfucka!" She yelled, locking the door behind him. "Goodbye!"

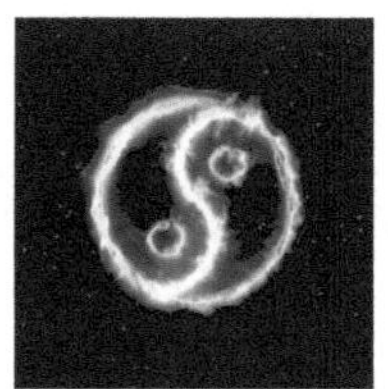

A FULL MOON.

The second Legend walked in his bedroom, his nose picked up on the sweet scent of January's natural fragrance and he knew she was near. Taking long strides towards the balcony, he froze in place when he saw her, completely naked, dancing under the light of the full moon.

Knowing that there was nothing that would stop him from what his body had already responded to, he quickly slipped out of his clothes and walked out to join her. Swaying gently against the breeze while humming the most seductively sweet melody, January didn't even know that he'd slipped up behind her, bending his head down a bit to take in a whiff of her hair.

"It's a full moon out tonight."

Before January could react, she felt warmth from Legend's body behind hers as he stepped in close against her. His breath on her neck, she closed her eyes, completely pouring all of her senses into him. Tingles in her belly danced sweetly, calming only when his hand wrapped around her, pressing against her stomach. He excited and calmed her at the same time. His ability to constantly produce competing sensations within her added to the mystique of their connection, making it impossible for her to see herself with anyone else.

January sucked in a breath, feeling the warmth of his fingertips brushing against her thigh. A trail of heat followed the trail he made on her skin. He created a pattern, as if writing something on her. The markings were permanent, whether they could be visibly seen or not. Legend's name had long before been burned into her soul.

As he pulled her back into him, January felt her sex stir, the sweetest honey dripping from her thighs as he pressed his hips against her backside, prying her cheeks apart with the girth of his dick. With his left hand on her hips, holding her in place, he lowered his right hand between her thighs, subtly using his thumb and forefinger to force her thighs apart. Breath spilled from her lips as tension built up inside of her.

"Relax..." he whispered into her neck. And, as if he were a magician, her body followed his command.

Her body softened into his strength. January gave him full permission to have his way with her. One finger, and then two, entered the space between her thighs. Her bottom lip dropped open, ecstasy filling her as he stirred her insides. A light breeze in the air danced across her nipples, adding increase to her sexual energy. It was nature's way of giving them her blessing.

"Bend over."

Nervous and excited energy coursed through January as she did as he asked. Keeping her legs straight, she slid her upper body forward. Legend assisted her with one hand, pushing her further and further down until she was grabbing onto her ankles. Night air tickled her exposed clit and she reveled in the sensation, shivering slightly from the cold, and then trembled when Legend pressed his face between her cheeks, sucking her pearl between his lips.

January gasped loudly, sucking in a sharp breath of surprise before groaning with pleasure. Her knees began to buckle under the intense pressure and ecstasy, and Legend grabbed her thighs to keep them straight. Once he was certain that she was stable, he pulled back his hands and then used them to pry her ass apart. Cold air blew into her, followed by the warmth of his tongue thrashing against her peach. She dripped honey down her thighs, gritting her teeth together, feeling as if she was going to spontaneously combust. The sensation was overwhelming. Legend sucked on her skin as if he wanted to swallow her whole, as if the elixir of everlasting life came from inside her cave.

"Le-Legend, I can't—"

Her protest only made him more aggressive. He gripped her ass tighter, sucked her harder, grunted louder. She reached out for something to keep her balance as he licked, sucked, and finger-fucked her savagely, seeking ultimate pleasure. He was hungry for her, and it felt like an insatiable desire. She felt her climax build up from the depths of her, rising up, as if it were going to explode up her spine.

"Legend...please, stop," January whispered, begging him profusely. "You gotta stop, please. Please!"

Her begging only made him go harder, sucking, thrashing, and fucking her with his tongue. She held her breath, trying to maintain control of her body, but it was no use. A rush of cold air washed over her and when it hit the fire Legend had kindled between her thighs, it was fireworks. The floodgates opened and she released sweetness from her lower lips. As if it were sugar water, Legend drank from her, moaning his satisfaction as she struggled to catch her breath.

It was maddening how much control he had over her—her body, her emotions, her entire life. Legend entered her life and transformed it in every way. It was the sweetest chaos; a feeling January wanted to rid herself of but couldn't shake.

Scooping her up into his arms, Legend cradled her with care, showing off a tender side of him that she rarely saw. She leaned into him, enjoying the moment of calm as the burning flame in her body simmered into a small flame. When Legend, still holding her in his arms, knelt down, placing her onto the dozens of stacked pillows in the center of the balcony, January became aware that this was only the calm before the storm.

He laid her on her back and then retreated back a bit, taking a moment to look her over. She wondered what was on his mind, what he was thinking as he looked at her body. Her insecurities were many; she wasn't absolved of them simply because she pretended to be. But now, everything she hid from the world was fully on display, staring Legend in the face. Suddenly feeling self-conscious by how deeply he was staring at her, January began to shrink away from him, moving to cloak her body with her arms.

"No," Legend said, grabbing her arms to pull them apart. "Don't hide from me."

What he was asking seemed so impossible to her, but she forced herself to do as he asked.

Still, January couldn't help but notice the obvious differences between them. Legend was the epitome of the appearance of the perfect man. Chiseled, washboard abs covered by smooth, golden-brown skin. Everything about him was rooted in strength and exuded absolute confidence. He seemed so sure of everything. The complete opposite of what she felt about herself.

Fighting against her natural instinct to look away, January held her attention on his face, reading into his expression. Despite what she felt, all she saw in his face was curiosity and pure love. Reaching out, he shifted her body as he knelt between her thighs, putting her closer. When he leaned over, closing the distance between their bodies, she was caught by his intense gaze. Looking into his eyes, she felt at home until she felt the bulge of his manhood pressing against her entrance. She tensed, bracing herself for pain.

"Relax," Legend said.

Leaning down, he sucked her bottom lip into his mouth, nibbling softly before transforming it into a kiss. He used his tongue to force her lips apart, deepening their kiss to the point that he felt like everything around them began to fade away. January totally forgot herself and completely surrendered to him.

"Relax. More."

Legend spoke his words directly into her mouth while simultaneously sucking on her tongue. Fingers pinched her nipples and the sweet sensation caused her thighs to fall open. Legend wasted no time responding to her soft retreat. With a gentle push forward, he was inside of her, entering slowly, giving her piece by piece.

His width forced her apart, forcing a sharp jolt up her spine.

"Ahh…"

January sucked in a breath to absorb the pain, squeezing her eyes closed as he eased forward. As the ache began to subside, she opened her eyes, greeted by the sight of Legend's eyes on her. He kept his eyes on hers as he continuously moved inside, seeming to fill her to max capacity until it got to the point where she thought she couldn't take any more.

"You should breathe," Legend spoke directly into her ear.

It wasn't until then that January realized she was even holding her breath. Exhaling, she relaxed her body and gave in to him, moving her legs to wrap them firmly around him. The pain subsided and she closed her eyes, releasing her will into the natural rhythm of their bodies as they flowed together, becoming one with each other.

"Oh my god..."

The sensation was overwhelming. Her juices flowed out of her like a fountain, saturating their movements. Legend's hands lowered from her hips and he grabbed her ass, once again spreading her apart so he could have better access.

"Damn, you feel so fuckin' good," he moaned into her ear. "Your pussy feels so fuckin' good to me."

January felt energy building up at the base of her spine that she couldn't control and suddenly, she found herself thrusting back into him. They fell into the natural flow of give and receive: a divine sexual reciprocity. She spread her thighs open wider, hungrily wanting even more of him. He was giving her the dick, but she was greedy, thrusting and thrashing even harder into him.

January wanted more.

Needed more.

He gave in to her desire.

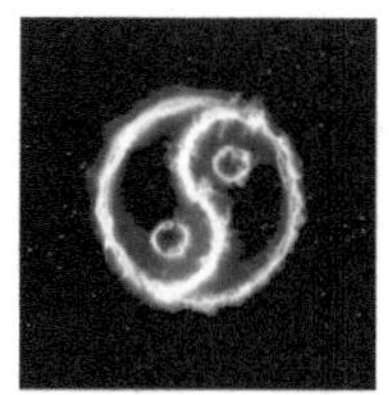

DANGEROUS.

Dangerous as fuck.

That was the only way Legend could describe what he was getting into with January. Danger was the only thing that would come out of making love to her. If he'd thought there was a chance on turning back before, it was becoming clear that all that was over. He wasn't prepared yet to admit it, but it seemed obvious that there was no longer a possibility that she wouldn't be his.

"Damn, Shorty... yo' ass gon' drive me fuckin' crazy."

Falling forward into her, Legend pressed his lips to hers, sucking and biting gently while she whined her hips against him. Heaven on Earth.

Losing himself in her was the easiest thing to do. January was more than willing to open up and receive him. This didn't even feel like their first time. They moved in rhythm with each other in a natural way, as souls that had made love many times over several lives though their bodies were just now catching up to the experience.

Gritting his teeth, Legend clenched his jaw and pulled out quickly, removing from her warmth so fast that it made her pussy pop. She groaned out in pleasure and he bricked up even more, swelling to the max.

Her eyes locked into his, and he hesitated. January was so fucking beautiful to him and she didn't even know how much. Just looking at her awakened something in him. Something he didn't know was there. She brought out emotions he'd never felt before.

"Legend..."

The softness in her voice mixed with the glitter in her eyes teased him. He felt like he could cum just from the sound of her voice. It was so fuckin' sexy to him. Flipping her over with ease, he twisted her body around and pulled her hips forward to lift her thighs. Twisting around, he ran his legs parallel outside her body so that her ass and swollen pussy were situated right in front of his face. The sight alone of her dripping wet peach made his mouth water.

Legend couldn't control himself. He pushed his entire face forward, spreading her body in two. He nearly swallowed her whole. He'd imagined this moment so many times before, but nothing he'd ever imagined could rival the real thing.

"Legend, oh my god!"

January's arm found her way behind her to push him away, and he responded fast. Grabbing it, he pinned her down to teeter her off balance and hold her in place. She gasped loudly as he went crazy, sucking and licking every part of her body that she couldn't even see.

Once he was certain that there was no way she could get any more wet, he pulled back, pointing his erection right at her opening. Releasing her arm, he placed both hands on each side of her ass and then snapped her hips down, driving his dick straight through her core, sending it home.

"Don't do that," Legend told her when she lifted her hand to push him away. "Trust me. Do you trust me?"

"Yes," she whispered, much too softly for his satisfaction. He jerked forward, pushing further into her while simultaneously slapping her ass. Hard.

"Ahh! Oh, shit! Legend?!" The way she screamed his name had him confused as to whether it was a statement or a question.

"I said, *do you trust me*?"

Another smack on the ass, this time much harder.

"Oh, *shit*!" she screamed. Her pussy throbbed, puckering repeatedly as she leaked warm honey on him.

"Yes, Legend," she gritted through her teeth. "Yes. I trust you!"

The intense emotions in her words ignited what felt like a motor inside of him, and everything around them faded away.

Before long, January matched his motion, giving in to the sweet ebb and flow rhythm that their bodies made. Her body was illuminated by the moonlight, glistening like chocolate diamonds under the sky. Shit had him feeling poetic and whatnot.

Legend had been with many women before January, but this one time had him ready to forget all the others.

They climaxed together under the night sky, setting off fireworks of their own that illuminated the dark shadows in Legend's heart. In that moment, there was no more sadness, no more hurt, no more pain. All he could feel was love.

And as he lost his strength, falling forward, colliding overtop January's skin, he opened his mouth and some shit that he'd never thought in a million years he would ever say.

"You better trust me, January. I fuckin' love you."

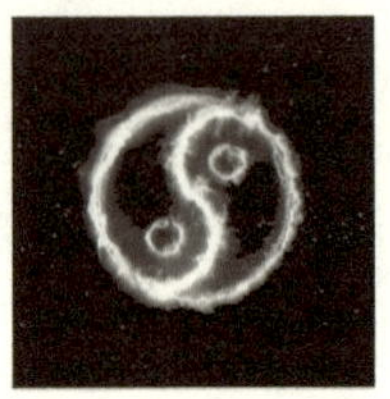

THE SHADOWS.

"I am destroying myself so other people can't. And it's the worst kind of control but it's the only form I know."

NOTHING BUT THE LIGHT OF THE MOON WAS PRESENT TO PROVIDE coverage over January's naked body as she slept soundly, cuddled up next to Legend, enjoying the warmth that his body provided. She was completely at peace, fully surrendered into sleep as he lay next to her, surrendering to the toxic thoughts in his mind.

Just as soon as he had allowed himself to give in to the one thing that he'd wanted so bad from the one woman on Earth he'd thought he'd never receive it from, he couldn't shake the feeling that he'd made a mistake. January made him feel open in ways that he wasn't prepared for. And like a rookie poker player, he'd exposed his hand. Completely caught up in the folds of love, caught off-guard by the potion she'd enraptured him into, he'd said too much. He admitted feelings to her that he wished she'd forget.

"The game changes once you fall in love," he remembered his father saying. *"So, even if you feel that shit, never admit to it. Once women know they got a nigga caught up, they use that shit to their advantage. Never let a woman know that she holds the strings to your heart, or she'll play you like a puppet. Have you with your nose wide open looking like fuckin' Pinnochio Jr. 'round here. Doing every fuckin' thing in the world, jumping through all kinds of hoops just so that you can be what she considers 'a real man.' Don't ever go out like a simp."*

Legend Sr. had been speaking out of anger, poisoning his son against Black women in the way that Black men sometimes did when they didn't know any better. In the days when his parents first came together, trying to make it work, it had been difficult. Legend's parents were like January's. Both of January's parents came from two-parent homes. No matter how difficult the trials were that they had to face, Outlaw and Janelle had one small advantage: they knew what it looked like when a man and a woman truly loved each other because they'd seen it first-hand. They knew the compromise that it took, the level of self-sacrifice needed, and the tremendous amount of love required to love someone unconditionally to the point that your love heals them past their individual pain.

Legend's parents never had that.

Legend's mother, Shanice, was the daughter of a dope fiend and she never knew her father. If it wasn't enough of a challenge trying to be in love, try doing it with daddy *and* mommy issues. And Legend's father had even deeper wounds stemming from molestation, abandonment, murder, and abuse. He'd learned how to be a man from the same streets that taught him that a woman's place was beneath his feet. Falling in love with Shanice had never been part of his plan, but it happened, and when it did, he had no idea how to deal with it. The start of their love was toxic in every way, riddled by broken promises, forced encounters, addiction, obsession, and the repetition of patterns that they'd inherited through trauma that had occurred before they'd even begun to live their lives.

Unfortunately for Legend, he was around when his father was learning his way through the painful part of the process. And the effect of that led him to spew into his son many lessons of hate and emotional distance when it came to how to be with a woman. By the time that Legend Sr. had learned the errors of his ways and had begun to love and treat his wife right, Legend was already gone, working for Outlaw in New York. It was too late for Legend to teach his son that the key to accessing a perfect love was to be committed to loving a woman through her pain.

No one on Earth could love a Black man like a Black woman could. And, on the contrary, no one could hate him just as much when he rejected the love she was eager to give. The single thing that made all the difference was the commitment level and loyalty of the man that she gave her heart to. If he was committed enough to be with her through the highs and lows, love her through the devastation and pain inflicted on her through generations and generations of feeling unloved, less than, set aside, and ignored, then his prize would be that he'd finally earn access to play a part in the greatest love story ever told.

But not many Black men were able to experience that level of love because they were too busy adding to the hurt that Black women had to endure instead of adding to the love. They were too busy living out the lessons their fathers had taught them in their times of hate. Too busy following behind the ones telling them to be players, to never commit, never show love, never beg, never chase. They were too busy learning how to play out their self-hatred by hurting the only women in their lives who wanted to do nothing but love them. And the cycle continued with heartless men creating bitter women until all that was left were loveless Black neighborhoods where every example of a 'loving relationship' involved betrayal, lying, abuse, or distrust.

Running his hand over his face, Legend couldn't hide his anger. He was sitting next to a woman that his heart said he needed but his mind told him no. He wasn't ready yet. Being with January meant that his entire life had to change, and he didn't want that. She'd only been in his life for few months as it was, and she'd totally came in and wrecked shit to the max. Each time they connected, their story ended with Legend creating new enemies of old acquaintances. Her presence required change, even if she wasn't the one forcing it on him. And he wasn't ready for that.

He didn't want responsibility. He didn't want to be selfless. He didn't want to think about the future. He didn't want to make plans. He liked being reckless. He liked living in the moment. He liked not giving a damn. And he loved having nothing to live for. Things were easier that way.

Reaching out, he grabbed the blanket from where it was pooled around January's hips and pulled it up, tucking it just under her chin. Being careful to not wake her, he slid his body away from hers, creating much-needed distance. Her aura was suffocating. It was all encompassing. He was addicted to it and repulsed by it at the same time. She was like air; you needed it to live but too much of it coming towards you at one time, and you couldn't breathe. January affected him in that way. He could only take her in small doses or it was overwhelming. He'd felt that way since the beginning, which was why he had tried so hard not to have sex with her, no matter how much he wanted it. But now they'd opened Pandora's box and there was no closing it. He didn't know what he was going to do about that, but he knew right now, he just needed some distance.

Hours after Legend had removed himself from her, January slowly blinked awake, finally noticing his absence. She felt cold in a way that she hadn't felt when he'd been nearby. Even with the comforter over her, there was a noticeable difference.

Her chest tightened in a fearful response that she couldn't place when she opened her eyes and noticed that he wasn't there. It was a sensation of instant panic, like he'd left her. Not like he'd gone to the bathroom or walked back inside, but like he'd *left* for good. Sitting up, January ran her hand over the top of her head, wondering about the reason for such a sudden and irrational emotional response. She then placed her hand to her chest, feeling the face-paced beating of her heart. Placing her hands to her cheeks, she closed her eyes, trying to calm herself down, wondering why she suddenly felt like she was having a panic attack. Something else had to be wrong. There was no way that her body was reacting like this simply because she'd opened her eyes and Legend wasn't there.

She heard a light buzzing sound and pulled up the covers, seeing that it was Legend's phone ringing. He had to be close, he'd left it behind. Lying back down on the pillow, she tried to calm herself, waiting to see if he was going to walk back in but the buzzing continued. Whoever was calling him was calling back-to-back.

Maybe it's an emergency? Maybe Nico? Or Onyx? she thought.

Flipping the covers up, this time she grabbed the phone and turned it around to look at the screen. The name 'Jessica' showed on top and the photo of the girl she saw accompanying the name must've been her. It was a full-body shot of a woman that wasn't what January would've ever thought was Legend's type, but then again, what did she know? The only one he'd shown interest in was her. Plus, Jessica was... cute. Big, large, bouncy breasts showed through the top of her tight, form-fitting black dress. She had long hair, dirty-blond in color, and big, bright eyes.

January's lips twisted a bit. A white girl. While January didn't have any issues at all with interracial dating on any level, it did put somewhat a sour taste in her mouth. Black women were the only women on the face of the Earth who had to wonder if the men who looked like them considered them to be their type. No other race or ethnicity, be it white, Hispanic, Indian or Asian, had to look at the men who shared their history and think *"I wonder if he'll like me"*.

Placing the phone down, she tried not to let her insecurities take over, but they were coming in full force. Especially now that Legend had disappeared. He was always disappearing. She was the only one stuck in his apartment. He came and went as he pleased. And now she couldn't help but wonder... was he going to be with Jessica? She'd just had sex with a man, for the first time, who wasn't *really* hers in any way. He wasn't committed to her at all. So, in all honesty, he could be fuckin' Jessica right now and there wasn't a damn thing she could say.

What is wrong with me?

Closing her eyes, she placed one hand to her chest and the other to her belly, repeating a method that her doctor had taught her when she was recovering from the shooting. Back then, she'd had panic attacks often, suddenly waking up in the middle of the night from dreams where someone was chasing her down, waving a gun in their hands. Even some where a gunman had killed one of her parents, permanently removing them from her life. The dreams may have been different, but certain elements were always the same: there was a gunman, and someone would be killed, whether it was her or her loved ones, leaving her in a state of panic once she realized that she was all alone, whether in life or in death. Each dream had seemed so vivid that she awoke in complete panic, with it taking several minutes for her to realize that it had only been a dream and not reality.

Blinking a few times to calm her nerves, she stood up and walked back inside the apartment, needing to move around to calm her nerves. Instead of going back to her room, she decided to make some tea and headed for the kitchen. When she stepped out of the hall and saw him, once again, sitting at the table, she stopped, frozen in place.

Legend lifted his head slowly, not hearing anything, but *feeling* something. When his eyes connected with January, he felt his chest get tight. Now he knew what he'd felt and why. And, for some reason, it angered him. They had an unexplainable connection that drew them to each other whether he wanted it or not. It was out of his control. And he *hated* feeling like he didn't have any control. It made him feel like his life lay totally in her hands.

"Is it okay if I come in and…" She lost her words. "I just want to get some tea."

So many questions ran through January's mind while Legend stared into her, not saying a thing. She felt scrutinized, small. As if he were standing somewhere up high and glaring down at her from his perch.

What's happened between us in the few minutes since we were together? She began to think, suddenly feeling insecure. *Did I do something wrong?*

His dark brown eyes didn't seem so brooding the longer she gazed into them, and in that moment, she could've sworn there was a ring of hazel around his iris that reminded her of a forest. It was so strange how the color of his eyes seemed to shift sometimes. His long locs were parted to one side, in a distinguished way, like the gentlemen of old who used to bust out cigars and bourbon during advertisement meetings. The scruff along his jawline was tailored and even, drawing her eyes to his chiseled bone structure and the fierceness of his features. She studied him. Really studied him. And she found a few things about him that were imperfect, yet perfectly him.

Like a barely noticeable scar that ran right through his right eyebrow, preventing the hair from growing.

Or the small line along the left side of his jaw. Another scar with hair that didn't grow there.

"What happened?" January asked.

Legend blinked. "To what?"

She pointed to her temple. "Your eyebrow. What happened?"

He chuckled. "Sure you want to know?"

She nodded. "And with your jaw."

"Seems I'm not the only one that's been staring."

She felt herself blush at his words. "Do you mind me asking?"

"Not at all. The one on my eyebrow I got in a training accident with Nico. We were sparring, and he split my eyebrow open with a punch."

"Ouch. That must've hurt."

He shrugged. "I've hurt worse. The one on my jawline actually extends all the way to the other side of my face, though."

"What happened? That seems like a pretty hefty scar to—"

"I was captured in the middle of a fight and held for a while. Back a few years ago. They ended up trying to slit my throat. That's how I got the scar."

January's eyes bulged. "You're kidding."

"Not one bit."

Her eyes fell to his outfit and she studied it. All black this time, and it suited him. He had this sun-kissed complexion that the black accented, and that brooding stare of his matched well. But the black also brought out the white of his teeth.

And she wondered if she could make him smile again.

Her jumbled thoughts kept scrambling around in her mind and she busied herself by making the tea. For some reason, he put her on edge. But he also made her curious. Very, very curious. And she couldn't deny the fact that he was incredibly handsome. Sexy in a way that captured her into him. She wanted him inside her again. And it was way beyond the sex.

She was seriously attracted to him. Like, crazy attracted, maybe even obsessed. It seemed as if this man dripped with sin, and not the kind that got someone killed. He was everything her father warned her about. He held every trait she'd told herself was ungodly, yet it only drew her to him more.

Legend was a bad man. A killer. Part of the mafia, for crying out loud. January *couldn't* be so into him. That wasn't an option.

But knowing she shouldn't like him wasn't helping.

"You should get back to bed. It's late."

She shook her head. "I'm not tired."

Sighing, she hugged her fingers around the mug of tea, interlacing them in the front. Her eyes were achy and swollen from crying herself to sleep for the couple hours she'd been able to accomplish what had initially felt impossible.

"This place is safe. No one can hurt you here. Even if I'm not around."

"What do you mean 'if you're not around?'" she asked, feeling an icy feeling come over her.

"I mean, *if I'm not around*," he repeated, this time more aggressively. Angrily. "I plan to leave soon. Maybe for a couple days. Maybe more. There will be guards stationed around to watch out for you if I do."

What?

This made no sense. She didn't understand it at all. What had she done in the brief moment of time since they'd been intimate to make him not want it—her—again?

Maybe he has to find someone else. Maybe you can't please him like the other girl can.

Briefly, January's mind fell on the woman who had been calling Legend's phone. Jessica. Was that who he was going to see? Long dark hair, olive skin, light blue eyes. She looked nothing like January in any way. Maybe she was more his type. Maybe he'd tried January out only to find that she didn't measure up.

A sharp, icy pain ripped through her heart, and she fought against the tears that were coming to her eyes. She wasn't worried about anyone breaking in and hurting her. The one who was hurting her was already inside. And, by some strange, merciless twist of fate, he was the only one available for her to talk to. She didn't want to be near him, but she didn't want to be alone with her thoughts driving her crazy either.

In some strange way, her torturer had become the only remedy for her pain. January was fully convinced that the Universe hated her. There was no other way. Regardless to how much she was trying to make the right decisions, all she was met with was more blocks. More pain. More disappointment. There was no other explanation that she could see. She had to be paying for some karmic sin she'd committed in another lifetime.

Legend eyed January curiously. He had unintentionally stepped on one of the many landmines that triggered her insecurities, and he didn't even know it.

"What's wrong with you now?" he asked as if annoyed.

"Nothing," January replied. Equally annoyed.

"Whatever," he said, running his hand over his face as he blew out an exasperated breath.

He looked tired, like he hadn't slept in days. It was then that she paused to actually scrutinize the entire scene in front of her. The clock on the oven showed it was well after 4 am and Legend was sitting alone, in the dark, at the kitchen table holding a full, untouched mug of coffee between his hands. The fact that no smoke came from the cup told her that it had gone completely cold.

There was no telling how long he'd been sitting there.

"Are you okay?" January asked, holding her attention on him as she asked the question. Legend was a mystery to most, mainly because he'd trained himself in the art of keeping his innermost feelings secret, but body language didn't lie.

"Yeah," he said with a slight shrug.

"No, you aren't," she replied.

Sliding into the chair across from him, January grabbed the mug from between his hands and took a sip.

Cold. Just as she'd thought.

"We have to turn in some of our report to Ms. Bey this Friday. Just an update on some things we've learned so far. This would be a good time to discuss some things we can include in it... don't you think?"

He responded with a barely audible grunt, which she chose to accept as a 'yes'.

"Okay," she said, forcing a cheerful tone as she adjusted in her seat. "How about we take turns asking and responding to questions?"

Legend didn't respond but his eyes lifted to meet hers, his unspoken interest sparkling through the darkness. He was a tortured soul, tumbling through life like a bruised warrior returning home. A victor, beaten down and emotionally scarred beyond repair, but a victor, nonetheless. Sometimes, January wondered if he truly enjoyed his life or if he'd just gotten used to living with his demons.

"So... I'll start," January began, pausing for a beat to lick her lips.

Just that quickly, Legend was beside himself. His body rebelled against his mental fortitude and his eyes slid downward, catching her tongue's trail. He shuffled his feet, adjusting in his chair, attempting to ease the tension building in his loins.

Where the hell was all this pressure when he was trying to mess around with Jessica? it was like his body had a will of its own, deciding that when it came to anything regarding January, it would betray him.

"What is your favorite..." January paused to think, her eyes casting upwards as she rocked side to side. "I got it!" she snapped her fingers, bringing her sparkling eyes down to meet his. "What's your favorite city?"

"Hell," Legend responded without blinking. Matter-of-factly, as if he were engaging in casual conversation.

"Hell?" January scoffed, rolling her eyes. "Hell isn't a place, Legend. It's a state of mind. A horrible, tortured state of being. And, from the looks of it, you've been there for a long time."

Instead of the snarky know-it-all tone that was her normal these days, Legend picked up on a touch of sympathy and sadness that made his chest burn. He didn't want her sympathy and definitely not her sadness. He forced a burst of air through his nostrils.

"Inaccurate," was all he said. "It's not horrible. I'm not tortured. I'm actually quite comfortable there. Hell feels like home."

January peered at him, seeing straight through his tough exterior to the man underneath. The one who was so used to being unloved. He wasn't totally aware of how to deal with someone who sincerely cared. She could see that the fact she did care annoyed him, but she didn't know how to be any other way. Her kindness made him more aggressive, which is why he acted like an asshole to push her away.

"What's your favorite food?"

"The kind you eat."

"Your favorite car?"

"Fast, sporty, expensive."

"Your favorite TV show?"

Legend frowned. "You see a TV in here?"

January paused, matching his frown. She hadn't even noticed in all this time that there wasn't a single television in any of the rooms she'd been in.

"Noted," she replied.

“How about you let me ask you some questions," Legend asked, leaning forward. His eyes pressed into hers, piercingly so, as if he were directing his question to her.

“Okay,” January said with apprehension.

Locking eyes with Legend caused flashes of heat at the base of her neck. And wetness between her legs. Just a few minutes ago, she had been completely devastated by him. How was it that he was able to cause such a drastic mood change? Especially when he didn't seem affected in the least by this moment. At least, not in any sexual way.

“Why don’t you dance anymore?” he asked. “What happened to the January who told me she wanted a dance studio one day? The one who couldn’t wait to go to that dance school in New York? Are we ever going to touch on that? Or are you going to keep poking around in my shit?”

January’s aura visibly dimmed, and her shoulders drooped right along with it.

Once again, Legend had been able to force a sudden mood change. Her spirits dampened but she forced herself not to respond to his hate with more hate. Somehow, she knew that he was fighting a battle inside that she just wasn’t able to understand just yet. He was stuck in the shadows, struggling to come up for air. He was fighting a battle in his mind and until he got the best of it, he would push everyone around him away until he was totally alone, being tortured by his own demons. Alone, in his personal hell.

“Trauma shaped you, Legend. You were young... too defenseless to stop it. Stop confusing who it made you become with the person you can now be. You are more than this. You don’t have to push everyone who loves you away just because you’re afraid of real intimacy. You can trust me.”

“You mean like how you trust me?” he retorted, voice dripping with sarcasm. They said hurt people hurt people, and that was nothing but the truth. Legend was a perfect example of that.

"If you keep treating people like this, you'll end up always being alone. You don't have to embrace your anger just because you feel it. There are other ways to handle things. You're not alone but you have to let down your guard enough to let someone in."

"I don't mind being alone." Legend shrugged. "It's quiet and I don't have to answer to anyone. I'm not responsible to anyone."

"You're not meant to be alone," January said, shaking her head. She was trying to get through to him because, somehow, she felt like she was the only one who could. Of all the people in his life, she felt like she had the most access, but he was a hard nut to crack, as the old folks would say. It was tiring. And it was hard to help another learn to love when you felt your own heart had a huge leak inside of it.

"I hear what you're sayin', love, but I work in the principle of 'mind over matter'," Legend stated, folding his hands together across the table. Which in laymen's terms means, if I don't mind, it don't matter."

"That's not what that means, Legend. It doesn't mean you avoid things that you don't like. It means that your mind state, your thoughts, the things you tell yourself, creates your reality. Your subconscious thoughts and emotions control every part of your everyday life. That's what it means. Dumbass."

"Yeah, whatever, smart ass," he replied. "Riddle me this. What do you think my mind is saying right now about you?"

January bit down hard on her bottom lip. She was losing her patience and also losing the battle. Legend was triggering her, which was exactly what he wanted. A person who was so traumatized and so tortured only found pleasure in getting under other people's skin to the point that they could push them away. He'd learned this tactic throughout his lifetime and it had served him well. Even in this instance.

"You know what? I hate you," she replied, rolling her eyes.

"Yep," Legend replied with a wink. "Maybe you are a genius, because you're exactly right."

Jumping up from the table, January's first move was to put as much distance as she could between them. It was obvious that Legend was fully intent on hurting her for some reason and he was succeeding. She wanted to believe he didn't mean it, that he was just acting out because of fear or avoidance of being pinned down into a commitment, something that would force him to be someone he'd never considered being before. But it was hard to think that way when you had eyes full of hate and anger staring you back in the face.

I don't even know why I bother, January thought, shutting herself in her room. She had no regrets with anything she'd decided to do that night but deep down, she wished she hadn't given her love away to him so soon.

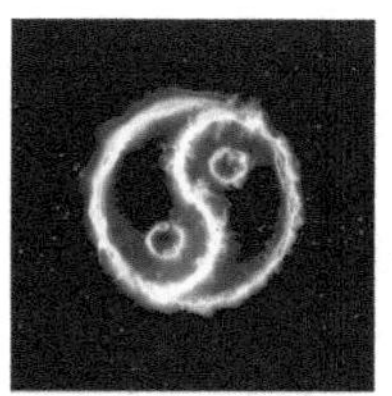

FIGHT CLUB.

The stuff you heard about me is a lie.

I'm way worse.

LEGEND

ONE FINAL BLOW STRAIGHT TO THE SIDE OF HIS JAW WAS ENOUGH TO lay Legend's opponent down. He was some white boy who was known around the city for knocking niggas out.

Not anymore.

The small arena was packed beyond the legal limits. But the owner didn't give a fuck about what was legal. The only thing that Luis cared about was the bread.

Nothing they did here followed the rules. Being here, doing what they were doing was enough to get Luis locked up and the club shut down for good.

This was a fight club, but it was known around the city as 'The Murder Den.' People didn't come here just to tap someone up right quick on their lunch break before going back to work. Or to blow off some steam before facing wifey at the crib. This was where motherfuckas like Legend came to tame the demons riding their backs. Shooters, serial killers, rapists, and whoever the fuck else was collecting bad karma like Pokémon cards came here in between time to feed the demons who'd become part of their entourage over time. Legend didn't personally know everybody's story—this place wasn't for talk therapy—but he could tell by looking a man in his eyes whether or not he'd caught a body before.

And here? There wasn't a single person who hadn't caught plenty. They were the devil's children. And Luis was like the devil himself, collecting payment for every soul he stole. The only difference was they handed theirs over to him freely.

"Legend!" Luis called, walking over to Legend with his lips curved into a greasy smile and his hands on top of his bulbous belly.

When Legend first met Luis, he was thin and gauntly in appearance with a scraggly beard that didn't completely fill in. Now he was one of the most finely dressed Italians Legend knew. His business survived off Legend's back. And business was always good.

"You made a lot of money tonight," Luis said, nearly singing a tune as he approached Legend with his arms wide. "I'll have your share delivered to your room, as usual," he added with a wink. In other words, he was going to have some chick come deliver the cash to Legend along with a shot of ass. He wasn't interested in either, honestly.

He didn't do this for the women. He didn't even do this for the money. He did this because he had no other choice.

When you grew up the way he had, lived the life he lived, and made more deals with the devil than you cared to count, it was hard to live in a way that didn't involve pain. Sometimes his, but specifically, someone else's.

Legend was miserable without it. Too much quiet made his demons bored. And if he wasn't entertaining them by beating the shit out of someone else, they decided to torture him. His body was free, but he was in prison. His mind belonged to them. But somehow, he got a thrill from it. He chased it like a junkie chased the feel of that first high. And he was just as addicted to it, too. He didn't want to live life any other way.

He was one crazy motherfucker, unapologetically. And when he told that to people, he meant it in the most fucked up way. They never believed him so it really made no difference.

"Did she sign?" Legend asked Luis as he unwrapped his hands.

They valued skin to skin contact, so they didn't fight using gloves of any kind. They only had one rule at the club: draw blood.

For that reason, any type of protective gear wasn't allowed. The exception was bandage tape to wrap your hands to minimize damage to the most crucial asset for them: their hands.

Trust, there were ways to provide someone with an agonizing death without them, but it was far messier.

"Of course, she signed." Luis grinned like a Cheshire cat before shoving a cigar between his lips. "She was happy to do it. Eager. They always are, even after seeing you in the ring, which surprises the hell out of me."

Legend didn't respond. Wasn't interested in small talk. Or any talk at all for that matter. Dugan was supposed to be a decent opponent, which was the reason Legend was so ready for the fight. He'd made a name for himself in his backwoods, country-ass, redneck town and Legend thought that since he'd already ran through all the city boys and delivered them their asses, that a steak-and-potatoes-eating hillbilly could pose a challenge for him. Turns out, he didn't. It wasn't long before he folded under the pain. The only problem was that Legend had an appetite to cause more.

And that's where Luis came in to save the day.

Like a dealer of sorts, he fed Legend's forbidden addictions in multiple ways. It was fucked up to only find pleasure in the creation of an immense amount of pain. It took a special type of crazy to be okay with that. Luis was that type of crazy.

"Tell Nico I'd like to see him in the ring one day," Luis called after Legend just as he was leaving to head back to his room.

Because of how much money Legend brought into Luis' club, Luis had an entire wing constructed specifically him. It was a suite, complete with a full bathroom and bed. He'd had it custom designed to Legend's specifications with all the necessities required to satisfy his darker appetites.

Entering his chambers, as Luis called it, Legend quickly stripped down and stepped right into the shower, not bothering to wait for the water to go hot from cold. He needed the shock to his system. He was eager for anything to curb his mood. He couldn't get January off the brain and it was driving him fucking insane. There was only one time in his life he could remember asking God for something. Only one person in the world who had been the reason for that.

After Outlaw forced him out of *BBM*, Legend couldn't figure out if he was more affected by being ousted from the group he saw as his family by the one nigga in the world who truly felt like his father, or by the fact that Outlaw had seen through him, picking up on what he felt for January and made him promise to stay away.

Outlaw didn't think Legend was good enough for her, and Legend could see why. Outlaw had raised him to be the more vicious and heartless version of himself. He could remember Outlaw joking around about how love would calm him down one day, same as it did him, but that whatever woman was destined to do it had a hell of a job in store for her. But Outlaw never expected that woman to be his own daughter. Shit, Legend didn't either. But he also couldn't deny the reality of it all. He wanted her. The one woman he couldn't have. Regardless to what he felt, he knew that he would never cross Outlaw no matter what the circumstances. Loyalty was everything and his word was bond.

And so, he asked God every night to help him stay away. Help him forget her face. Take the guilt of his failure to protect her away. None of those requests were answered, but there was enough physical distance between them to help him pretend that they were worlds apart. But now, years later, and they'd collided again, smashing into each other like shooting stars. Somehow, their destinies were connected, drawing them together like magnets. But also, like magnets, the same force that pulled them towards each other also pushed them away.

The scalding hot water thundered on Legend's back, so hot it felt as if it were searing his skin, beating straight to the bone. He was so caught in his thoughts; he couldn't bring himself to feel it. He was lost in the visions in his head, remembering every bit of her soft skin that smelled like a mixture of shea butter and coconut oil. Her eyes that looked at him as if she could see into his soul. It was unsettling. Unrattling. Shit, it was fucking addicting, but he wouldn't have her any other way. *If* he could allow himself to have her. But he couldn't.

It suddenly came back to his mind that Luis was sending someone to the room to bring his payment from the fight. He finished up in the shower and started to get dressed. He wasn't interested in having sex with whatever random Luis had chosen for him. Whoever she was would be disappointed to hear that, but it wasn't his problem, and he gave no fucks. The more he was around January, the more he was cock-blocking himself. He didn't want anyone else.

Crossing the room to find a t-shirt decent enough to toss over his head so he could leave for the night, Legend passed by the full-length mirror in the room and glanced up, catching his reflection.

The man he appeared to be now didn't look a damn thing like the one he'd been the other day with January. If she saw him now, there was no way she'd recognize him. And it didn't have anything to do with the fight; his opponent hadn't had a chance to get a decent punch in to make that kind of impact. He just looked like a fuckin' monster.

Something about being around January brought out another side of him; someone he didn't think he could be anymore. TV shows and movies make the life of a hitta glamorous, but there is nothing glamorous about it. In a way, they are like highly paid, highly trained garbagemen. They do the dirty work that every criminal organization needed but people rarely wanted to do. And it was mostly because of the cost that came along with it.

Working for Outlaw, Legend did things that could get him locked up —executed even—but he could reason with himself that it was always for a good cause. The lives that Outlaw ordered to be ended were of people who hurt others for personal gain and for little regard. Dirty politicians, racists cops...people in high positions who used their power to the detriment of others. Legend didn't have any issues carrying out Outlaw's commands. Especially since he was being paid for it. Hell, he would've done it for free.

But when he was removed from his position with *BBM*, word traveled fast that he was back on the streets. He started to receive contracts from people offering to pay whatever price he could come up with to handle their problems, with the same stealth and precision as he had for Outlaw. Every contract came from some shady, immoral, low life motherfucka who he wouldn't have normally dealt with. No reputable person would fuck with him on any level because the rumor was that he was Outlaw's enemy and the reason his entire family was almost killed. Everyone who knew anything about what went down blamed him for the fact that January had been shot, and he never bothered to correct anyone who said it because he believed it himself.

Legend accepted every job presented to him as a matter of escape from suffering through the guilt that he felt and the misery that came along with going from being at the top to swiftly falling to the bottom. His character was shot; everyone saw him as a traitor. In the criminal life, illegal crimes were overlooked, but betrayal was never forgiven and usually punishable by death. The only reason he was afforded any grace at all was because he'd supposedly betrayed *BBM* to save his family. Therefore, being regarded as a traitor led him to find respect another way: through fear.

Legend took contract after contract, racking up bad karma and more money than he could ever spend. Eventually, he became numb, terrorizing the streets like a zombie, without regard for anyone's life as long as whoever wanted it to end could pay the price. He would've gone on forever, not thinking anything about it, until he saw the way his mom looked at him one day.

One day Legend went to visit her, and she couldn't even look him in his face. She said his eyes were cold and dark and that the second he entered the room, she felt something evil in the air. He asked her to look at him and when she finally did, all he saw was her fear. The shit almost broke him. That day, she'd seen a part of him he never wanted her to see. He never wanted January to see it either.

When January looked at him, love oozed from her eyes. Whether she knew it or not, he saw it clear. Her face was so expressive, whatever she felt showed and she wasn't able to hide it. She wore her heart on her sleeve. The way she looked at him made him feel like he wasn't the demon he thought he was. When she was around, he was able to be the person he'd been before he'd sold his soul to the devil.

Legend heard someone knock on the door and he felt his body tense. Whoever it was that Luis had sent, he hoped she'd go away without putting up much of a fuss. He wasn't in the mood to hear it, which meant he was incapable of saying some shit that wouldn't hurt her feelings.

"Give me a minute," he mumbled to the person at the door, crossing the room to grab a t-shirt that he'd left the last time he was there. He took a sniff to make sure it was clean and then pulled it over his head, only to see there was a big ass hole in the center. Obviously, the reason why he'd left it.

Fuck.

Pulling the shirt from over his head, he tossed it to the side and rushed to answer the door, prepared to grab the money and tell whoever it was to fuck off. If she tried to whine about it, he'd just slam the door in her face. Simple solution for a simple situation.

More knocks on the door and it only pissed him off more than normal. With clenched teeth, he snatched the door open.

"I told you to give me a fuckin'—"

Legend stopped the moment his eyes fell on Jessica. Her hair was pulled up in a ponytail, accentuating her long neck, which had a spiked collar cuffed around it, in her mouth was a ball gag, secured by straps clasped at the back of her head. She wore a long leather trench coat that was open, showing that she was completely naked underneath.

The jacket was custom made with snaps that had various objects used for various sexual acts one might call sadistic: nipple clamps, whips, handcuffs, all of which were clearly shown, and a few others which were hidden, but he knew were there. How? Because the jacket she was wearing, he'd designed it.

"The fuck are you doin' here?" Legend looked off behind her. "Did Luis send you?"

She shook her head. "No, he doesn't know. Can I come in?"

"Drop off the money and tell me how the fuck you found me and got back here," he said, turning back to walk inside. Grabbing the shirt he'd had on before the fight, he pulled it on, along with a hooded jacket as Jessica did what he'd asked.

"Everyone knows what you do here. You're almost famous. Didn't you see the crowd out there? Everyone was here to see you."

He shrugged, not caring whether or not that was a fact. All he came here to do was fight and Luis handled the details. He didn't know who came here for who.

"How'd you get back here?" He asked, moving on to the next subject.

"Oh, *that* was easy." Jessica shrugged her shoulder, cocking her head to the side. "Luis sent some other bitch, but I got Sway to let me back instead. He's dating one of my friends."

Legend made a mental note to make sure Sway was fired by the end of the night. His only fuckin' job was to make sure that no one got back here unless they'd been cleared by him or Luis.

"Well, you did your job so now you can go," he said and slid his feet into his shoes. Sitting on the bed, he leaned over to tie them up, ignoring all the sounds of frustration that Jessica was making next to him.

"What? Why?" She stood in front of him and pulled the jacket open to reveal her body. "I'm not dressed like this for nothing. You won your fight and now it's time to claim your prize. We can kick it like old times."

Sitting back on the bed, propped up on his elbows, Legend let his eyes wash over her, looking from head to toe. She was crazy as fuck, mentally ill to the point that she probably needed a prescription, but Jessica's body was *sick.* It was her way of life, so naturally, it was her greatest, and only, asset. She wasn't smart or ambitious enough to do anything else; her entire life came by way of her perky tits and fat ass.

"Take off the jacket and get on the bed."

Legend stood up and watched as she did exactly as he asked, finishing up the command by lying spread eagle on top of the bed. Her eyes widened as she waited for the next instruction.

"Put the straps on your ankles," he ordered. "Tight."

"Yes, Da—"

"Don't speak!"

Jessica's mouth clamped shut and she followed his instructions to the letter, placing each strap on her ankles. Turning around, he walked to a cabinet in the far corner of the room with contents inside that were the reason for the contracts Luis made every girl sign before sending them to him.

Opening one of the doors, Legend paused and observed each tool before making his selection. Behind him, he heard Jessica's heavy breathing, getting even heavier at the sight of him holding each tool in his hand, inspecting it as he decided whether he would use it on her or not.

In some parallel world, Jessica and Legend could've been the perfect match. Neither one of them had any interest in making love. She craved pain and he had a hunger for inflicting it. Most women wouldn't admit to it, but they liked a little BDSM in their life—hair pulling, having his hand around their neck, choking them while he hit it from the back or slapping their ass until it stung and turned red.

The problem with Jessica was that she'd always wanted more. The more pain she felt, the more she was convinced it was love. She wanted to be brutalized, but he wasn't like that with chicks. The things she had wanted him to do to her required a little help from a bottle of Hennessy. Once the liquor kicked in, he slipped into full demon-mode and all inhibitions were tossed to the side. It brought out the worst in him. Jessica was the reason he didn't drink anymore. She hated when he stopped and that's when he had to get rid of her. They leached off each other's sickness in order to feed their own. They enabled each other.

With the whip in his hand, Legend walked towards where she was lying with her legs spread open on the bed. Placing the whip down for a quick moment, he grabbed her wrists and secured each one into the straps at the bottom of the headboard, tightening them until she winced from the leather digging into her skin. He then tightened the straps she'd fastened around her ankles until they were so tight, he couldn't pull them anymore. Once that was done, he took a step back to admire the sight.

This wouldn't be like last time. Jessica had been trying to pleasure him, but he couldn't because it seemed impossible to remove January from his mind. It wouldn't happen this time. Love couldn't exist where there was enormous pain, because there simply was no room for it. And no pleasure would happen in here without a good amount of torture. By the time he got started doing all the merciless things he was about to do, January would be the last thing on his mind.

Legend was about to cater to his demons.

Angels couldn't coexist in the places where demons roamed.

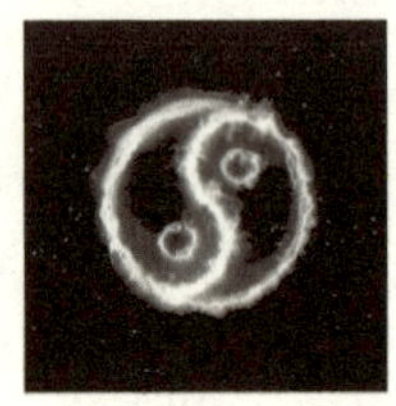

DECEPTION.

The problem with love is: You can love who you want…

But so can they.

"January… I have something to tell you. And, I just—I just want to first tell you that I'm sorry."

Blinking hard, January sat up on the bed, gripping the phone in her hand, wondering what in the world Brooke needed to tell her that she had to apologize for. Placing the phone on speaker, she placed it down on the bed and then rubbed at her eyes before peering through the darkness surrounding her, the only glimmer of light being what was shining from the screen of her phone.

"What time is it?" she mumbled, yawning loudly. "What are you doing awake?"

"Forget all that and just listen to me," Brooke said, in somewhat of a harsh whisper.

Frowning, January sighed, running her hand over her face. What was going on? And most importantly, what was Brooke whispering for?

"Alright," January said and then fell back on the bed, closing her eyes again the moment that her head hit the pillow. "I'm listening. What do you need to tell me?"

"Well, first, I want to apologize," Brooke began, biting down on her bottom lip for a brief second as she contemplated her thoughts before continuing. "I want to apologize for telling you to ignore what you were saying about Legend and to give him a chance."

At the mention of Legend, January's eyes shot open. She placed her hand on her chest, feeling a burning sensation all of a sudden that she couldn't explain. The feeling seemed to be at her heart's center, like an early reaction to whatever it was that Brooke was about to say. She didn't need to hear anything further to know that the words that would come next would be painful. Her body was already reacting to words that she hadn't even yet heard.

"What happened?" she asked, forcing the words out. Her voice was ragged and raw as it seemed to scrape across what had become a dry tongue. Reaching out, she grabbed the bottle of water on her nightstand and took a quick swig, hoping that the water would refresh her mind, body, and spirit. Or at least push away the feeling of pending doom that had settled over her.

"I went out with Onyx last night even though I said I wasn't going to go because I didn't want to run into Nico's bitch ass." Although Brooke was trying to play it strong, January could hear the pain in her friend's voice in relation to Nico, and something about it intensified the pain in her chest even more. "At the last minute, I changed my mind. I've never been one to let a nigga stop me from having a good time and I'm not about to start now." Pausing, she snorted a burst of air out of her nose and then sighed. "Or that's what I thought anyways. He ended up being there… sitting up in V.I.P. with some bitch I've never seen before. I guess she's whoever he wants to be with."

"Aww, Brooke," January started, placing her hand over her chest. She knew exactly how her friend might feel, even if she tried to deny it. Brooke had very deep feelings for Nico and it had to hurt her to see him with someone else.

"But that's not it, January," Brooke continued, about to drop the hammer on the nail that was prepped and ready to pierce into January's heart. She didn't want to tell her the next part of what occurred during her night but at the same time, she knew there was no way that she couldn't. January was her friend and she would be doing her a disservice to not share with her what she'd seen, no matter how hurtful it could be.

"Nico was there with another girl… and so was Legend."

"He was?"

January felt sick to her stomach. Like she was going to vomit. Legend had been gone for over a week and every day she chose to focus on her studies, busy herself with school while tell herself that he hadn't left her to be with another woman instead.

"Yeah, but I wasn't going to bring it up because the first time I saw her, it was obvious she wasn't nobody special. But then I saw her again. And it was different."

When Brooke said it, in some odd way, she appeared green in the face. Green in the Black girl way, where her face looked a little peckish and drained of blood. Like she was about to be forced to say something she really didn't want to say.

"Different, like how?" January asked, though she wasn't sure she really wanted the answer to her question.

"Well, it was last night. Legend had just had a fight and Nico called me after on FaceTime. He was waiting, I guess. For Legend to… finish up."

January's stomach lurched forward. "I think I'm going to be sick," she muttered.

"I don't think he knew Legend was with Jessica. Because when he noticed I could see Legend and the girl behind him, he said 'Oh shit!' and hung up. He called back later, asking me not to tell you, but…" Brooke shrugged. "Nico knows what's up."

Still fighting against what she was hearing and what she felt she knew in her heart to be true, January tried to give it one last fight.

"Well, how do you know he was doing something with her? Was she just around? And… what does she look like?"

Brooke sighed, knowing she was about to deliver the final blow.

"White girl, dark brown and blondish colored hair. And the reason I'm telling you this time is because they came out of Legend's back room holding hands, her hair was all over the place and she had that 'freshly fucked' face. Also, she was wearing a long trench coat with heels even though it was hot as hell. I'm positive she didn't have any clothes under it."

Hanging her head, January sniffed a tear from her eyes. She was devastated. Didn't even have the will to speak on the phone anymore. Her heart was completely broken. Seemingly beyond any kind of repair. Never in life she ever think she would give a man the power to hurt her in this way… and he actually do it.

"Thank you, Brooke," she whispered. It took all the strength she had left to do simply that. "I don't feel good. I just wanna lie down for a while. I'll call you later."

Silent for a while, Brooke wondered if she had done the right thing. It felt like she hadn't; January had been so upbeat when she had first called and now it was like she had ruined her day. But at the same time, January was her best friend. She would be doing her a disservice if she stood by and let her friend's emotions get played like that.

"I understand. Call me any time, it don't matter when," Brooke replied. She was about to hang up and then stopped. "And if you want me to creep up on that nigga and stab him or even just slash his tires, I'm here. I know you can't go nowhere and you definitely can't do nothing in that house without being the obvious suspect. But I'm still out here in these streets and I'm ready."

By some miracle, that was able to pull a small giggle out of January.

"Thank you, girl," she said. "Who knows? I might have to take you up on your offer one day."

"And I will be totally motherfuckin' ready."

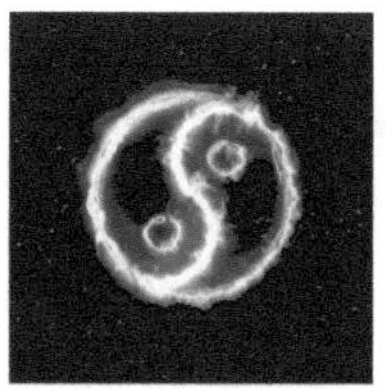

PRINCE OF DARKNESS.

"If you know not that the prince of darkness is also the king of light, then you know not me."

January's face clouded with confusion. Here was Professor Bey talking in riddles again when all she wanted was a straight answer. Could she turn in her paper early so that she could skip town and never have to see Legend's face again? He didn't know how but someway she was leaving. She wanted it too deeply for her wish to not come true. But instead of understanding her frustration, Professor Bey wanted to flex her knowledge and talk her through her issues. As usual.

Yes, I totally understand that your partner is an asshole. He's the jerk of all jerks. No one in the world could be a worse partner than mine.

That's all she needed to hear but instead, here she was getting another philosophical lesson that she didn't have the time or patience for.

"I'm sorry, Professor Bey, but I have no idea what that means. Really, I just want to—"

"It means that we were all created with dual natures—both good and evil. I brought it up because you said your reasoning for not wanting to partner with Legend on the final paper is 'because he's evil'."

January flinched. She'd actually forgotten that she'd said that.

"But no one is all one or the other. We classify 'evil' as things that cause human suffering and 'good' as things that stop human suffering. But no person is evil. Their *attachment* to evil behaviors is evil but beyond the attachment is only a person, like you and me. A person who has to figure out how to stop being attached to things that make them act in evil ways."

January blinked at the image of Professor Bey's face through the computer screen. completely lost as to how this related to her question, to her project and to Legend.

"Legend has an attachment to ways of thinking based on how and where he was raised. You didn't grow up where he did. The streets give you an entirely different way of thinking and processing. It's a dog eat dog world out there and it's hard on the psyche to meet someone who doesn't act that way and expects you to be different. He's sincerely clueless about how to deal with you. He's slowly learning as life moves along. You're healing him in a way but healing is a low process. But, the fact that he's moving at all means he's trying. Remember the story of the tortoise and the hare… 'slow and steady wins the race'."

Shit, January thought, sulking. If slow and steady was what Legend was, he wasn't a tortoise at all. He was a fuckin' snail. She had fallen in love with a damn snail.

"As people mature, they begin to see others in the world in terms of 'us' and not 'them.' They feel connected to others, so they don't want to hurt them. But when people haven't matured to that level, or when they are stuck in survival mode, their thinking is in terms of 'us vs. them' or 'me vs. you.' They don't understand the act of karma—that everything you do, whether good or bad, has an equal and opposite effect back onto you. Maybe not in the *exact* way that you inflicted that pain on others, but it *always* comes back.

People who think this way are okay with doing evil to others because their thinking is 'that's not *me*, that's them. And 'I'm only concerned with me.' That's the reality Legend has lived in. He only existed in an us and them mentality. 'Us' included the people important to him and 'them' was everyone else. And he developed attachments to behaviors based on those things. One attachment he developed is that he prioritizes his time, attention, and focus on material things. He was loyal only to what brought him money and prestige. Then you came along. He has to change. And it's hard as hell to change the way you think. It's literally a rebirth. You're watching a man die. He's losing his old identity and creating a new one that includes many exceptions that he has to make to include you. You have to be patient and keep sending him love. If you don't, you'll end up being just like everyone else in his life who has left him when he needed them most. But still… the only way for you to be there for him is to be there for yourself *first*. Which means, love him, but don't swallow his bullshit."

Pausing, Professor Bey took a moment to shake her head and laugh, obviously seeing and understanding something that January couldn't for herself.

"There comes a time in every man's life when he runs into the one thing that shows him there is something more important than himself. And that moment usually happens at the same time when a woman realizes that the most important thing in the world is herself."

January crinkled her nose. "Huh?"

"Girl!" Professor Bey said, laughing. "Must I explain everything to you?"

Lifting a finger, January scratched the top of her head.

Apparently so, because my ass is lost again, she thought.

"Okay, let me break it down like this." Professor Bey sat back in her chair, allowing her eyes to lift to the ceiling as she thought about the best way to illustrate a concept that she was so excited about. "From the beginning of life, right at the start of childhood, little boys are taught that they are the most important beings on Earth and what are little girls taught? That they are on Earth to serve men. Men are taught to put themselves first and that they are defined by their possessions and money. And women are taught to do everything in her power to attract and keep a man. In essence, men are taught to gain power at all costs and women are taught to hand her power over to him. It's not until a man falls in love with a woman who has fallen in love with herself that this changes. She will stop being a martyr for love and realizes that she deserves to get back the love she gives. And that man, if he loves her, will realizes that he's willing to do whatever it takes, even if it means sacrificing the things that he once put above everyone, to be with her."

It was a lesson in love that January hadn't even been prepared for. At the same time, it made perfect sense.

"So... When a woman loves herself first, then a man learns how to love her?"

"That's when he learns to love her properly," Professor Bey corrected her. "He can love her before but as long as she's sacrificing herself to make him happy, he will take without really giving back anything. Once she loves herself and demands more, he will either level up or move on out."

Swallowing hard, January pushed through the mental urging telling her not to ask the next question.

"What happens if he doesn't? What do you do if he never levels up or decides to level up and treat her better?"

"Well..." Professor Bey sighed. "The thing about love is that you can't love anyone unless you love yourself first. Which means you establish boundaries around anyone and anything who makes you feel unworthy or less than. Sometimes that means creating distance between you and the person you love, even if they do love you."

Clapping her hands together once, January leaned forward in her chair. That was exactly what she wanted to hear.

"Right. So, then you agree that I can't work with Legend anymore. That I should just do our project on my own."

"No," Professor Bey replied, shaking her head. "Actually, I think the exact opposite."

"What?!" January's eyes nearly busted out of her skull. "I thought you just said..."

"I said that you should establish boundaries," she clarified. "You can't cut people out of your life or heart. Life is about acknowledging the good and the bad in people and learning how to punish the bad while also inviting in the good. It's how you learn to love yourself while also teaching someone else how to properly love you."

January fell into a full-on sulk, bottom-lip dropping and all. Obviously, Professor Bey had picked up on more about her situation than she'd told her. There was more to this than a simple need to keep them together for a class project.

"I really must've been a matchmaker in another life," Professor Bey said, almost as if she were talking to herself. "I'm fucking good at this shit."

"Yeah, but where does that leave me?" January mumbled, thinking about the reality of her present situation. She couldn't fathom dealing with Legend anymore. She couldn't get over his lies, all the secrecy, and his inability to just be a regular human being. Dealing with him required too much energy. It opened her up to too much heartache. She didn't want to learn how to establish boundaries by dealing with him. And she definitely didn't want to teach him how to love a woman. She didn't want to teach him a damn thing.

I'm not his parent, she thought. *I'm barely even his friend.*

"There are both good and bad in everyone. The same person who can make you feel the purest love can also cause you the sharpest pain. You have to accept these things for what they are, adjust, and move forward in grace."

"But can't I just—"

"No." Professor Bey cut her off, but her tone was softer, more understanding. "I know you can't. I can see how much this is bothering you and, as your teacher and mentor in this, I can't force you to be with someone who is creating this much of an issue, especially not when you have so much going on in your life. You can do the project alone and submit it to me when you're ready. Take all the time you need to."

"Thank you," January whispered, wiping tears from her eyes. She hadn't even known that she had gotten that worked up. It all happened before she even knew it.

"No problem," Professor Bey let out with a sigh. "I'm sorry you had to go through this. I really thought you two were the perfect pairing for this project. I wish you the best and I'll miss speaking with you like this. Call me any time you feel the need to!"

With a nod of her head, January gave Professor Bey a final goodbye and laid back down on her bed. All she had the energy to do in the moment is just stay in bed and cry.

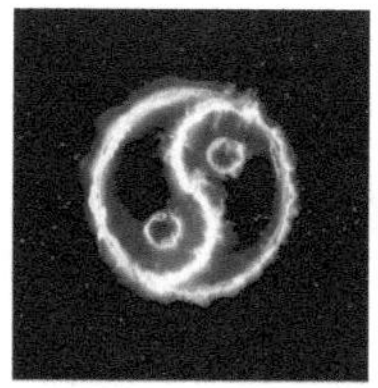

THE 3 FS.

"YOU SEEN JANUARY YET?"

"Nah."

"You avoiding her because I told you about Brooke seeing you and Jessica?"

Legend mired, pausing for a bit to consider the question. "Somewhat. I mean, I hadn't been back over there in about a week before that happened. But…" Sighing, he placed his elbows on the island in Nico's kitchen and clasped his hands together. "That said, it ain't like I'm in no hurry to see what's about to happen when I do go back. Shit's different between me and her now."

Nico's brows bunched on his forehead as he stopped making their before gym smoothie to look at him.

"Oh? How different."

"Different, different." Legend ran his hand over his face and sighed heavily once again. "I did some shit with her I knew so shouldn't have done. Now I'm just trying to fix it."

Slamming down the container he was holding onto the countertop and looked his cousin square in the eyes.

"Nigga! I *told* you the shit I'm fuckin' with and you went and did the same thing? It's voodoo. All the girls doing it now. Got us thinking it's just good pussy and they done really hit a nigga off with some other-worldly shit."

Legend couldn't say anything to that because Nico definitely had a point. Everything he had said the other night that Legend had thought was just the crazy ravings of a man who hadn't ran up in nothing decent in a while was actually starting to make sense.

Leaning over on the counter, Nico lowered his voice to ask him another question to confirm one other thing that had been happening to him since he had sex with Brooke.

"Tell me this, you did anything with Jessica?"

Sliding back in his chair, Legend took a deep breath and then nudged his nose with his finger before shaking his head.

"Nah, wasn't happening. I tried like hell but wasn't in the mood. Everything Jessica did turned me off. I just wasn't feeling it like that. It felt fake, like I was missing something."

"I knew it," Nico said, slapping the tabletop with his hand. "A spell."

"Ain't no fuckin' spell," Legend said, laughing this time. Nico was crazy as hell. He would come up with any reason, even claiming Brooke was poisoning his ass in some way, rather than to admit he'd caught feelings.

"Well, what you think it is then?"

Pausing, Legend took a moment to consider it. Their homeboys in the hood would be fully with the shits for what he was about to say, having all the jokes.

Growing up, it was common knowledge that a real nigga wasn't supposed to have feelings. But Nico and Legend were raised differently. Many boys growing in the hood never had fathers to show them how fulfilling it could be to really love a woman and get the best of her love back. Or if they did have fathers, them niggas were too busy playing the field, fucking anything in the streets and bringing her back his fucked up energy along with whatever vibes he'd caught with the hoes he was dealing with. And that's not even talking about the abuse.

Though it had a rocky start, Legend's parents learned to battle their own traumatic upbringings and heal together into what was now the most perfect love. So did Nico's parents. Shit was different with them; though they tried to fit in with their surroundings, deep down, they knew there was nothing weak about loving a woman. A woman's love was how a man found his true strength. And loving her the right way was what helped him to manifest his greatest dreams. Fucking a woman over brought along God's greatest wrath.

"I don't think. I know what it is. And so do you," he cut his eyes at Nico. "Lovesick ass nigga."

Sitting up, Nico threw his hands in the air. "Here you go with this bullshit, bruh. I'm better off thinking she puts roots on me or some shit."

Laughing, Legend started tying up his locs, getting into gym mode.

"Well, the better question is, love or voodoo magic, what you gon' do about it?"

Nico shrugged his shoulders a little. "Chicks be on some afferent shit. That's also why I can't fuck with Brooke right now. She want attention, wine and dines, picnics at the park." He shook his head. "I ain't on that shit right now. I got too much going on. Trying to stack as much bread as I can so I can jump out of this shit and jump into something else."

"And then what?" Legend asked, leaning back in his seat.

He shrugged again. "And then I guess I'll find out where Brooke at and scoop her. She givin' me wifey vibes but it's coming at the wrong time. I ain't on that shit right now. Don't got time for it. She want too much from me and, to be honest, I can't say she don't deserve it. I'm just not the nigga who can give it to her right now."

Legend's eyes widened. "Wifey vibes, huh? That's part of the spell too, huh?"

Scrunching up his nose into a frown, as if it pained him to admit it, Nico nodded his head.

That was shocking for Legend to hear. Nico and Legend weren't the type of niggas who didn't know how to talk about shit that most niggas would call 'soft.' They were raised by men who didn't have any problem telling the world how they felt about the woman they decided to live their life with. So it wasn't like they had issues with admitting or discussing their feelings about loving a woman when the time came. The problem was that they never thought the time would come. Never was it a thought that they'd experience the shit to begin with. It was weird as hell to be even having a conversation about it.

"You tell her that?" Legend asked, sincerely just wondering for his own benefit. "You ask her to wait?"

"Nah," he admitted. Leaning over onto the counter, he balanced his weight on his elbows. "I can't ask her to do no shit like that. I can't give her what she wants, so how can I expect her to not wanna move on?"

Legend nodded, made sense to him. Grabbing his phone, he thumbed through it, checking for a message from January. Of course, there was none. Her ass was stubborn as hell. Clenching his jaw, he stuffed the phone back in his pocket.

"That said…" Nico began with a smirk. "I know she won't."

"You better hope not. You already been a shitty ass sparring partner and she ain't even with nobody," Legend replied and stood up. "If she decides to move on, you ain't gon' take it well. Yo' ass gon' be sick."

Nico didn't deny it and instead grabbed his own phone from off the counter, pecking in it with a tight expression on his face. Legend eyed him for a moment, knowing exactly who he was hitting up. And in that moment, his own problems came to mind. He had some shit going on in his own world of pain and pleasure that he was creating with January. He couldn't run from the confrontation he knew was coming. It was time to face it.

"Listen, I'm 'bout to head out," Legend said, walking around the counter. Nico looked up from his phone in time to clasp hands as they said their goodbyes.

"Raincheck on the gym, huh?" Nico grinned as he said it, knowing full well the reason for Legend's sudden change in plans.

"I'mma just work out at the crib. Gotta check on something right quick," Legend told him, chucking the deuces.

"Yeah, I feel ya. So do I."

Legend looked back at Nico before he walked away, not at all surprised to see his attention back on his phone.

Imagine this shit, Legend thought.

Legend never thought he'd see the day, to be honest. It wasn't like they deliberately avoided having something real with a woman, it just wasn't something they could see. Their parents had been able to do it, but they saw them as an anomaly. In their minds, their fathers had been able to find the last decent women in the world and God just didn't make 'em like that no more.

Regarded as 'young rich niggas,' they had their pick of any woman on the planet. And that's exactly how they spent their teens—picking every woman on the planet that caught their eyes. After a few years of doing that shit, it became clear that wasn't nothing fulfilling about it. From Instagram models to some of your favorite celebrities, they dealt with them all and came to the same conclusion: behind every pretty face was a lot of bullshit for a nigga to deal with. And, honestly speaking, neither one of them felt like the chick they were with was worth putting up with all of it. It was easier to move on and start over again with someone else until that went sour, too.

January was the first woman in the world that Legend actually considered fighting to keep *in* his life rather than fighting to get her *out* of it.

At the same time, he had to ask himself, he was fighting to give her what? What glory was in it for her to be the mafia hitta's girl? She didn't even want that life, which she'd said plenty of times before. And Legend was stuck in it. Being in the streets was all he knew; it was all he'd considered for his life. He hadn't thought behind it to anything else. What could he *really* give her out of all the things she wanted?

Honestly, he didn't know the answer to that.

Legend stepped through the door of his apartment, not quite knowing what would greet him on the other side, but he was prepared for it. He wasn't sure how much of what went down with Jessica that January knew about but, knowing what he knew about Brooke, she definitely gave her all the details she saw and probably even some shit she had only *thought* she'd seen. Brooke meant well but she was a sucker for some gossip and that kinda shit Legend didn't have the patience for. That 'he said, she said' shit could get a nigga killed. Having that kinda strife between him and January was too much for him. He needed her to be at peace. She meant too much to him. That was the biggest reason he'd decided to skip the gym and come back home.

"January?" He called out when he saw that all the lights in the entire house were off.

Walking towards the hall, he stopped in front of her room door and looked down, noticing that her light was off too. He looked at his watch. It was nearly noon. There was no way she was still sleeping.

"January?"

"Go away!"

Fuck.

She was crying. He could hear it all in her voice. Scratching the top of his head, he began to pace back and forth in front of her door, trying to figure out what the hell he was going to do. His stomach twisted in knots, his legs felt like they had somehow transformed into rubber. But worst of all, he didn't have a single fuckin' idea as to what to do.

"The secret to calming a woman down is to always remember the three F's: Food, Fuck, and Find. First you give her food, then you fuck her. If neither one of those work, nigga, you better find yourself some other place to be."

That was wisdom given to him courtesy his Uncle Murk, Nico's father. But in this instance, he didn't think any of the three would apply. January had already proven that he couldn't make her eat shit, he was scared as hell to fuck her, especially if she thought he'd just been with another woman, and finding another place to be wouldn't solve anything. He was at a loss for what to do.

Before he could decide whether to try again to speak to her or just go to his room until she calmed down, her door was unlocked, yanked open and the next thing he saw was January's puffy face, tear-stained cheeks and red-rimmed eyes looking back at him.

"What do you want, Legend?"

Clearing his throat as if somehow someone above would send him down the words to say, he just stood there, waiting. And looking.

"Yes?" January asked, again. "You're here, at my door. You knocked, I responded. I even opened the door. What else do you want from me?"

In that moment, Legend fully understood the phrase 'cat got your tongue'. He literally was caught between a rock and a hard place. He couldn't bypass the fact that she had been crying because it was obvious. But to speak on that would be to ask her what was wrong. And that would open another can of worms. With no other advice to lean on, Legend decided to take a page out of Uncle Murk's book, starting with the first of the 3 Fs.

"Um… you hungry? I was thinking I could make you something to eat."

Something to eat?

Something about how she perceived his question, how careless, heartless and avoidant it sounded to her ears, set January's emotions into overdrive. The last part of control that she had over them folded and all that was left was a raging fire of pure emotion. A ball of unavoidable anguish and pain, all brought on by the many faces of love.

January was hysterical. Her emotions and thoughts merged into one, making her a complete, inconsolable mess. Legend watched her with curious eyes, somewhat horrified, a pinch of devastation burning inside. So many emotions, and so little experience on how to deal with them. Everything about this situation was a hot, fuckin' mess. By nature, he was aggressive. He was a fighter, and that's the only way he knew how to handle his problems.

"What the *fuck* is wrong with you?" he said, hoping that she would just make this easy on him and get everything out in the open so it could be dealt with. With any hope, it wouldn't be what he already thought it was and they could move forward in another way. But, of course, one thing was certain about January; she was anything but easy.

"Is this because I left you here alone?" he asked, hoping it was. "Because if that was it, the problem has been solved. I did all the shit I needed to do while I was gone. I was *working*. So if you choose to leave, I can secure a flight for you. If it'll make you happy, you can be out of this bitch today."

And now he wants to get rid of me. I've become a complication in his life… of course.

She was thinking from hurt and Legend was speaking from his own pain. They were caught up in the illusions of love and emotions, and it was only sending them both deeper down the rabbit hole. Neither one wanted to separate but they were too stubborn to do anything but push each other away.

January wanted to speak, to tell him what was wrong, curse, shout, yell, explain, but her capacity to express anything in real words wasn't working. At the moment, all she could do was feel. The problem was feeling was the last thing she wanted to do. If she had the capacity to go numb, it would be much more preferred than the immense amount of pain she felt. The worst part of it was that she couldn't even explain why. There were so many things wrong with how she was feeling, but she felt them all the same.

Legend *wasn't hers* to stake claim on. He *wasn't hers* to be jealous of.

When it came to ownership, it was painfully obvious that shit only went one way. She was the one perpetually stuck in her feelings, seemingly cockblocked by the universe into being faithful to a nigga who wasn't even hers to begin with. She opened her mouth to tell him the words that she'd formed in her mind. The ones she had rehearsed over and over again for the next time she saw him, hoping that the rehearsal would give her the nerve to say it all to his face. She wanted to let him know that she never wanted to see him again. He was none of her concern and she wasn't really his.

They needed to go back to being strangers. She wanted the life she had before she had run into him the second time around. Every collision with Legend seemed to send her completely off course. Like a bookmark in a book, there was a before and after him, but the after always seemed to leave her wounded in some way.

Trying to force herself to speak, she opened her mouth to let him know all the things she wanted to say but the second she opened it, the only thing that came out was more tears. Eyes narrowed, Legend allowed his arms to hang by his side, feeling awkward as hell. He scratched his head, staring at her, wondering what on Earth he was going to do about this woman in front of him who was quite literally about two seconds away from flipping the fuck out.

"January, I swear if you don't fuckin' talk..."

"Then what?" she shouted, suddenly finding her voice as her emotions quickly shifted into anger. "Then you'll go back and fuck the bitch you've been with? The one you've been fuckin' already because I couldn't do it good enough for you?"

Legend's eyes bugged and his hand swiped the top of his head as he stared at her, standing in the official 'ain't shit nigga' pose: legs wide, hand on head, eyes squinted, mouth prepared to tell a lie that his brain hadn't quite concocted yet. January waited with hands on her hips, eyes narrowed, for him to go ahead and say whatever was coming next so she could go in for the kill.

"What the hell are you talkin' about? I don't have no—"

Before he could finish, he had to duck, just barely moving out of the way of some object she had thrown at his head. It wasn't until he turned to look that he realized it was the pocketknife. One he he'd given her to protect herself. Protect herself against other mother-fuckas… not *him.* She was out of control.

Legend sucked in a breath, suddenly realizing that he'd greatly underestimated the situation. January wasn't only mad, she was mad *as fuck.* This shit was quickly working its way up to a whole other level.

She really tryin' to kill my ass, he thought, finessing the facial hair on his chin as he looked back at the knife once more, noticing the blade was out.

Damn, he thought again, feeling an unsettling feeling in the pit of his stomach. Did she really want him dead?

"What the fuck goin' on with you?" He steeled his voice with the question, trying to stay calm to hopefully lower the level of her aggression. "You're trippin' right now. We both know I don't have no—"

Once again, his statement was left unfinished. Like something wild, vicious and untamed, January charged at him full-speed, as if she doubled as an NFL line-backer in her free time. He braced himself for the collision but was completely caught off-guard when she launched in the air and pirouetted on his ass like a little ass ballerina ninja, tackling him straight to the ground.

"You're a fuckin' liar and I hate you!" she yelled, pummeling him with punch after punch.

Stunned, Legend was rendered speechless and unable to move for a moment, until a smooth right-hook nearly caught him in the jaw.

"Whoa, shit!" he said, jerking back out of the way.

January wasn't playing around. Grabbing both of her arms, he stretched them apart to restrain her. She was seething, suspended in the air and unable to move, unable to release the aggression she felt onto the object of her misery.

"What the hell is going on with you?" he asked, searching his mind for the answer himself. "When I left here, you were all good. Now you trippin'. What the fuck? Speak... say whatever it is that you want to say. Put that shit out on the table so we can deal with it."

Pausing for a moment, January frowned, realizing that the ball was in her court. But now she was even more conflicted. She wanted to tell him the reason for everything, but realized she couldn't. She wasn't his girl; they hadn't even talked about how they felt about each other or if they felt anything at all. She was just the girl he was fucking. That position came with nothing. No expectations, no guarantees, no accountability, and no responsibilities. The only thing it came with was occasional dick and, as much as she loved it, she knew she didn't need any more of that. It only further complicated things.

When their bodies merged, the effect was intoxicating. It only compounded all of the emotions she already knew shouldn't be felt. As much as she wanted to feel him in that moment, and every moment, she knew she couldn't take it there with Legend any longer. But unfortunately, he had other plans.

As Legend lay under January, restraining her, something took a sudden shift. A vision of a sweet fantasy erupted in his mind and his body went warm with heat building up straight from his center. His eyes connected with hers and in that moment, she could read his thoughts clearly. He didn't have to say a word, she knew exactly what he was thinking.

"Legend, *no*," she said, with force.

He didn't respond to her, barely paid attention. The thing about their connection is that he could read her like a book that he'd written himself. He knew when January's 'no' was really a 'no' and he also knew when her 'no' was really a 'yes'. In this moment, she was playing it hard but she really wanted what was coming next as bad as she did.

She was a warrior, the same as him. A pretty one. A gentle one. But a warrior nonetheless. Her father had made sure that she could defend herself, if it came down to it. Besides being in ballet, before the accident, she also had a background in taekwondo and judo. She couldn't fuck with guns before he taught her to hold one. But if she really wanted to, she could flip a nigga on his shit. The fact that she wasn't fighting him, barely doing anything but somewhat pushing him away told him everything he needed to know about how she *really* felt.

Time to go to the second of the 3 Fs, Legend thought.

If this one didn't work, he'd give her what she wanted. He'd let her have her space. But tomorrow, same time, he'd be back at it again.

Offering the first of the 3 Fs. And if she knew like he knew, she better eat his motherfuckin' food.

"I can't do this… not when you've been with someone else," January told him, a tear falling from the corner of her eyes. "Brooke saw you with a girl…"

Legend was sliding her shorts down, along with her panties, positioning himself right between her legs, using his legs to force her thighs apart so that he could access her happy place.

"I didn't fuck her. That was an old situation… some bullshit that I had to deal with right quick. Not a concern."

Leaning down, he kissed her cheek as he pulled down his sweatpants with one hand, his other one still wrapped around both of January's wrists, holding her in place. She was still putting up a struggle but that wasn't shit he couldn't deal with. The only thing that was making it all hard was his dick. He was bricked up to the max. This was the side effect of real chemistry. Jessica had done all kinds of tricks and could barely get him from being half-flaccid. January, on the other hand, didn't even have to try.

"But I love you, Legend," January admitted, unable to say anything that didn't come straight from the heart. She was telling him too much, much more than she ever really wanted to tell anyone. But she was so tired that she could barely fight against anything that wasn't real. Couldn't even force him off of her when everything was telling her that she should push him away for breaking her heart. For leaving her alone to share time with another. But she couldn't even do that because she loved him that much. Unconditionally. No matter what.

"I love you too," Legend said, leaning down, speaking sweetly right into her ear.

She wasn't the only one who couldn't escape the realness in between them in that moment. Somehow, a moment that had begun in utter chaos had suddenly become the perfect atmosphere to release everything inside of them that was pure. All the things that needed to be said.

Letting go of all resistance, January relaxed her body totally, allowing Legend into her. Whatever the situation was the night before, whatever had happened, hadn't happened or almost happened was no longer a concern of hers. All that she had was this moment, and in *this* moment, Legend had confessed his love for her. She honestly couldn't say that she wanted anything more.

But, even still, with all the love she had in her heart, and how content she was in this moment. She knew that was all it was… a moment. Once they left it, things would return back to the chaos, the questions, the lack of clarity that she had felt before. She needed to leave. She needed peace. She needed to get back in control of her life. She couldn't allow the things happening with Legend to crowd her mind anymore.

Heavy is the crown and yet she wears it as if it were a feather, There is strength in her heart, determination in her eyes and the will to survive resides within her soul.

She is you. A warrior. A Champion. A fighter. A Queen.

R.H. SIN

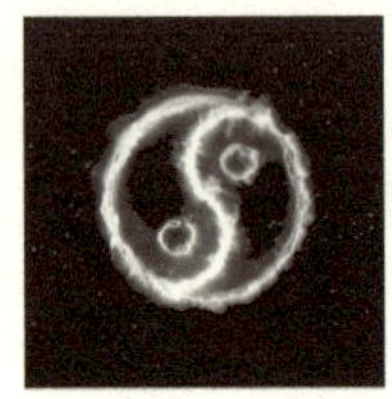

TIME TO GO.

They said heavy was the head that wears the crown, but what did they say about the heart?

JANUARY WAS ESCORTED TO THE LOS ANGELES INTERNATIONAL Airport in true mafia princess style, with a motorcade of cars that fit the requirement for the President of the United States. Truth be told, even the first family didn't have security as thick as hers or with half as much advanced technology. She was guarded beyond measure, totally and completely unreachable. Untouchable.

The only problem was that the true damage had already been done. In her ignorance of experience about love and life, she'd already let the enemy in. Now, although on the outside no evidence could be seen, she felt like she would spend a lifetime nursing the scars on her heart.

"Are you okay?"

Brooke's voice called her attention but, though she knew her friend wanted more, all she could manage to give her was a quick nod.

Like a Band-Aid placed over a bleeding wound, she forced her lips into a smile, hoping that Brooke was able to pull more warmth from it than she felt in delivering it. Regardless of the warm autumn LA breeze, January felt a constant chill in the air. The cold nature of how Legend had dismissed her left her soul permanently frostbitten beyond repair. The only thing left for her to do now was wait until that part of her broke away over time.

Being abandoned by him was different from the last time. They'd bonded on a level that was much more than a simple conversation in the park. He was more to her now than a childhood fantasy. A possibility. A potential lover somewhat possibility. He'd explored her body in ways no one ever had. Fused with her soul, they merged into one other.

Two parts had become one.

She'd thought after experiencing her first heartbreak that she was wiser now. More cunning, more prepared and more apt to see through a surface layer of truth down to the lies beneath. Unfortunately, she was learning that when it came to real life, there was no mastering love. The issues of the heart were no fairytale. No romance novel could fully and accurately describe the type of pain a woman felt when she let down her walls to give her love away, only to find out that she'd chosen to give it to the wrong nigga.

"It'll get better with time," Brooke said, reaching out to touch January lightly on her knee.

If anyone on Earth understood what her girl was going through, she did. It was a cruel, cold world for a woman who had yet to receive her first love scar. Heartbreak was inevitable and when it came to love, only the strong survived. Unfortunately, strength of heart only came through the suffering of experience. Rarely did a woman escape that. You had to deal with a few bad eggs before you learned how to spot a good one.

Growing up sheltered from the pain of life that was commonplace in the life of so many others gave January a heart of gold. One would think that witnessing a heart so pure would make a man consider it unfuckwitable. That any man with any type of decency would either come correct or not come at all. But, apparently, Legend wasn't a decent man at all.

"I'll be fine," January said, keeping it one hundred. "I don't know how. But I will, eventually."

She didn't have the strength to play it hard like she would have in her life before. Dealing with Legend had opened her up. He'd gotten her used to exposing her vulnerability, relaxing into her honesty. He'd made her see the value in taking off her armor, even though he'd made her regret it anyway. She hated to admit it, but he'd changed her, and she would never again be the same. Her life would be forever split into two parts: before Legend and the time after. He'd marked her heart, written his name all over her soul. She would never be more than 'okay' again.

"Thank you for riding with me to the airport," January said, sniffing as tears came to her eyes.

She'd cried so much in the past few months that she didn't even bother to fight them back anymore. They felt so natural in her eyes now. Just like the pain ripping through her chest, it seemed to all belonged there.

"Are you sure you're making the right decision?" Brooke asked in a soft voice, somewhat apprehensive about speaking on a sensitive topic.

"Yes," January said matter-of-factly, as if she knew it to be a Biblical truth.

Brooke stared at her, loving how sure of things January seemed to be in the moment. She wasn't sure what it was, but she wanted some of that for herself.

"We don't want the same things from life. We don't want the same things from each other. Legend is restless. He's searching for something to make him feel fulfilled. Never satisfied about his life because he's always searching for the next best thing. Always on the move, always looking for something to add an extra layer of spice to his life."

January shrugged and swallowed hard, forcing away the tears from her eyes. "I want something solid, practical, exciting but real. I'm not trying to lock him down. Being honest, marriage sounds disgusting to me." She giggled lightly at the thought. "At least in the way people currently make it."

As wonderful as her parents' marriage appeared to be, she wasn't sure that a traditional relationship appealed at all to her. January valued her freedom; she never wanted to exchange love for that.

However, in being free, she still knew that she deserved a stable love. She deserved someone willing to commit to her. Someone who saw a future with her in whatever way they defined it. Someone who knew his soul as intimately as she knew hers. Highly intuitive and creative, January had always been incredibly insightful, even as a child. She always knew that she wanted to achieve a lot in life; her plate would always be full. She didn't want to involve herself in a future of drama and fighting with future lovers. She wanted to fall for someone, and allow their worlds to collide.

"He's just not ready for me yet. And he may never be." January shrugged, trying to wave away the void inside that came along with her admission of that. "But I have to be okay with what he's choosing. No one can fight against what their soul wants and still be happy. So if he's happiest without me… then that must be what he needs."

"Damn," Brooke said, shaking her head. "Listen, I knew you was a little older than me and all… but that was some real deep shit you just said."

As they pulled up to the area for boarding the private jets, January leaned over and gave Brooke a big hug, holding her as tightly as she could. She hated that they had to be apart in this moment but somehow, she knew this wasn't the end and that their paths would cross again. Closer to her than any of her cousins, Brooke was like the sister that January always wanted and never had. They would always stay in contact with each other.

"Love you, J."

"Love you, B."

The car came to a stop and the driver stepped out to open January's door. The second her heeled shoe hit the cement and she fully stepped outside, she noticed there was a slight chill in the air. Not at all what was expected for L.A., even in the late fall.

"I'll grab your bags," the driver stated and January nodded her head before turning off to look in the distance, feeling as though she were being watched.

And it turned out that she was.

Side-by-side in the distance was Nico and Legend, both standing tall like soldiers on command, watching her with eagle eyes. January's heart skipped a few beats when her eyes connected with Legend's. His expression never broke, he didn't move to wave or even say a word, but she felt so much inside of her that she felt he wanted to say.

Tears blurred her eyes. As much as she wanted to fold up in her feelings and run away towards the plane, pretending that he wasn't there, she found that she couldn't. But she also couldn't trust herself to leave if she closed the distance between them. There was something about being close to him that was intoxicating. The closer she was to him, the more impossible it would be to go.

Lifting her hand, she gave him a quick wave, to which Legend responded with a slight nod of his head. Though his expression was blank and showed nothing of his true feelings, Legend's heart was hurting. Inside, he felt like a piece of his soul was being ripped away. January was his everything, and there was nothing he wouldn't do to get her to understand that. But in this moment, he just couldn't. He was all tied up by circumstance. He had too many issues that he needed to lay to rest first. He had to get his life together, straight up the shit with his family… there was so much he had to do first before he could accommodate her.

"You good, nigga?" Nico asked, looking straight ahead.

"I'm solid," Legend replied, watching January ascend the stairs to the jet.

There was so much to say that he wasn't ready to say yet. And so, it seemed best to just stick with the basics.

"You can go ahead and go," he told Nico. "I might stay here for a minute."

"Bet," Nico replied. Pulling his hands from where they were clasped behind his back, he turned to his cousin and gave him a quick hug. He knew Legend was a G but every thug needed a hug sometimes. In this moment, he understood completely how his cousin felt—it would be the same way he felt if roles were reversed and it was Brooke that was leaving. And what was worst than January leaving was the fact that she going to a city that it was forbidden for Legend to even step foot in. It was a fucked up situation, saying the least, and Nico knew his cousin just needed some time alone.

"Don't stay out here too long. We got practice at 8," Nico said before walking away.

Not saying a word, Legend simply nodded his head.

The jet's engine began, the strip was cleared, and the take-off was approved. Legend sat in the distance, watching every bit of the exchange and didn't move a muscle to leave even when January's plane had lifted off into the air. He stood in the same place even after he could no longer see it cutting through the skies, taking her father and father away from he stood.

"Fuck," he whispered, bending down to take a seat. Something inside told him that he wasn't ready to leave that space yet. And if there was anything that he knew about that voice inside of him, it was that he should listen to it.

The sun set, it got dark and when Legend looked at his watch, it read a quarter to eight. It was time to go. Standing to his feet, he noted a very noticeable difference in him than the moment when he'd came. The void inside him, the one he'd always carried around, seemed much bigger. It was as if some of the space there had been taken by January but, now that she was gone, nothing but the emptiness she'd left behind remained.

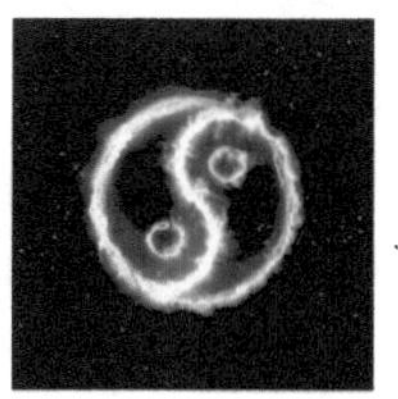

DATING GAMES.

It's hard to wait around for something you know might never happen; but it's harder to give up when you know its everything you want.

"You know, they say the best way to get over one nigga is to get up under a new nigga. Maybe you should give it a try?"

"Really?" January said, rolling her eyes. "Do you really think I should give that a try… considering how well that worked for you?"

Brooke's jaw dropped wide before she was able to gather it back up and then flip January a quick middle finger, placing it square in front of the camera so there would be no missing it on her phone screen.

"Touché, bitch," Brooke said. "You're petty as hell for sayin' the shit, but you got a point, I guess."

"Yeah, but you have a point, too," January had to admit as she considered for a moment what Brooke had said. "Maybe I should be open to dating. Honestly, I've never had a real boyfriend. Just..."

"Situationships," Brooke filled in for her without missing a beat.

January's nose crinkled into a frown. "Huh?"

"That's what they are called," Brooke explained. Lifting her wet, freshly painted nails in the air, she blew hard over the surface of her blood red nails. "Situationships are when there is no commitment, no labels on it. Y'all might even fuck every now and then but it's just a... situation."

Bowing her head, January thought to herself for a moment, considering all of the minor details in her life that people normally considered when assessing whether their lives were happy and fulfilled or not. She was in her twenties. Had somewhat of a foggy idea as to what she wanted to do with her life. She had friends and family who loved her, health, security, financial stability, shelter... pretty much everything that was required to live a satisfied and healthy life.

The only thing that she was missing out on was passion. Passion in the form of romantic love or passion in the form of anything else. Dancing was no longer part of her life, no matter how much she felt the pull to go back to it, she couldn't. Legend wasn't no longer part of her reality. And no matter how much she felt the pull to go back to him, she couldn't bring herself to do that either. Her heart was literally closed to all of the things she really wanted to bring into her life, and she was at a loss on how to fix that. The only remedy seemed to be that she had to confront those things directly. The problem was that she wasn't ready to do that directly just yet.

"What about that one guy you told me about that one time? Your high school boyfriend. What was his name? Keith?"

"Kyle?" January's brows bent low. "That's funny you mentioned him," she said, sitting up in the bed, noticing the first few bits of sunlight peeking through her blinds.

It was early as hell—it seemed that more and more Brooke was calling her at ungodly hours of the morning, waking her up far before her alarm clock did, but January was starting to like how these conversations seemed to bring clarity on what she should focus on for the rest of that day.

"What's so funny about it?"

"My mom mentioned him the other day," she thought as she picked up her phone, scrolling to the screenshot her mom had sent her of a text exchange. In it, Kyle had been as polite as ever, asking Janelle how she was doing, giving off all the pleasantries that a young man raised with the perfect amount of manners should give, before finally getting to the reason for the contact, asking about January.

I hope you don't mind me asking… I heard that she was back in the city and I was just wondering how she was doing.

January stared at the screenshot for the second time that day, this time feeling as though she should actually take action on it.

"She sent me a message that he'd sent to her. Asking how I was doing."

"You should go out with him. Nothing serious," Brooke added as a warning. "You're still getting over the bullshit with Legend, so you don't want to rebound. But it would be good to just get your mind off the drama."

"Yeah… I think you're right," January said, speaking slowly as she began to get used to the idea of reaching out to her past some-what-kinda boyfriend. "I'll send a message and… if he asked me out, we'll just go from there."

January twiddled her thumbs, ignoring the swirling sick feeling in the pit of her stomach as she sat in the backseat of one of her family's heavily armored SUVs. She was gorgeous from her head down to her toes, ice dripping from her ears, neck, and wrists, designer dress, and designer shoes on her feet. She was the mafia princess, royalty in every sense of the word, and she wore it well. She exuded power from the crown of her head to the soles of her feet. Money, power, and prestige.

The only problem was that she didn't feel powerful at all. She felt trapped, like she was liable to burst at any time under the immense pressure she felt but had to keep inside. She was fighting a war in her mind that she felt forbidden to speak about.

Legend still cycled through her thoughts, day and night. He haunted her like a tortured soul she was responsible for. It felt karmic in nature; as if she were receiving payment for wrongs she had to make right. Even now, she was trying to move on from him, but she wasn't able to, and she couldn't understand why.

"This is it," her driver said, pulling up to the restaurant. "Are you ready to get out?"

"No," January said, shaking her head. "I want to sit here for a bit."

With a nod of his head, he slid in curbside, right in front of the building, nonchalantly blocking the flow of traffic to the restaurant. None of the valet even batted an eye to tell him or the two SUVs flanking their front and back to move. There had undoubtedly been a call made ahead to inform them that Outlaw's daughter was arriving.

I don't know about this, January texted Brooke.

Once she'd hit send, she took a deep breath and then let it out slowly, trying to force herself into relaxing. Not even five seconds later, a text from Brooke came through.

Girl, it's just a date. And with a man who is damn near perfect. What are you so afraid of?

January pursed her lips into a straight line after reading the message, but she didn't reply. She was right. It was just a date. A date with a guy who was absolutely perfect. Everything any woman wanted.

But therein lay the problem.

Kyle may have been perfect, but he wasn't what she wanted. January didn't want perfect because it was too much pressure. *She* wasn't perfect. She had flaws and it wasn't a bad thing. She loved her flaws. Through heartache and pain, she'd learned how to love herself in spite of them. She didn't identify with perfect. She wanted someone who was flawed, too. She wanted someone who knew and had experienced the power of healing themselves through some major shit. Someone who had been through hell, but realized they were stronger because of it.

She wanted Legend.

But he wasn't ready yet. Instead of conquering his demons, he was still walking hand-in-hand with them, traipsing through hell and admiring the wallpaper. He'd made peace with his scars without fully acknowledging them or his tortured emotions. He hadn't learned how to love yet, so all he could bring her was his pain. And January knew she wasn't strong enough to bear it any longer. No one was strong enough to take on the wounds of another. Everyone had to carry their load for themselves. He had to face his own karma. Unfortunately, he wasn't ready to do that yet. And so… here she was on a date with Kyle.

"I'll get out now," January finally said with a long sigh.

The driver looked at her through the rearview mirror under lifted brows.

"You sure? I'll be here the entire time, so you don't have to get out until you're ready."

I'll never be ready, she thought, but "Yes, I'm ready," was what she said instead.

With her clutch in hand, she exited the car and walked into the Michelin-star rated restaurant pretending as if she didn't have an armed member of BBM walking behind and ahead of her. She was back in New York City and BBM presence was part of her normal life. She was always heavily protected. Apparently, even when she didn't know that she was. She was escorted into the restaurant and taken up to the top floor to a seating area for VIPs. As soon as she entered the space, she felt all eyes on her. But only one pair in particular caught her focus.

Wow, she thought as soon as her eyes came in focus on Kyle.

He was *not* the little high school boy that she'd dated. Clean cut, nicely dressed in a collared polo shirt that fit snuggly as if his muscles had been poured into it. His eyes sparkled as he looked her over, openly appreciating everything he saw. January immediately relaxed into his presence, feeling like she was the only girl in the room. His eyes were on her and her alone, zeroed in as if nothing else mattered. Such a clear difference from the way Legend had peered at her with disgust when they first saw each other in the bookstore. He looked at her with a mixture of curiosity and disdain whereas Kyle stared at her with pure awe and fascination.

"You're beautiful."

The first words that passed through his lips put a bright smile on her face that she couldn't hold back.

"Thank you," January said, feeling her cheeks warm.

"I should be thanking you," he replied. "Let me show you to our table."

With that said, he placed his hand in the curve of her lower back to lead the way. A slight motion from January's security team briefly caught her attention, but she motioned for them to calm down. They weren't too happy about her being touched, especially during a first date, but January felt completely at ease.

Kyle was a perfect gentleman, just as she'd always known him to be. He pulled out her chair as she sat down, helped her into her sweater when she got cold, and even allowed her to order first when the time came. In every way possible, he treated her like a queen, never once forgetting to put her first. Their conversation came easily and without force, flowing naturally like they'd never had a break in their friendship. January even found herself laughing on more than one occasion, something that she hadn't really done in a long time. It was like having the clouds part and the sun shine through on a dark and gloomy day. Finally, it was as if her spirits were lifted, and she was able to feel a small bit like the person she used to be.

"So, how do you like it at NYU?" Kyle asked, suddenly changing the subject to something January would rather avoid.

"NYU is..." she paused and took a deep breath. "…is great so far. I mean, I would much rather be in Cali, but I had to transfer to be closer to home."

"Yeah, I heard about the move back. But no one ever said why. Did you want to come back home?" Kyle asked, not missing a beat.

January paused, cycling through her thoughts. A familiar thumping in her stomach was her first signal of discomfort and then her chest went tight.

"Well… it was a matter of politics," she said, using the excuse that her parents had trained her to use when something mafia-related affected their lives. "It was just better for me to be home. So, I had to come back."

"Makes perfect sense," Kyle said, wiping at his mouth with a napkin. "We don't have to talk about that anymore if it makes you uncomfortable."

"Ahh, thank you," January replied with a slight nod of her head. "I appreciate you saying that."

The gleam in Kyle's eyes said that he understood what she was saying but also what she was *not* saying. He would make a great partner in that way. He understood how to be discrete in the way that her lifestyle demanded. He was able to protect her in the way that mattered. However, there was something missing. It was one thing to be able to tolerate her lifestyle, but it was another thing to actually be a part of it. There was a level of intimacy that came with it that Kyle was lacking. She didn't feel with him like she did with Legend.

When it came to Legend, there was undeniable passion. It didn't matter whether they were on good terms or not, talking or not, near each other or not, the feelings she had for him remained the same. She couldn't ignore that.

"You finished eating?" Kyle asked, watching January shove around the food left on her plate with her fork. Her appetite was gone, she couldn't stomach another bite. Although the date had started out promising, the second her mind went to Legend and she thought about all the things that were lacking with Kyle in comparison to the chemistry she had with him, she knew there was no way she could continue going out with Kyle again. She wasn't ready. Her heart still longed for Legend and as long as that was happening, there was no way that she could love anyone else. Or even pretend to.

Reaching across the table, Kyle grabbed January's right hand, enclosing it in between the two of his. She resisted the urge to pull away. She wanted to be nice, but she also didn't want to be touched.

"January, I know it might be too soon to say this but... honestly, I've thought about you a lot over the last few years that we've been apart, and I just don't want to continue wasting time."

Stirring in her seat, January bit down on her bottom lip, struggling against stopping Kyle from saying what he wanted to say. He was a good guy. Safe and reliable. She wanted to give him a chance. She didn't want to push him away just because Legend's memory was in the back of her mind fucking up her energy. However, he was coming on too strong. Moving way too fast. This was only a first date.

"We had a good thing going before, even though we were young—"

January suppressed a snort. *Young? We were in high school for God's sake. Babies.*

"I just want to continue that. I'm not asking for you to take my hand in marriage or anything... yet," he added, chuckling a little as he said it. "But I do want to move forward with you into something solid. I don't wanna waste no time and risk you getting away again."

January shifted in her chair before she drew back, slowly sliding her hand away from his. "Getting away *again*?" she repeated, allowing the frown on her face to deepen. "That's not exactly how I remember it. I got shot. Whole life destroyed in an instance. You visited me twice... maybe three times. Promised you would be there with me as a friend and then stopped coming. The next thing I knew, I heard you were dating Brennan."

Her nose curled at the memory. It was high school shit. Immature shit. Kyle's eyes widened in shock, as if he were surprised she'd remembered that and then he began to laugh.

"Oh yeah... I almost forgot about that. But Brennan and I didn't date all that long. I know they said your memory was a little spotty at the time. Maybe you don't remember everything

clearly."

January's gut twisted. It was another lie. Coupled with a petty dig at her 'spotty memory'. Such a narcissistic move.

"You're right. My memory was a little spotty at the time. But now it's all coming back to me," she said as she began collecting her things. "You dated Brennan for almost two years. You broke up with her when it went public that her family went bankrupt. so, I guess it's your normal thing to abandon people you so-called 'love' when their situation is no longer benefits you."

Small details began to come back to her, the more and more she thought about the circumstances surrounding their parting as well as the many encounters he'd had with other girls afterwards. She hadn't paid too much attention to it then because Kyle and his romantic endeavors were the least of her concerns but now, she saw and understood him clearly. *Kyle* was the opportunist. Not Legend.

January had accused Legend of using her… of only being around because of his own personal gain. But when it really came down to it, deep down, she knew that wasn't it at all. He proved himself through his actions. He'd held her down and protected her even to his own detriment. He'd sacrificed himself and his reputation, even the respect of his father, for her. *Kyle* was user. He was the selfish one and it was clear that the Universe was giving her this example in this moment to show her how to tell the difference.

With her last words said, January gathered her purse, phone, and sweater before standing up to leave.

"January, wait. That wasn't what happened—I mean, where are you going?" Kyle said, standing up in attempt to stop her.

"I'm leaving," January replied, speaking to the head of the security team. "And Kyle?" she said, facing him.

Eyes glancing to the side at the bulky, muscular security officers ready to pounce if he neared a muscle, Kyle decided to sit back down in his chair.

"Yes, January?"

"Thank you for the date. I truly mean that. Because if you'd never asked me out, I would've never realized what it was that I truly needed."

Those last words said, January swiveled around with complete grace and left without ever turning back. Kyle may have been everything she thought she wanted on the surface, but he was missing one quality that she needed: Loyalty. It was the trump card that trumped all.

Legend wasn't the type that you took home to mom and he wasn't the type of a man that a father would pick for his daughter. He wasn't the easiest guy to understand or to deal with. He was a complexity that she still wasn't sure she had the patience, will or right to figure out. But, at the same time, some part of her said that he was everything she needed.

What they had was so toxic. Such an addiction. A trauma bond formed between two people who had met under the worst circumstances. They weren't supposed to be together. They hurt each other when they were together. They hurt each other when they were apart.

It was a beautifully, toxic love story in every way but in some sickening, sad way January knew it was the love she wanted. She was addicted to Legend and she didn't know if she'd ever be able to let him go.

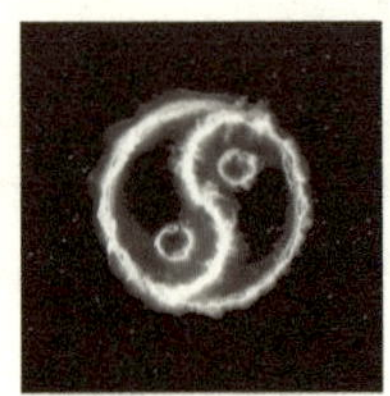

NIGGAS STILL AIN'T SHIT.

"I knew it. Didn't I tell you, January?"

Turning around, Brooke looked through the phone at January with her eyes spread wide, the expression on her face making it perfectly clear that although she was there, via FaceTime, to 'chaperone' Brooke and Nico, she didn't want nothing to do with this drama shit.

"Huh?" January asked, stuffing a gingerbread cookie in her mouth as if she hadn't heard her.

"You heard what he just said. Talking 'bout that girl I saw sitting on his lap, who alo happens to *live in his place*, is 'just a friend' he help out every now and then. That's what he told me. Like I'm dumb." She rolled her eyes. "I told you… it's like I always said. Niggas ain't shit."

Once Brooke finally let what she really wanted to say fly out her mouth, she felt like she'd finally learned how to summon the strength she needed to speak her mind. Every single bit of it. January's scary ass, on the other hand, didn't even respond. Cramming the rest of her cookie into her mouth, she snatched up the whole box, along with her books and laptop, and bolted from the room faster than Brooke had ever seen anyone move their legs. Brooke's mouth almost fell open. She didn't even bother disconnecting the FaceTime so it was obvious that she had only left so she couldn't be talked to. Her nosey ass was definitely still listening.

What happened to all that shit January was just talking about always having my back? Brooke thought, rolling her eyes.

"Niggas ain't shit, huh?" Nico said, drawing her attention away from Judas-January, her traitor of a best friend.

Standing up straight, Brooke placed her hands on her waist and leveled with him, staring straight into his eyes.

"That's what the fuck I said. And I stand by that. Niggas ain't shit. And *your* ass ain't no different."

Nico nudged his nose with his index finger, making some kind of sound that resembled a low chuckle, although it was clear from the expression on his face that he didn't think a damn thing was funny.

"Nah, shorty, that logic don't apply. What you should say is the niggas *you* been picking ain't shit. But riddle me this, have you ever stopped to ask yourself why you keep layin' up with ain't-shit niggas?"

This time, Brooke's mouth really did drop open and, from somewhere behind her, she heard a loud gasp through the phone followed by a just barely audible 'oh, *shit*!'

Just as she'd thought, January's lurking ass hadn't gone no damn where but right around the corner to listen. Brooke made a mental note to give her a piece of her mind later but, at the moment, she couldn't say a thing. Normally, there were a lot of words swirling around in her mind, but what Nico had just said to her had all bits of her mental twisted. This was happening much too often... him laying down something real that had her thoughts too fucked up to even begin to respond. How in the world did that keep happening when *he* was the one on the bullshit?

"I keep telling you that I'm not like any other nigga you've met. And real shit, I ain't trying to say that I'm the only man like me because it wouldn't be true. I was raised by men like me. And Legend is more like my twin than Onyx even is. We're cut from the same cloth, so I know for a fact that every man in the world ain't 'bout bullshit. But I can tell by what comes out your mouth that you ain't never dealt with a man like me. If you had, you wouldn't be spitting that toxic shit. I love you, Brooke, you're real important to me. But I just gotta shoot this shit to you straight."

Damn. Now that he'd put it that way… Brooke could kinda, maybe possibly understand what he meant, but her pride wouldn't let her fold so easily.

"Well, based on *your* logic," Brooke battled back, "What does that say about you for claiming that you love a chick that's so toxic?"

For whatever reason, he found that funny and started to laugh. "Yo, you don't listen. Your birthday coming up, right? Remind me to buy you some Q-tips for your ears."

Cute.

Brooke folded her arms across her chest and tried to fight against the pout threatening to form on her lips.

"Listen, Brooke, I didn't say *you* were toxic. I said you were spitting toxic *shit*," he clarified, speaking slowly and with his usual flare of dramatic emphasis when he called himself 'learning her shit.' "There is a difference. If I thought you were toxic, I wouldn't have ever fucked with you on the level that I fuck with you."

Something about the way he was speaking, with such blunt, raw honesty, calmed her roaring lioness inside. Which was saying a lot because she didn't have a lil' baby cub Nala inside of her. Brooke's lioness was a whole lion queen. Wasn't nothing calm about her, she stayed on go. But Nico was always putting something real in her ears that had her purring and shit.

Fuck it. She couldn't even be mad at January because her ass was a traitor, too. She hadn't been out of the room for two whole minutes yet and Brooke was folding even harder than January did. Nico had her like a lawn chair in this bitch.

"If I'm always saying toxic shit, then how you know *I'm* not toxic?" Brooke asked, speaking sincerely and genuinely.

The question was to him but really it was for herself. If what she thought and said was toxic and she reacted based on that… didn't that make her toxic?

"I'm not an expert in physics and not too boss with equations, but it doesn't take a rocket scientist to know if A=C and B=D, then A+B= C+D… minus X, or however that shit goes." She shook her head, losing her train of thought. "Listen, I ain't no chemist. Basically, what I'm trying to say is… if I'm thinking and saying toxic shit, wouldn't that make me a toxic bitch?"

"Nah, I knew you wasn't toxic the second I first laid eyes on you," Nico replied with a shrug as if that just explained it all.

Brooke gave him a blank stare, waiting for him to elaborate. His words made about as much sense to her as that bogus ass equation she had just come up with.

"Look me in my eyes."

He waited and she did just as he asked, with a little bit of residual attitude added, like a cherry on top.

"Nah, not like that," he said, chuckling. "Relax your body, drop all that extra shit, take a deep breath and look me in the eyes. Directly in them. And don't just glance at me. Like really, *really* stare into me."

"Is this going to end with us being naked or no?" Brooke asked, with one curious brow lifted.

He laughed again and she pinched her lips. Hell, she was serious.

"Yo, just do what I said. I'm trying to show you something."

Sighing, Brooke rolled her eyes. "Here you go trying to *learn me something* again," she toyed with him.

"I'm trying to remind you about something you forgot you already know. Stop saying that. I'm not trying to *learn* you shit."

Whatever.

Doing as he asked, Brooke took a deep breath and relaxed her body and then her mind. Pushing every other thought away, she connected with him completely and looked him right in his eyes. He stood there, saying nothing, standing totally still with his sexy brown eyes focused in on her. Never faltering, never once wavering. Hell… she wasn't sure whether or not he even blinked. They stood there for what felt like an infinite, unknown, and unmeasurable moment in time. Him watching her, and her watching him… watching her.

Brooke wasn't totally sure when it happened, but she felt the atmosphere shift and her entire body went into another layer of relaxation. Complete and deep relaxation. An ultimate peace. Something she'd never once in her life ever felt before. Whoever was the first person to say 'be her peace,' this feeling right here was it.

"What's your body telling you about me?"

"Huh?" Brooke asked, not comprehending him completely. He had her ass *that* far gone. Her brain had gone on vacation. She wished that she could bottle up whatever this was and sell it. She would be richer than Oprah. Every asshole on the planet would pipe the hell down. Niggas in the hood would be sprinkling it on the weed, lacing blunts with a new drug called *Nico*.

"What is your body saying? What do you feel in my presence?"

She frowned slightly. "Um… well, I feel at peace. I feel relaxed."

A smirk edged up from the corner of his lips and slowly took over, giving way to a full and beautiful smile.

"That's how you read someone—anyone you first meet. Look them in their eyes, quiet your mind, don't give a fuck about what they're saying, pay attention to how your body responds to their presence as you stand in it," he explained, speaking seriously. "Whatever your body is telling you, trust it. Your body understands vibes. Your mind just responds off whatever shit you been telling it."

"Uh huh," Brooke said, barely paying him any attention. Her body was still talking but right then, it was saying some other shit. Nico had sparked a fire in her loins, as her granny would say, and it was growing wild, rising steadily up her spine. It was a magic fire, and he had the special kind of elixir that she needed in order to put it out. Cocking her head to the side, she continued to look at him and reached out to hold him and bring him closer into her.

"Aye, what you doing?" he said, chuckling as he tried to step away. "Nah, we ain't doing that. I told you about this the other day."

Ignoring him, Brooke twisted around and pressed her ass against his dick while forcing his arms around her waist. He continued to attempt to back away, but she was on him like glue. When he moved, she moved.

"You told me to trust what my body is saying so I'm doing that." Brooke shrugged.

"See, that's why I told you to get January on FaceTime before I came over. I already knew you was gon' be on some crazy shit."

Turning, Brooke frowned at him, looking into his eyes just as deeply as she had been before so he could really feel her.

"Do you *really* think January being here on FaceTime means a thing to me?" As if to illustrate her point, Brooke walked right over to the phone and positioned her finger above the red button. "Bye, January, I gotta go. I love you, bitch!" Pressing her finger against the trigger, she ended the call and then turned to Nico, smiling wide.

"All done, problem solved," she said, wrapping her arms back around his waist. "Now, let's get to it."

"Yo, you wildin'," Nico replied, laughing. He kissed her on the forehead, his way of telling her goodbye, but it only made Brooke increase her grip around him. Laughing even harder, he began to twist away.

"Shorty, you crazy right now. Let me loose. I gotta go."

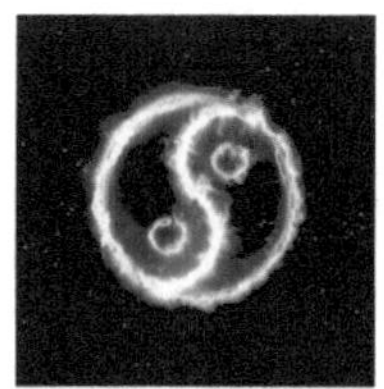

LOVE ISN'T POSSESSION.

"If you love a flower, you don't pick it, because it'll die. You leave it right where it is and you let it grow. Love isn't about possession."

SITTING WITH HIS HEAD IN HIS HANDS, LEGEND KNEW HE WAS DOING the right thing when it came to January. The only thing he couldn't understand was why it was so fucking hard to do.

"Man, how long you gone sit over there looking miserable?" Nico asked, walking into the room as he emerged from down the hall. He really couldn't judge Legend because, truthfully, he was dealing with the same thing when it came to Brooke. Both wanted women that, deep-down, they felt they weren't good enough to have.

"Listen," Nico said when Legend made no movement at all to answer him. "Let's go to the gym, fuck shit up, and then you can come back here and cry some more. You can cry all night if you want to but, right now, you gotta get your ass up. We can't be late."

"Ain't no fuckin' crying," Legend said, dragging his ass up from off the floor. Bending slightly, he grabbed up the bag he would need and took off behind Nico.

"I can't tell," Nico replied as he walked in-step behind Legend. Nico paused for Legend to exit out his front door so that they could lock up and put in place all the alarm codes. It was a hassle to do and took forever but, in their lifestyle, you couldn't take anything for granted.

Especially not life.

"I DON'T CARE what the circumstances are. You never run from a fuckin' fight, boy. You hear me? I don't care who it is. You always make sure that you're the last motherfucka standin'."

Standing in the middle of the ring, Legend clamped down hard on the guard in between his teeth and stared at his opponent as his father's words echoed in his ears. Words that he'd said to Legend when he was no more than six years old. Words he probably didn't even remember he'd said. However, those words stuck with Legend for the rest of his life. In fact, the words and the situation surrounding when he'd spoke them totally affected how Legend lived his life. Call it childhood trauma. Call it unhealed wounds. Call it whatever the fuck you wanted to. All Legend knew was that he was one fucked up individual because of it.

"Okay, we want this to be a fair fight. No hits to the groin. No cheap shots... Y'all niggas know the rules. The people in here paid a lot of money to see this match, so don't make me have to stop you."

Although he was supposedly speaking to them both, his warning seemed almost fully directed at Legend.

"You got me, Legend?" he asked, further clarifying who he was really talking to. Legend wasn't one to throw a cheap shot, and no parts of his body would ever purposely come into contact with a nigga's dick, so that wasn't really the part directed at him. He was known to go in hard during fights—that was his vice. When he got into fight mode, he got in a zone. He was liable to black the fuck out and pulverize his opponent way past the point of when they'd rung the bell. A few times, the vet had to dive on him and pull him off. It wasn't intentional. Fighting was his way of battling his demons. From the time he threw his first punch, all his sins were all he could see. The pain he'd inflicted on others was all that he felt. In essence, Legend was fighting himself. And he'd been taught to never back down. To fight 'til death.

"I got you, Chief," Legend replied with a nod of his head.

The referee returned Legend's words with a nod of his own and then backed away to prepare for the start of the fight. Legend's heart tripled its beats, sending blood and adrenaline coursing through him. He'd been around junkies and alcoholics all his life but never once felt the need for drugs. This was how he got high. What a paradox it was to hide one's pain by inflicting more pain.

"Fuck you, nigga," Cease, Legend's opponent, gritted through his teeth as they stood facing each other with only about a foot between them. "I don't give a fuck what your record is, what the hype is surrounding ya. I'mma fuck yo' ass up."

Not saying a word, Legend simply stood in place maintaining his stance. It was a normal thing to shit talk. In fact, most trainers encouraged it to hype yourself up and also throw off your opponent. But he'd never had a trainer, and he never felt the need to talk shit. He let his hands do all the talking instead.

"Good game, champs," was the last thing the referee said before he made them

bump fists and take a couple steps back for the fight to begin.

In that instance, Legend allowed all the anger, rage, and grief that he'd been holding back to come rushing in. All the thoughts, words, emotions, and feelings that January was always saying he suppressed came swarming to the surface preparing to be released.

"Fight!" the referee yelled, and with the chime of a bell, it was on.

The crowd around them roared as they circled the ring, sizing each other up.

They were probably wondering who would throw the first punch. That usually wasn't Legend's style. He preferred to let his opponent waste their energy trying to hit an unhittable target. He was quick on his feet and hard to catch. By the time they realized how fast he was, he would've already had them frustrated and tired from dancing around the ring. The only thing was, Cease was a decent fighter, and Legend knew he'd studied him. A lot of niggas Legend met in the ring didn't take the shit seriously. They were just known for knocking niggas out in the hood and figured they could make money from it. But Legend had seen Cease fight before, and he was nice. Unlike most, he was legit.

After less than a minute of circling around the ring, it became clear that Cease was waiting for Legend to make the first move. He peeped it and, normally, he wouldn't allow a nigga to fuck with his strategy in that way. Usually, he wouldn't allow his opponent to take him out of his element. But he was working with a fucked up mental. His head hadn't been right since he and January parted ways. He was desperate to release the pressure. He needed to transmute that shit and it couldn't wait.

Cease continued to toy with him, coming in close just to slide back out, but after a few times of that, Legend took the bait.

Swoosh!

His right fist sliced through air, connecting with the side of Cease's face but what he didn't see was that Cease had a left hook headed straight for his chin.

"Oof!" Legend groaned, feeling the wind nearly get knocked out him.

"Ah, shit!"

Nico's ass was loud as hell. Legend could hear his voice over the crowd, which had picked up the volume a few more octaves after Cease made contact.

I'm dizzy as fuck, Legend thought, struggling to regain his eyesight. He'd underestimated Cease's strength. His fist hit like a fucking brick straight to Legend's face. Arrogant to the max, Cease took a few steps back to allow him to get himself together. And once he was able to see straight, the first thing Legend focused on was his cocky ass grin.

"Told you I'mma fuck you up, lil' nigga," Cease said, smiling maliciously. "Let's go."

Instead of focusing on him, Legend's eyes slid somewhere behind him to the crowd and he could've sworn he saw January in the stands staring back at him. Worry filled her face. Tears in her eyes. Then he blinked once and she was gone.

Fuck.

She was haunting him.

One deep breath and Legend put his focus back on Cease, determined to end this match as quickly as possible. It was either that or Cease was going to end him. Legend usually drew fights out because he loved to inflict punishment. But he couldn't do it this time. His head wasn't in it.

They danced around the ring but, this time, Legend didn't make a move. The crowd was pissed, but Legend didn't care. He needed to take back control of this fight. And the only way to do it was to draw Cease into his element.

The first round ended with quite the anti-climax, but Legend wasn't moved by it. He knew what he was doing. A nigga like Cease had a big ass ego. Though he didn't show it, Legend knew it was fucking him up inside to not give the crowd a good fight.

"This time you better fuckin' fight, pussies!" some guy yelled, and Legend chuckled a little as Nico walked up to hand him water.

"I know what you doin'," Nico said, squeezing the bottle to shoot a burst of water into Legend's mouth. "It's genius. That nigga's strong, but his skull is thick as hell. Once his big ass ego fills it, he ain't gone be able to think out shit."

"And that's when I'mma go in," Legend replied.

Nico nodded. "I'm already knowin' it, cuz." He bumped his fist against Legend's glove before turning to leave. "Put all that other shit to the side right now and focus. You can't do anything about that, but you can handle this."

Legend nodded his head.

It was true.

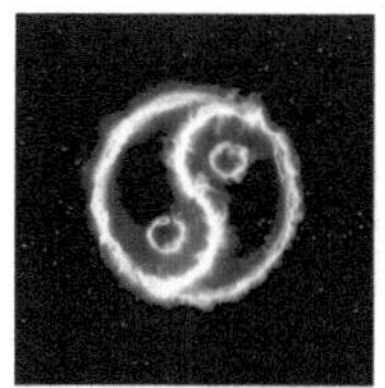

WINS & LOSSES.

"Damn, nigga, you beat the fuckin' charcoal black off that motherfucka! You should be ashamed. You probably... you probably sent his ass to the hospital. I hope somebody called his mama!"

Legend chuckled to himself as he and Nico cut out of the building through the back doors to avoid the crowd. For him, fights were all about the mental high. It wasn't about the people screaming his name or even the money. He didn't give a damn about the chicks offering up their pussy after fights or the respect that thorough niggas gave when they recognized a real one. To Legend, it was all about the mental high. It was about the release that came after inflicting pain. Maybe it was shit like this that classified him as a fucked-up individual.

It was shit like this that didn't make him husband material.

"So now that you handled your business like a man, let me get you back home so you can go back to crying on the couch like a big ass, ugly baby," Nico said as they got in the car.

His old school, fully restored, and pimped-out Chevy Capri was parked curbside right at the back door, mixing the back-alley street with some down south Florida-boy flavor. Once they settled into the seats, Nico hit the push-start to the ignition and the engine roared to life. An old soul in all ways, he had a thing about antiques when it came to most things. Except his women, he'd always said. He preferred them young, dumb, and full of cum. Easy to get and easy to throw away. He worked hard for everything in his life but refused to do the same for a woman. Although, deep down, he knew a woman was the only thing in his life he was missing. He couldn't help it; he was a walking paradox.

"Nigga, fuck you for life," Legend replied. "It's easy to talk shit when the shoe's on the other foot. "What's going on with you and Brooke? You ain't hit her back yet?"

Eyes on the road, Nico shrugged. "Hit her back, why?"

Legend paused for a beat before chuckling and shaking his head. Nico was still sleeping in the bed of denial.

"Hit her back because you feeling her. You ain't fooling nobody, bruh."

"Nah." Nico shook his head. "Last time I spoke to her, she said some foul shit."

The way Nico's face folded up with disgust made it clear that he was sincerely bothered by whatever it was that Brooke had said. That alone piqued Legend's curiosity. He'd never known Nico to give a fuck about what anybody had to say.

"What she said to you?" Legend asked, truly curious.

"Man... the motherfucker called me toxic."

A few moments of silence passed by as Legend waited for whatever else was supposed to come next. When Nico continued to drive in silence, still frowning at the thought of what Brooke had said, it became clear that he was done.

"Wait..." Legend began slowly. "That was it?"

"What the fuck else there gotta be? Her ass called me toxic. That shit right there is bad enough."

Legend blinked, wondering if he had to state the obvious. "Nigga, you *are* toxic!"

"I'm not toxic. I just do toxic shit. From time-to-time," he made sure to add. "But my intentions are pure." Legend couldn't do a damn thing but laugh at that. Nico was on one for real.

"How the fuck you do toxic shit with pure intentions? Ain't there some universal law about that?"

"Universal law?" Nico smirked, cutting his eyes at his cousin. "Aww, don't you sound like your boo?"

"Nigga, fuck you."

The fun was immediately sucked from the moment the second Nico mentioned January. He didn't want to think of her. The whole reason for agreeing to this impromptu fight tonight was so he wouldn't think about her. He'd never had a problem erasing a chick from his mind, but this one had him caught up in a headlock.

Witchy ass probably put a spell on me, he thought, running his hand over his face.

It was like the shit was unheard of. Especially, when it came to chicks back home in Miami. Voodoo queens in the south were always mixing up some home remedy that would have a nigga's head sprung. Even the smoothest motherfuckas would take a leap of faith on a life change, throwing their playa card away. All because some chick mixed a spell on some black magic shit. Legend ain't know if it was real or fake, but he definitely ain't want no parts of it.

"I was gone let it slide, but well, I need you to explain this shit to me, man. How the hell you do toxic shit with good intentions?"

Taking a quick right turn, Nico decelerated and took a moment to fire up a blunt before answering Legend's question. It wasn't to get his explanation together, because he had that part down put. After

Brooke had called him toxic, it hit deep, made him really consider his ways in regard to how he treated her. He'd definitely been toxic to other bitches before because he didn't give a damn. But he'd never been that way with her, so when she put that label on him, it had him really questioning why.

"See, it's like this," Nico began in the way hood niggas did when they were about to spit some 'logic' that really didn't make sense. "I'm feeling Brooke... like on a real level. But she ain't ready for a nigga like me yet. Her mind still fucked up by that lame ass dude she was messing with. So, I'm just giving her space to get her mind right."

Legend smirked, giving Nico a sideways look, as if waiting for the punchline. But it was clear that his cousin really believed the bullshit coming from his mouth.

"So, to help her get her mind right, you wait until it looks like she's made some progress to pop up in her life with all the lovey-dovey shit, maybe even fuck her to seal the deal so she won't let another nigga in to take her attention away from you. And then you fuck up her vibe by disappearing when she pressures you for commitment?"

Nico's brows furrowed into a hard frown. "Well, when you put it that way..."

"Nigga, you toxic as fuck!"

Weed smoke in the air, Nico swerved through the streets smooth as a Snoop Dogg song while they both took liberty with the blunt.

This short time off from real life was something they both needed. Wasn't nothing more priceless to a street nigga than a peaceful mind. It was a hot commodity because the one sure thing about running the streets was that it robbed you of peace. In spite of all the sacrifices Legend made to stack paper, that was the one thing he wanted back.

I'm your peace.

He heard January's voice so clearly in his head that it made him want to put the blunt down. He frowned, squinting his eyes at the juicy, fat roach in his hand, wondering what the hell kind of weed Nico had in it.

"Here you go, nigga," he said, giving it back. "I'm good."

Nico smiled, giving him a knowing look. Smoking weed always made Legend sentimental. And he didn't even have to ask about his cousin's thoughts at that moment. He knew them just as clearly as if they'd come out his mouth.

"It ain't gone stop," Nico said, shaking his head. "Trust me, man. I'm trying to fight the shit, but I know it won't."

"What won't?" Legend asked, lifting his head from the phone he was holding in his hand. Lots of missed calls, plenty unanswered texts.

None from the one woman on Earth he was dying to hear from. Literally. He felt like his organs were decaying inside. Mainly his heart.

"Thinking 'bout her," Nico replied.

"Nah, nigga," Legend chuckled, finessing his chin hair. "The only reason I got this sappy shit running through my mind is because you keep fuckin' me up with this Cali weed."

"It ain't the weed." Nico shook his head and leaned back in his seat as he slid into his covered parking space. "The thoughts are always there under the surface. The weed just quiets your mind so you can hear them. It's like my nigga, Osho, be sayin'..."

"Ah, here you go, nigga, with this philosophical shit."

Laughing hard, Legend leaned back in his own seat to hear what Nico had to say. He was teasing him about it, but the shit that had been coming out his mouth lately had been pretty deep. He liked to hear from Master-Sensei-Prophet Nico every now and then.

"Don't trip off my nigga, Osho. He be speaking real shit," Nico said, making Legend laugh even harder. "Anyways, he says 'Get out of your head and get into your heart. Think less. Feel more.' So, in other words, stop overthinkin' shit. Whatever you feel is all you need to know. If you know you want somebody, then want them. All of them other details and shit don't matter."

Nico went silent, going into his own thoughts. It felt more and more these days like the more he gave advice to Legend, the more the things he was saying could be applied to himself. All he was doing when it came to Brooke was thinking with his head. He knew he wanted her, but he also knew he wasn't ready to invest in what he knew would be the real thing.

The real thing was hard. The real thing could expose you to hurt and pain. The real thing was a risk, and Nico's life already exposed him to a lot of risks. The main difference was that these were the risks he was open to taking. Physical pain was a small thing. He had learned easy ways to take care of that. No one had ever taught him about how to deal with heart pain.

"It's not as easy as that. I wish it was," Legend replied. "January's got a life that would be all fucked up if I tried to combine it with mine. I have to think with my head. I ain't really got no other choice."

It seemed Outlaw's stance hadn't changed in any way. After the handoff happened with Legend delivering January to safety, there was no additional communication, no nothing.

"You gotta do what you gotta do. No regrets. Figure out what you want and go after that shit." Nico lifted his fist and Legend nodded his head before bumping it with his fist.

"Yolo, right? You only live once, my nigga. So let's get it."

"Nah," Legend replied, shaking his head. "You only die once. You live every motherfuckin' day. But you're right… let's get it."

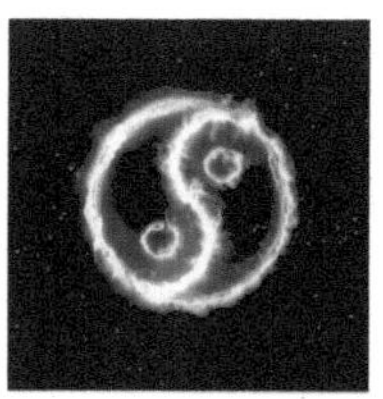

PLAYIN' GAMES.

"Nico said he would always be there if I needed a shoulder to cry on. What a player."

"Huh? How does that make him a player?"

"Girl, everybody knows the moment you need a man, the shoulder he offers you to cry on becomes the dick he expects you to ride. He must think I'm stupid."

"Who hurt you and how can we begin to fix this?"

Rolling her eyes towards the window, Brooke pressed the palms of her hands against the top of her thighs and let out a deep breath. It felt like the longest possible sigh. Carried the weight of the world in it. Who hurt her? Hell, the list was so long, she felt like she had these niggas out here picking numbers and getting in line. Who wanted a chance to fuck up Brooke's mind? Take a number and step right up.

"She's got too much water. Too emotional. That's dangerous."

Brooke had never really understood what her grandmother meant when she said that. How could emotions make you dangerous? She didn't understand that her grandmother didn't mean that her emotions made *her dangerous. She meant that they were dangerous for* her.

Brooke played it hard on the outside, but she wasn't hard. Nothing close to it. The tough exterior was a defense mechanism. A mask she wore to protect herself from men like Trevor. And apparently men like Nico, too.

"Girl… ain't nothing wrong with me," she told January, waving her hand with her answer. "It's just the normal shit. The normal nigga shit. He did all this stuff in the beginning to get my attention and as soon as I started to kinda show interest, he bounced. All of these niggas scared of commitment, but I bet as soon as I start looking at someone else, he'll swoop back on the scene with his Captain Save-a-Hoe cape on, acting like he's trying to save me from fucking with a lame."

Scoffing, Brooke rolled her eyes and pulled her legs up on the sofa to place her chin on top of her knees. With her arms wrapped around her legs, she sat there in silence feeling all the fucking feels. She was happy as hell to see January, even if it was only via FaceTime. She missed her—definitely had needed a friend like her around lately. However, the fact that she hadn't seen or even really spoken to Nico at all before today had her feeling some type of way.

"Get dressed. You got somewhere to be."

That's how he'd greeted her when she opened the door. No 'Hey, how you doing? I know it's been a minute since I've popped over here to see you after sticking my dick in you the last time. My bad, I was out and about doing fuck nigga shit, but I promise I'm all done with that now.'

Nothing. No explanation. No apology. Nothing at all. Just like the arrogant, selfish, and self-absorbed prick that he is, he didn't think she was deserving of an explanation.

"Excuse me?" was her response. She wanted to come with something harder, but she was so caught off-guard, she couldn't even react properly.

"Get dressed," Nico repeated, taking a moment to pause and look her over slowly from head to toe.

Brooke saw a sparkle of heat in his eyes as he observed her 'barely there' attire. Of course, he'd been the last person she'd expected to be standing there when she opened the door, so she didn't have anything on but some itty-bitty pajama shorts and a tank top. No bra at all, so she knew her nipples were peeking through. Actually, she was most certain of that, judging by the way Nico's eyes seemed to linger there for a little longer than he'd probably meant for them to. She straightened her back, sitting the girls up even higher, adding to the pressure. She wanted his ass to know every bit of what he was missing out on while he had been out doing whatever the hell it was that niggas did when they were playing games.

"This the kinda shit you wear to open the fuckin' door?" he said, the upper corner of his lip curling with… disgust?

Damn. Well, that isn't the response I would've expected.

She batted her eyes, trying to hold her expression. Once again, she was caught off-guard for the second time in less than five minutes.

"Man, get the fuck in there and put on some clothes."

Pushing by Brooke, Nico walked into the apartment like he owned the place, as usual, not waiting at all for permission. Everything about him said that he just didn't give a damn.

"First of all, you can't tell me what to do, when to do it or what to wear. I'm a grown ass woman and I make my own decisions. And furthermore," she added, forcing on a little extra emphasis. "You are not my man."

"No, I'm not your man," Nico replied, turning around to look at her. "I'm just a motherfucka who cares about you and I don't want you out here looking like a fuckin' T.H.O.T. Go put some damn clothes on, anyways. I'm about to take you out."

Brooke's neck jerked back, and her brows formed a deep and dark frown on her face. Had she just heard him correctly? He most certainly had to be kidding.

"Oh, no, you're not! I'm not going anywhere with you. And, like I said, I feel perfectly comfortable dressed like this. So, if your reasoning for coming over here was to treat me to a quick meal so that you could drop off some dick, I'll pass."

Nico threw his arms in the air, totally confused about what to do next. His feelings for Brooke were overwhelming. Overwhelming to the point that he had no fuckin' idea what to do. On one hand, he wanted to please her—needed to figure out a way to make her open up to him. But, on the other hand, he felt like the things that he could offer her would never be good enough. He was fighting a battle in his head that he couldn't comprehend and it only manifested in him fighting the same nonsensical battle with her.

"Man, love is some fuckin' confusing shit," he grumbled under his breath, feeling like he was about to come down with a migraine.

Brooke craned her head to the side, straining to hear with her good ear.

Did this nigga just say the word 'love'? I know I didn't hear him right.

"What did you say?" she asked. For some reason, she knew he wouldn't repeat it. And she was right.

"Why the fuck you gotta be so difficult all the damn time? You wanted me to take you out, now I'm ready to take you out. Let's fuckin' go. I ain't got time for this bullshit."

Rubbing at his temples, he was beginning to lose his patience. But the craziest thing was that he wasn't losing his patience with her, he was losing it with himself. He knew what she wanted him to do, he knew why, and he also knew why she felt it was needed, but for some reason he just couldn't force himself to be that man. She wanted him to be on the romantic shit, wine and dine her, impress her. She wanted to be chased. But Nico was a G and the OGs he knew didn't get down like that.

"Nico, you want me to be solid while you're out here on some fuck shit. Who do you think I am that I would go anywhere with you based on how you're acting right now? How about you go to the nearest hell and sit the fuck down in time out? I'm sick and tired of this!"

Before Brooke knew it, tears were stinging her eyes and she could barely see straight. Which might have been a good thing because, honestly speaking, she really didn't even want to see his face. Nico was the most selfish kind of lover. She'd thought Trevor was, but it turned out that she'd been wrong about that. At least Trevor stayed away from her while he was on his bullshit. He avoided her completely and simply refused to come around her with his fucked-up energy.

Nico, on the other hand? He brought her all the bullshit. He did whatever the fuck he wanted, when he wanted it and how he wanted to do it, and all he gave her in exchange was some dick and his ass to kiss when she asked for something solid. How was it possible for him to, on one hand, tell her he loved her but then through his actions show that he really didn't give a damn about her? It was insane.

"Man, Brooke, I'm tired of explainin' this shit to you," Nico said, speaking in a low tone. He was trying his hardest to keep his cool and explain a concept to her that she was refusing to see. "It's not what you think. I want you. I just… I really just need time."

Crossing her arms, Brooke looked him square in the eyes, fully understanding what he was saying and fully accepting it. If time was what Nico wanted, time was what he would have. However, something about her dealings with Trevor made her aware of how she'd been fuckin' up when it came to letting men fuck her over. This time around, she wasn't about to make accommodations for anyone to be comfortable at the expense of herself.

"Fine," she began, looking at Nico with all seriousness and all intensity. "You can have all the time you want to do whatever you need to do. Just don't think you're going to spend your time, wasting mine. Goodbye."

And with that said, she walked straight out of the room, grabbing her shoes along the way. Somehow, something in her had changed. And, though it had taken forever, the change had finally taken place. She was done being shoved around by men who wanted to take and never wanted to give. She'd been so willing to love, thinking that the intensity of her passion meant something. That it would make a difference. That it would force them to treat her according to her worth. Turned out, giving so much wasn't doing a damn thing. It was like peeling off the best pieces of herself and just tossing it away.

The right lover would involve her in an equal exchange. The right lover wouldn't only take. He'd replenish what he'd gotten from her by giving her his love back. It would be an equal relationship that would make her feel valued and worthy in every way. Nico cared for her, of that, she was sure. But what he was giving to her wasn't the love she was worthy of. He had a sense of entitlement to her that he never earned. He felt entitled to her body, her heart. Even her space. The audacity of him to just walk into her room as if he owned it.

I've got to get my own place back asap. Like… now.

She made a mental note to call Trevor and formally break things off with him that night. He needed to get out of her space, her heart, and her mind. All the shit that he was using, and abusing was hers and she wanted it all back. In fact, there were a lot of pieces of her that he and Nico were using and abusing. But she was done with letting them get over at her expense.

Brooke wanted it all back.

"The bad thing is, as much as I can't stand him, when he's away all I do is think about him," Brooke continued her conversation with January, wanting to put the entire last altercation that she'd had with Nico behind her.

In truth, she felt like a failure. Because as strong as she'd thought she was and as much as she'd tried to push him away, what she really wanted was to have him back. She said she didn't but she wanted to go out with him. Brooke felt alive in his presence. But the life he gave her was always short-lived. Because the second he left, she was all alone wondering who he was really spending his time with in the major gaps of space between that moment and when she would see him again. There was so much distance in between them and everything in Brooke's mind told her that Nico was filling that space with other women.

"You don't have to tell me a damn thing," January began, letting out a sigh. "You already know I understand. Fully and totally. Not a day goes by that I don't think about Legend. Especially after my terrible date with Kyle." She rolled her eyes the moment she was reminded of it.

"Oh yeah!" Brooke sat up, feeling upbeat as soon as the opportunity presented itself for her to escape from her own problems. "How did that go?"

Flopping back on her bed, January held the phone in front of her face and let out another long, heavy sigh. "Girl, let's just say I'm glad it's over. Kyle's an opportunist. He's just looking for a trophy. Some chick from a family with money would can look good on his arm. Probably don't even have to have money. He just wants someone he can brag about."

Brooke shrugged. "Maybe he should ask Nico if he can borrow that bitch, Dru."

The giggle came so fast from January's throat that she almost choked on it.

"You know what, Brooke?" she laughed. "Maybe he should!"

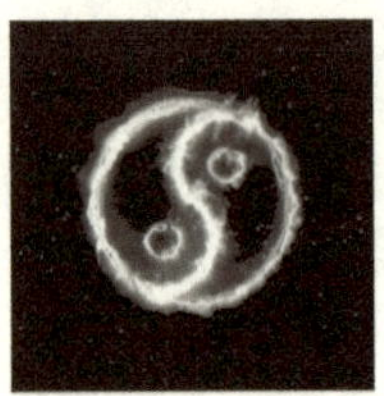

POWER STRUGGLE.

"A good woman who truly loves a man… she becomes the best part of his soul. And what does it profit a man to gain the whole world and lose his soul? Nothing at all."

LEGEND

ONCE AGAIN, LEGEND WALKED INTO NICO'S HOUSE AND CAUGHT HIM blasting some sad shit over the surround sound speakers. This time he'd swapped out Ed Sheeran's "Thinking Out Loud" for "End of the Road" by Boyz II Men.

"Nigga, what the fuck?" Legend said, reaching out to the wall panel to turn the volume down.

"Nah, man, turn my shit up," Legend heard Nico say from somewhere in the living room. "Let that shit play."

"Hell no, I ain't turnin' it up. You got it on ear-bleedin' status already," Legend said, walking into the living room, eyes running around, looking for Nico. When he finally saw him, he couldn't fuckin' believe what he was seeing.

"Nigga, what in the *fuck* you got goin' on right now?"

Nico was lying on the couch with his arms wrapped around the teddy bear that he'd bought for Brooke. The same one she'd thrown right in his damn face the night before after popping up by his place and catching him and Dru together. Squinting to make sure that he was seeing shit the right way, Legend watched as Nico sat up, still holding the teddy bear against his bare chest while shaking his head sadly.

"I'm fucked up right now, nigga," he said, speaking somberly.

Legend's eyes bugged.

"Yeah, I can see *that* shit. What the hell is goin' on with you?" he stuck his hand out to check Nico's forehead. "My dude, is you sick?"

"Lovesick, homie," he replied, shaking his head. "I think Brooke put roots on me."

In spite of the bullshit he was seeing before his eyes, Legend had to laugh. If he wasn't here witnessing this for himself, he would've never believed it.

"She ain't put no fuckin' roots on you," Legend told him. "You played your cards wrong and now you gotta deal with that shit."

Nico shook his head, finally releasing the stuffed animal from his chest to allow it to fall to the side.

"It's fucked up." Dropping his head into his hands, he shook his head before looking back up at Legend. "I'm not supposed to be going through this shit right now. I'm a young, rich nigga in my twenties. I ain't ready to settle down with no bitch. I ain't got time to have fuckin' feelings. I still got shit to do. It don't make no sense."

Legend couldn't resist smiling at what Nico was saying. Shit, to be honest, he'd said the same damn thing to himself plenty of times.

"It don't make no sense for you to be fuckin' around with Dru's dumb ass either. You probably killing brain cells just by being next to her."

Nico sniffed, nudging his nose with his hand. "Dru serves a purpose. I ain't lonely but I can still keep my head in the game while she's around. She don't give me no shit."

"You fuckin' right about that," Legend said, nodding his head.

"What's that mean?"

Legend shook his head, deciding not to answer. Mainly because Nico already knew what the hell he meant. Dru didn't give him drama, but she didn't give him anything else either. Girl was nothing but a fuckin' waste of space. Which might be okay for some nigga cut from the same cloth she was torn from, but not for Nico. They were predestined to reach a certain level in life that required for them to have a woman with them who was the perfect match.

Most men in the world didn't realize their potential until they met a woman with the ability to pull it out of him and sit it right in his face. Until she came along, he would be walking through life with his eyes closed, slumming it with women like Dru who ain't put up no challenge, and didn't make him uncomfortable. But it was discomfort that forced you to rise to another level. As long as Nico dealt with a chick like Dru, he would be wallowing in the same shit, even though both of them knew he was tired of it.

The problem was, he was too busy trying to live a life that society said he should've been living. Young and rich, he was supposed to be club hopping and enjoying life, filling his bed with different women every single night. But Nico and Legend grew up in the streets. They matured fast, lived fast, and experienced things in their teens that the typical nigga did in his twenties. The phase of life Nico was trying to stay in was already behind them. Fucking random chicks for the sake of doing it didn't excite them anymore.

"Man, I can't believe I'm sayin' this but..." Nico paused. Looking behind Legend somewhere in the distance, he swallowed hard as if trying his hardest to pull out the words for what he wanted to say.

"But what?" Legend pushed with a frown.

"I think I want to... settle down," he finished, making a face as if he'd eaten something bitter. "Damn, nigga. My chest hurt." Wincing, he placed his hand to his chest and let out a heavy breath.

Before Legend could stop it, he found himself laughing hard as hell. He'd been trying to hold it in, but what he was seeing was too funny. Honestly speaking, it wasn't too long ago that he was acting the same way Nico was, but Legend handled his shit in private. Granted, had Legend not barged in on Nico, he would've been dealing with his alone, too.

"Man, stop laughing. I'm serious. My chest hurts... bad," he said, twisting his face up in pain. "I don't know what to do."

"Call her," Legend heard a voice say, immediately recognizing it as Onyx.

Turning around, Legend was greeted by the sight of his cousin, walking through the front entrance with several bags in her hands. He jumped up to help her.

"Yo' boy in his feelings," I told her, smiling as she handed over the bags to me.

"Both of y'all in your feelings," she corrected, rolling her eyes before giving Legend a quick kiss on the cheek. "But that's why I'm over here to talk some sense in both of you."

"Onyx, ain't nobody told you to bring yo' judgy ass over here!" Nico shouted, sitting up straight on the couch to glare at her. "The last thing I need in my life right now is another woman talking shit."

"That's *exactly* what you need right now." She placed her hands on her hips. "That's what *both* of y'all need actually. That's why I told

Legend to meet me here. I needed to talk to both of y'all because you're being stupid as hell."

Frowning, Legend pushed his index finger into his chest. "Wait… me?" he asked, confused. "The fuck did *I* do?"

"The same thing Nico's dumb self is doing," Onyx replied, pulling food and other items out of the grocery bags that she'd brought in. "I'm sick of both of you being stubborn and acting like you're not making the dumbest decision in your life. You know you love January—" She cut her eyes at me. "—and you know you love Brooke," she said, glaring at Nico. "But both of you are being stubborn and you're going to end up losing out on what it is that you really want."

Neither Nico nor Legend responded. Both of them sat in their separate thoughts, not saying too much as the radio went to the next track, "When Can I See You" by Babyface.

"Man, cut this sad shit off," Legend grumbled, looking at Nico.

Nico shook his head. "No can do," he replied. "It makes me feel better on the inside."

"Soft dick ass nigga."

"It ain't soft!" he shouted, getting in his feelings all over again. "It takes a real man to express his feelings genuinely. We all got emotions, Legend. I'm just man enough to be real 'bout mine." All extra defensive, he pressed his finger into his chest, pointing at himself. "I ain't tryin' to be round here actin' like I'm made of steel or some shit. I'mma let these shits out like I'm 'posed to. Just like my nigga, Osho, been tellin' me."

Legend groaned, running his hand over his face. "Here you go with this Osho shit again."

"Osho said disease comes from dis-ease, which comes from not releasing what you feeling when you feel it. If you happy, be happy. If you said, be sad. He said anger really comes from not dealing with your grief." Swallowing hard, the corners of Nico's eyes dipped low. "And, nigga, I been angry for a real long time. I don't wanna do that shit no more."

Wrinkling his nose, Legend looked at Nico sideways.

This nigga better not cry.

"Legend, you could learn a lot from him," Onyx said as she pulled out pots and sat them on the island. Just like his aunt, Onyx solved problems the way her mother did, over a spread of good food. His aunt Maliah always thought that everything could be solved over food as long as it was made with love.

"I ain't learning *shit* from this nigga. Look at his ass!" Legend replied, holding his hands out at Nico, who had the teddy bear in his arms, pressed against his chest again. "Sitting here hugging a fuckin' teddy bear with his bottom lip trembling and shit. All because he let Dru's dumb ass fuck up what he had going on with Brooke. I ain't did no shit like that. January knows I ain't choosing no other bitch over her. Her ass is just being difficult and I ain't with that shit."

Onyx rolled her eyes. "The way I see it, what you and Nico are doing is one and the same. Both of you are trying to hold on to some past shit and you're stopping it from letting you move forward. Nico is trying to hold on to his past life of being a player…as if that bullshit was fulfilling at all." She stopped to roll her eyes. "And you, Legend, you're trying to hold on to the illusion of power that came along with acting like you don't give a shit about anything or anyone. You like to walk around here like you're unimpressed by everything. Like nobody matters to you. You pride yourself in not having feelings, never being vulnerable or really caring about anything because you see that as a weakness."

"That's what I been tellin' that nigga," Nico's dumb ass jumped in. "I been tellin' him that ain't nothing weak about feeling shit. It takes a real man to—"

"Nico, shut your dumb ass up, because ain't nothing 'real' about feeling whatever the hell you're feeling but ignoring it at the same time. At least Legend is in denial and that's why he's not dealing with it. Your ass sitting on the couch, clutching a damn bear and about to cry when all you gotta do is go to Brooke and tell her how you really feel."

Pausing for a beat, Nico let that run through his mind for a minute before shaking his head. "I ain't doing that soft shit."

"My point exactly," Onyx laughed. "Both of y'all big-headed asses are stubborn."

Blowing a burst of air out his nostrils, Legend turned and sat down on one of the barstools where Onyx was prepping her meal and clasped his hands together. His eyes were focused on her prepping the food, but his mind was somewhere else as he considered what she was saying.

Was he in denial?

It didn't seem like it. Legend knew how he felt about January. Shit… she did, too. He never thought he'd ever tell a girl he loved her. And now the impossible finally happened but she didn't give a damn.

"You spoke to her?" Onyx asked, finally.

Legend shrugged. "She stopped answering my calls a while ago. She flipped on me about not calling her and then the second I tried to do the shit, I found out I was blocked."

For some reason, Onyx found that funny. "Both of y'all are literally the same person."

Frowning, Legend gave her a look. She caught it and cleared her throat before beginning to clarify herself.

"Neither one of you want to admit how you feel, but it's obvious to everyone around you. And it's even more obvious to each other. You both are doing the exact same thing but how you direct it to each other is in different ways."

Staring at her with a blank expression, Legend waited for her to explain this one to him in a way that made some sense. From where he was sitting, they weren't anything alike. January was an emotional tornado of inconsistency when they were dealing with each other. One day she wanted him to pay attention to her, the next day she was pushing him away. One day she was talking shit about how he never called her, the next day she was blocking him. The shit didn't add up and she was too caught up in her feelings to even see that shit.

"Both of y'all want each other. She wants you, but you're keeping her at a distance, so your words and actions don't line up. You're coming off as inconsistent. You say you love her but then you don't do shit to show it. And this makes her react emotionally inconsistent —wanting you to call but blocking you and telling you never to call her again when she picks up on *your* inconsistent actions. Don't you see that you're both doing the same thing?"

Legend blinked. "No."

"Both of you are afraid that the other one will let you down so you're pulling back on really giving yourself to the other one. She's pulling back by blocking you physically and you're blocking her emotionally by not really being there for her how you should."

Gritting his teeth, Legend took a moment to weigh what Onyx was saying in his mind and then shook his head. He wasn't afraid of January in any way. He feared nothing.

"I hear what you're saying but you're wrong. I don't fear her letting me down. I'm from the streets—been there, done that. I've dealt with many let downs. Why would I be afraid of something that I know is coming?"

Lifting her head, Onyx stopped what she was doing and looked Legend right in the eyes, not saying a word. Somehow, without her even saying anything, he slowly started to pick up on the shit he'd just said.

"Why would I be afraid of something that I know is coming?"

"Damn…" Legend said, pressing his hand to his chest.

Maybe he was tripping, but he suddenly felt the same chest pains that Nico might have been talking about. His words ran over and over in his mind as he slowly began to process them. It was like a 'which came first, the chicken or the egg' situation. Was January letting him down because he expected it, or did he expect it and was keeping her at a distance which led to her letting him down? Was he losing her because he never trusted that she would stay to begin with and was pushing her away?

"If you didn't feel that way—that she would let you down in the end—you wouldn't have held back to begin with. You would've gone into the situation with her with all your guards down. You wouldn't be so caught up on not wanting to be soft, not wanting to admit to people that you love her or that you want her. You wouldn't be afraid to chase her. The only reason you don't want to do that is because you're afraid that really giving yourself to her will blow up in your face."

Lifting a spoon that she'd been stirring inside of a pot, she pointed to Nico. "Same as Nico. He'd rather sit over there listening to sad songs and holding on to that teddy bear because he's afraid to go over there and be real with Brooke. He's afraid that once he does that, she'll break him. He'd rather break himself."

Swallowing the bitter taste on his tongue, Legend felt his chest ache even more. He cleared his throat, trying to ignore it, but it only started to ache even more.

"Fuck it," Legend heard Nico say from behind him. "You're right, Onyx. I'mma call her—nah, she probably got me blocked so I'mma just go over there. Grab her up and tell her that we gon' stop this stupid shit."

Legend turned around, watching as Nico acted out how he thought the moment would play out in his mind.

"I'mma grab her like this, by her arm, and tell her the real. Look her dead in her eyes and talk some real shit." Shrugging, he tossed his hands in the air. "I mean, she can believe it or not. But at least a nigga can say I tried."

That said, Nico began to walk away but then paused as if he forgot something. Doubling back, he grabbed the teddy bear from the couch and cradled it in his arms as he walked towards his bedroom. It was comical to watch and, prior to Onyx getting on his ass, Legend might have been laughing at him, but something about this entire situation was hitting him different.

Legend had to admit that Onyx was right—he loved January, that much he knew, but he hadn't really given her the chance to actually *feel* his love. That might have worked with any other woman on the planet, but January had the ability to always see through his bullshit. She wasn't a Dru—she wasn't easily enamored with surface-level shit. She could see straight through the smoke and mirrors to the reality that lay under the surface.

I know you love me, Legend. But it doesn't matter anymore.

The last words she said to him echoed through his mind, fucking with him even more than they had when she'd first said them. He'd thought she was doing the usual shit she always did. Being stubborn, trying to control a nigga. Trying to force him into being someone he wasn't. This was the first time he was starting to see how he was responsible for how she was feeling.

She might have been trying to control the situation, but he was too. By holding back on her, Legend was trying to control his reaction to the only outcome he saw coming from all of this. He was trying to minimize the impact of being hurt once she left him. He'd sabotaged himself in the process because the truth was, if he'd been himself, January wouldn't have ever felt the need to leave.

"I gotta get home," Legend said, pushing away from the island as he lifted out of his seat.

He felt sick as hell. Nauseated, like he was going to throw up. He eyed the shrimp that Onyx had washed and was deveining. Maybe that was the reason for it. Somehow, though he was telling himself that, he knew it was a lie.

"Leaving already? You're not even going to stay for food?" Onyx pouted with her bottom lip poked out. "I came over here to cook for y'all and now both of you leaving."

"I'll come over here later to grab a plate," Legend told her, walking over to where she was. Planting a kiss on the side of her forehead, he grabbed his keys off the counter and then turned around to leave. His mind was heavy with some shit he hadn't considered at all.

It was easy for him to admit that he wanted January in his life, but he'd never once thought about how any of his actions may have been the reason why she currently wasn't there. He'd thought that telling her he loved her, especially when he'd never once told anyone that before, should have been enough for her to see what she meant to him. He thought being real was enough.

Real? You're not real, Legend. You don't know what 'real' is. Real means that you stand by your word, regardless of anything else.

Sitting in the car, Legend didn't start the ignition as he began to replay all of their most intense conversations back through his mind. Everything that January was saying to him, he hadn't once considered that there was weight to it. All he could see was how much she was projecting her shit onto him. In his mind, *she* wasn't being real. *She* was the one saying she would always be there for him but threatening to be done with him as soon as she got mad. He never once considered that he may have been doing the same thing in a different way. He never considered that saying he felt a way about her but stopping himself from showing it to her in an authentic way was his version of doing the same exact thing.

You're not real, Legend. Why can't you be real with me?

"I thought I was doing that, shorty," Legend mumbled to himself as he sat in the driver's seat.

He didn't make it a habit to regret much, but in that moment, he was full of regrets. The queasiness in his stomach intensified. The last time wasn't the first time, or even the tenth time, that January had gotten mad at him. She found a reason to remind him of a fuck up every two weeks, like clockwork she cycled through her emotions so often, he'd gotten used to it. But this time was different. Something was off.

Starting his ignition finally, Legend was pulling out of Nico's parking lot when he picked up on the lyrics from a song that was playing.

See, I used to give a fuck, now I'm jaded.

I'm allergic to the bullshit.

Alright, orange soda, Deepak Chopra

Versace robe and my Gucci loafer

Sex on the sofa, that's my yoga

"Ain't listening to this shit," Legend muttered, changing the station.

Setting his thoughts onto something else, he bobbed his head to the music, not really paying attention to the lyrics until something caught his attention.

First I blame you, then I want you

Fucking hate you, then I love you

I can't help myself, no

When I have you, wanna leave you

If you go, that's when I need you

I can't help myself, no

You come in waves, waves, waves

Every hour, every day, day, day

You come in waves, yeah…

"Shit."

Legend changed the station again.

This time he waited to see what the song was. If it was anything that seemed to apply to his situation with January, he was gonna have to apologize to Nico. Maybe the nigga was right when he said voodoo was involved.

Don't worry about who it is I'm fucking

Or who I am loving

Just know that it is not you

This isn't up for discussion

I wish you good luck man

When it comes to you

It's none of my concern anymore

None of my concern

I know that I'm deserving of more

I know what I deserve

Blowing out a breath, Legend turned the radio off, deciding to ride the rest of the way home in silence instead. Looking out the window as he drove, he felt his jaw clench when he was drawn to look at the clock, noting the time.

2:22

He expelled air from his lips, immediately thinking to January and her fucking obsession with numbers. He shook his head and continued driving, forcing his mind to stay in the present. Dampening his lips with his tongue, he found himself looking at a flashing sign to his right.

Diesel. $4.44 per gallon.

"The fuck?"

Stopping at a red light, Legend covered his face with his hands, pressing hard against his eyes. He felt like he was losing it. Like he was literally going fucking insane. He was caught in some weird loop that he couldn't get out of. Everything was suddenly directing his attention to January, making sure that she stayed on his mind. It was like the Universe was telling him that he needed to right his wrongs, set things straight with her. As if now that he finally realized the part he'd played in their situation, he was being pushed to correct it.

The problem was… he wasn't ready yet.

Call it fear.

Call it boundaries.

Call it some other shit… he didn't really know how to refer to it. All he did know was that something was stopping him from wanting to go to her with his tail hanging between his legs. It was bad enough that she already had him doing shit he'd never done before. This was where he crossed the line. And the fact of the matter was that it didn't matter anyways. She was happily living her life in New York, doing her thing and moving on.

The only thing that was left was for Legend to do the same.

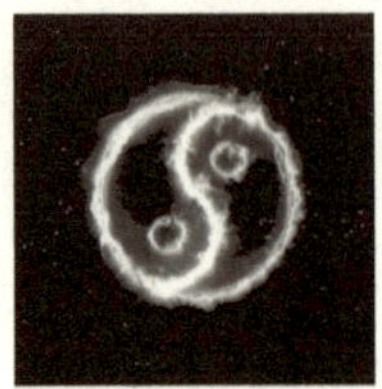

TEAM NO SLEEP.

"A rolling stone gathers no moss. Legend, as long as you keep moving around, you'll never sit still enough to grow."

JANUARY

It was some ungodly hour of the night and Legend was still awake. Lying in the bed with his arm propped over his face, he reveled in the complete, pitch-black darkness behind his closed eyelids. More often than not, he was finding himself spending his nights like this.

Usually alone.

But sometimes not.

"Why can't you sleep? Do you need anything?"

Do I need anything.

His thoughts echoed the question as if it were a statement because he knew the answer. He needed many things. Nothing that was easy to get.

"I do trust you, Legend," January had said. *"I didn't before, but now I do. My father always says, 'When people tell you who they are, trust them.' You told me that you were a monster. You told me you were a bad guy. A heartbreaker. Someone incapable of real love. Someone with no feelings. I didn't believe you because I was caught up in the fantasy. But I believe you now."*

"So you're going to run from me then?" Legend posed, narrowing his eyes. "Just because it's hard to deal with who I am?"

"The only person running from you is you," January replied calmly. "You say I only see the good in people... that I'm naive because I only see the good and not the bad. But you're the same way."

Legend's thought froze for a moment. Were they talking about the same nigga? Didn't seem that way.

"You've never had intimate relationships with anyone because you would be forced into something real. Something with depth. You are all good when we're joking around and having a good time, but you're closed off from me when my mood is sour or I'm going through a rough time. Or when I'm angry. You only like my light. You run away from dealing with my darkness."

January wanted to stop talking because she didn't want to hurt his feelings. She truly loved Legend in every way. And she felt he truly loved her back, but he could only love her as deeply as he loved himself, and it was clear that all his ego and arrogance was a facade because he didn't love himself very much.

"I'll always love you, Legend. Because you taught me how to embrace and love both sides of myself. I only cared to love the best parts of me. But through you, I learned how to see, love, and accept my bad. And I see the good in you and I fell in love with that side of you, too. But you only see, love, and accept your bad side and you're comfortable living in it. Until you can see, love, and accept the good inside of you, you'll never understand how to be good for me."

She let out a heavy sigh, her shoulders drooping as she finally was able to let out the truth she'd been holding in. "Because, honestly, you're not even good to your-

self. Maybe physically...but definitely not emotionally. And not mentally. I might fuck up when it comes to my physical body—which I'm working on—but my emotional body is in check. I know how to love myself and so I know how to love someone else. You're not capable of doing that."

Legend sat up in the bed and dropped his head into his hands.

Did she have a point?

"Go to sleep," the person next to him whined. It put him in an instant bad mood.

"Shut up," he replied.

Yeah, January definitely had a fuckin' point. Lifting his head, he glanced at the clock.

4:44

January would've had an entire fit. Her obsession with numbers was on a whole other level. Somehow, seeing the synchronicity made him smile. She was so far away but it was like a soft reminder that she was always with him.

"We're the same person. The same energy but in two different bodies, so we act out in different ways. We both get toxic when we're restless." January stopped, smiling a little as she thought about it. "I have a thing for emotional drama. I may not go and do as much as you do, but my mind is always on the next emotional adventure. I avoid feeling sad by searching for my next high. Even if that means starting an argument with you."

They both had to laugh at that one.

"But you're the same," she then added. "Always on the go. Always searching for the next high. We both have our addictions. Adrenaline junkies... fueling our obsessions into various things. But I can't do it anymore. I'm okay with embracing the exciting but also the mundane. I just want balance."

January had said some real shit to him that day. Dropped jewels so heavy that he wasn't sure if she knew the depths they hit. Before he met her, physically he was on point but emotionally, he had always been fucked up. He knew that wasn't how life was supposed to be for him, but it worked, so there was no point to changing it. Not until meeting January again. Not until developing whatever this attraction he had towards her was. Was it love? It could've been. Quite frankly, he didn't know. He was too cut off from that side of him to really understand. And now that he actually considered what January had said, he was beginning to understand why.

Standing up, he walked into the bathroom and stared at himself in the mirror. Finally desiring to be truthful to himself the way he told Nico to be.

Why was Jessica here? Why did he let her sleep next to him when he never let January that close? Why was he comfortable being there for Jessica in ways that he never had for January?

You got 'Captain Save-a-Ho' complex. You keep that lame ass broad around to make you feel good... because she's easy.

Those were the words he spoke to Nico. Shit... did he need to eat them, too? Jessica didn't give much. Wasn't demanding, wasn't a challenge, and he obviously didn't consider her his equal, so it was easy screwing her around. She looked at him like he was her blessing because, quite frankly, he was. There wasn't a damn thing that he did for her that she could do for herself.

With January that wasn't the case. And even if there was something she couldn't do, she always had Outlaw in the background to pick up the slack. Outlaw's influence and money was incomparable; he could handle things for January better than any man could. Honestly, Legend just didn't know where he fit in her life. He needed to have a purpose in every situation he involved himself in. Now that she didn't need him for anything, what purpose did he have for being in her life?

The only thing I want from you is your love, Legend. Being with someone isn't about material fulfillment. It's about commitment and connection. Giving to others the same love you give yourself.

Maybe that was the problem. The only love Legend had ever given himself were things. All he knew was material fulfillment. And, unfortunately, that kind of love was quick to leave, and at his current level of wealth, he could see that it wasn't fulfilling at all. It was a magnet for chicks like Jessica: all body and no brains. He desired a woman who had both. So, what the fuck was he doing dealing with Jessica for when January had it all?

As soon as the question came to mind, he knew it was time to make a move.

"Aye," he said, tossing Jessica's dress at the lump her body formed on his bed. "You gotta go."

"Huh?" She sat up, swiping her hair from her face. Blinking hard, she looked at him through tired eyes. "What are you talking about? What time is it?" Legend glanced at the clock.

5:55.

Had he really been thinking about this shit for an entire hour?

"Time for you to go. Don't come back," he replied, feeling nothing.

"What? Why?" Jessica asked, tears pooling in her eyes.

Legend felt nothing. It wasn't anything like when January cried. He was completely void of emotion. If ever he needed a sign that he had the wrong woman in his bed, that was it.

The only problem was, did he truly *deserve* someone as good as January in his bed? And if she were, would she be happy to be there?

He led the exact life she said she didn't want. He was the exact man she spent her life running away from. He wasn't the good guy type. She saw all good things when she looked at him but when he stared in the mirror, the side she saw wasn't there. All that stared back at him was the man he currently was. And it was impossible to aspire to a vision of someone you couldn't see.

She saw a man in him he couldn't yet visualize for himself because that man existed only in the future. And for street niggas, the future didn't exist. The streets taught him to only live in the moment because, with the life he lived, your next breath could easily be taken away. The future wasn't real for him yet. But he did know one thing: his future would look 100% better if January were in it. So maybe it was best to just start there.

"I don't have time to wait around for you," Legend said, grabbing his keys off the dresser. "Onyx will be over here in a couple hours to check that you've left. You better be gone by then."

Stopping only to make sure that his cameras were turned on in case Jessica decided to get brave and roam where she didn't belong, Legend left out the front door. With his intentions set on going to a city he hadn't been to since Outlaw ordered him to leave it, he prepared his mind to face whatever lay ahead.

Outlaw didn't believe in grace, mercy, or forgiveness. Once spoken, he rarely went back on his word. He'd asked Legend to protect January, fully expecting that he would risk his life for hers, but Outlaw never suggested that he would lift Legend's current status as enemy of the state as part of the deal. There was no conversation as to whether or not his sins were forgiven. Per Outlaw's last instructions to the Black Bag Mafia team of hitters, shown to protect and serve at a level that far surpassed the policy, Legend was to be killed on sight if he ever returned. But as Legend threw his car into gear and tore out of the covered parking deck, he couldn't bring himself to care about that.

"What the hell, man? It's early as hell and I got... company," Nico complained once he'd answered Legend's call.

Turning slightly in the bed, he glanced at the beautiful woman sitting next to him to check if she was awake.

Nah, her sexy ass still asleep, Nico thought, resisting the urge to reach out and palm the soft ass cheek that was peeking out of the covers, giving him a tease. As soon as he got Legend's worrisome ass off the phone, he was going to give her a tease of his own—big dick style.

"Aye, just wanted to let you know I'm headed out."

"Nigga, I don't need a play by play of your life! You sad as hell but you ain't suicidal. If you goin' to the store or some shit, you ain't gotta call me and—"

"Nah," Legend interrupted him, "Not to the store. I'm headed to the airport. Going to New York."

A long pause followed and then Nico finally spoke up.

"Something change with Outlaw?"

"Not at all," Legend replied with ease. As if he wasn't talking about a price on his head.

"Aw, damn. This nigga *is* suicidal," Nico whispered, taking to himself.

"Negative," Legend said. "I'm just clear on some shit and I know this the best way to go about it. I'm not letting anyone or anything get in my way."

Glancing once over at the woman next to him sleeping soundly, he reached out and lightly grazed his finger across her soft skin. Cupping her right at the bend of her ass, Nico thought about Legend's words as he stared at Brooke while she slept, fully understanding Legend's willingness to take the risk he was poised to take.

"You need me to ride shotgun?" Nico asked, his question taking on a double meaning. If anything went bad with Legend's trip, it would be better if he had another shooter by his side.

"No need. You stay," Legend replied, taking the interstate towards LAX. He was instantly hit with nostalgia, thinking about the last time he'd been here. The last time he'd seen January.

"On second thought, I do need a favor though," he added once another thought came to mind. "Give it a couple hours and then go to my place in Malibu to make sure Jessica left."

"Damn, bro. We switched sides," Nico said, alluding to the fact that he'd finally kicked his habit for having Drew around to make it work with Brooke while Legend had doubled back to Jessica.

"I fucked up because I was fucked up. But I'm about to get it right."

"I hope so," Nico added with honesty. "For your benefit."

"LEGEND, what the fuck do you think you're doing? Nico told me that you're talking about going to New York. Boy, are you crazy? Outlaw will *kill* you."

"Well, that's just the risk I'll have to take."

Driving through the city to the airport never seemed to take so long but Legend wasn't fazed by it. He was a patient man and didn't pay any attention to the delays and blocks when it came to getting to what he wanted. And right now, the only thing on his mind that he wanted was January.

"Legend! Are you listening to yourself? There is a better way to handle this. Like, a text. Or at least a phone call. Don't you think it's a better idea to at least talk to this man over the phone about what you're planning to do before you go flying into his city?"

Onyx was desperate for Legend to listen, even though she knew there was most likely no point in her pleas. One thing about her cousin, when he was dead set on doing something, there was nothing anyone could do to stop him. He was relentless when it came to getting what he wanted.

"The best way to talk to a man is face-to-face. What I look like calling him and asking for permission to enter the state?"

Holding the phone in her hand, Onyx paused to blink a few times. Legend couldn't be serious.

"What do you look like? You look like a man who has a price on his head and order to have him killed if he's seen in a city where he doesn't belong. I know you are trying to do the right thing about January, but do you really think this is the way to handle this?"

"Yes."

Onyx groaned and rolled her eyes. "Obviously, I asked you the wrong question."

Taking a moment, Legend tried to pause and see things Onyx's way. She was his cousin and, just like he was to her, she was very protective. She was worried about him and she truly had a reason to be. He was preparing himself to challenge one of the most unchallengeable men on the planet. And if that wasn't bad enough, the subject at hand would be about the man's daughter of all people.

"I'm going to be safe, Onyx. Ya cousin ain't no dummy. Stop worrying about me, I know what I'm doing," Legend said to calm her spirits. "Outlaw and I got some shit that went down in the past, but he knows I wasn't really behind it or I wouldn't be here talking to you today. He also knows that I'm a real nigga and loyal to the end. If he didn't, he wouldn't have ever hit me up to get January to safety. It's bad but, trust, it's not as bad as you think."

"I hope not," was all Onyx could say, wanting so badly to hold on to what Legend was saying as truth.

It was one thing for Outlaw to ask Legend to complete a task privately, but it was another for him to publicly overlook Legend disobeying an order that every mafia member in the country remembered him putting in place. Outlaw had killed many men who were close to him for lesser disrespect. He didn't take it lightly when people went against a law he'd set. For someone named 'Outlaw' who made an entire reputation around not following the law, he got merciless when someone didn't follow his.

"Don't hope. Trust," Legend told her, speaking plainly as he pulled up to the airport, sliding into a parking space. "Enough about me anyways. I want you to keep safe while I'm gone. I won't be able to make it this week to the club so Nico will have to fill in for me."

"That's fine," Onyx replied. "I'm feeling like you may not need to come any longer. I'm getting over my fear of being found. Deep down, I think we both know why I should."

She let her words linger, pausing for affect more than anything because she knew Legend wasn't going to say anything about it. She'd had a feeling for quite some time that her ex would never be a problem again and that Legend had made sure of that but somehow, she'd still clung on to the fear that his presence in her life had left. After talking about it with the girls, however, she felt stronger. Like, in some strange way, speaking on it had helped her to release it. She felt freedom like never before, even a renewed feeling about dating. She wasn't afraid to open up to another man anymore. Somehow, in some way, speaking on what had happened to her helped her to heal.

"I'll still come by if you want me to. You're still dating that square ass motherfucka, right? The lawyer?"

Onyx giggled. To the men in her family, any nigga who wasn't in the streets was a square. Deep down, they appreciated the fact that she'd chosen someone different from them even though they teased her for it. It helped them relax a small bit. There were battles they would've had to face with street niggas that with squares they wouldn't have to face. Her present selection of men made things easier on them.

"Yeah, I'm still dating him but it's moving along fine. He respects me. Treats me right. He's thoughtful and he's careful about everything he does. He makes obvious efforts not to hurt me." Onyx smiled as she spoke. There was such a warm, loving vibe that she was giving off that Legend could feel it through her voice.

"Sounds like you love this lil peanut head nigga," he replied, chuckling to himself.

"Maybe," Onyx said. "I can't say I've ever been in love before, but this feels like it."

"If it feels like it, it probably is," Legend told her. Reaching to the back seat, he snatched up his duffle bag, the only thing he'd packed up to take with him, and then stepped out of the car.

"I'll text you when I get there—"

"And you'll also text me every night before I go to bed, so I know you're safe," Onyx instructed him, speaking with intensity.

"Yes, mama. I mean, Onyx," he joked and they both laughed.

"Promise me," she said in all seriousness once the laughter died down.

"You know I don't ever make any promises," he replied, saying exactly what she'd expected him to. "But I will do the best that I can."

"WOULD YOU LIKE ANYTHING? Snacks? A drink from the bar?" the stewardess asked Legend, with an expression that seemed to imply that there was much more she wanted to offer him than what was on the menu. With a shake of his head, he promptly dismissed her, not at all apologetic about the fact that she seemed to take offense at his blunt nature. Legend had limited patience and at the moment, it was reserved for dealing with one woman in particular.

His thoughts ruminated with apologies unsaid and questions unasked. Would she want to see him? Would she hear him out? Would she forgive him for…?

Fuck, Legend thought, shaking his head.

To be honest, he really ain't have no idea what exactly he should be apologizing for. The fact that he didn't give her better when he knew she deserved better? Being the type of man January wanted and needed required him to step up in a way that he never had before. It required him to be unselfish. It required him to think of her first and himself last. The rules of relationships built on love were different from the rules of the streets. Legend had been in survival mode for so long, he wasn't sure he had what it took to turn off the switch. And, to be frank, he needed to keep that motherfucker on until he dealt with whatever would come once he saw Outlaw.

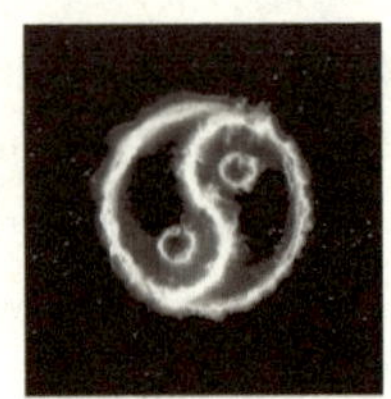

MOOD TRANSMUTED.

I SHOULD'VE KNOWN BETTER, JANUARY THOUGHT AS SHE HELD HER phone in her hand.

"Are you sure?" she questioned, wanting full reinsurance before she fully gave in to the stabbing pains in her chest.

"Yes," Brooke replied with a sigh. "Nico thought I was sleeping, but I heard Legend ask him to go check on her or something. He left her at his place."

Biting her bottom lip, Brooke wondered if she should tell her about the fact that Legend was on his way to see her. Part of her wanted to give January a heads up, but the other side of her said she should let things play out naturally in that regard. The only reason she told her about the girl was because she wouldn't be a friend if she let her girl be blind-sided by a nigga who was just lying up in bed with his ex-bitch. Brooke thought the best of Legend, and she knew that he had the capacity to be right for January, but if he wasn't at that point to do right, then he just wasn't ready yet. And January needed to know all the details before she let down her walls for him again.

"I feel so stupid," January admitted, a dry, dark chuckle falling from her lips to mask the sharpness of the pain in her chest. "I actually thought that maybe..." she paused, not wanting to voice her true thoughts. She'd thought Legend would be her hero. She'd fantasized about it multiple times, daydreaming when she should've been focused in class. She thought he would come to his senses and one day come back and save her. Unfortunately, life didn't work like the fairytales.

"I just thought he cared," she finished, dropping her head. Tears filled her eyes and she bit down hard on her lip to stop them from falling. Her mind told her that there was no point in crying over the fact that Legend turned out to be the liar she had already suspected him to be. But her heart wanted to grieve for the man she'd hoped him to be.

"I really feel like he *does* care," Brooke told her.

"How can you say that?" January shot back, unable to hold back the tears any longer. "He was just with someone else. He told me she was a nobody but now they are together. She's in his bed and I'm not. They sleep together. Literally, sleep together, not fuck. That's some intimate shit that you only do with someone you love and trust. We've never *slept* together. Not even once."

"Yes, but..." Brooke paused to sigh. "January, you're new to love, but what he's doing is just the dumb shit niggas do when they are trying to get over how they feel about the girl they lost. They try to bury that shit between the legs of the next bitch. It's not all what you're thinking it to be."

Rubbing her face, January sniffed and shook her head. That sounded like some backwards reasoning if she'd ever heard any before. She *needed* him in her life. She'd made that part perfectly clear. He knew she wanted him. Why would he bury the fact that he felt the same way by deciding to be with someone else?

"Don't try to understand it," Brooke said, already knowing that January was trying to piece things together in her mind.

“I won’t,” she replied.

Reaching out, she grabbed her ballet slippers and flipped them around in her hand. A rush of energy to the chest, straight to her heart center, confirmed what she needed to do to heal the pain she felt. The same thing she’d always done when she needed to release, rebuild, and repair herself.

After ending her call with Brooke, she placed her phone on the charger with the desire to take a break from being accessible in any way for the time being. As she laid it on the top of her small night-stand, she lowered down, squatting so that she could pull out the lowest drawer. Tucked inside of it in the farthest corner in the back were her leotards and tights. Without giving herself enough time to change her mind, she reached in and grabbed what used to be her favorite set to practice in and rushed to put it on.

Her father had built her a custom-designed dance studio for her thirteenth birthday and, though she hadn’t stepped foot in it in almost a decade, he hadn’t allowed any changes to be made to it. Somehow, it was like he knew that one day she would come back.

And here she was.

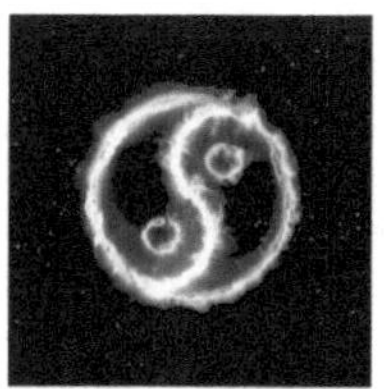

A HOUSE DIVIDED.

In a house divided, those still dwelling inside will become each other's enemies.

JANELLE

"You know I should be having you killed, right?" Outlaw said, using a carefully controlled tone.

Looking down over his nose at Legend, sitting right across from him, spine straight and head high like he owned every fuckin' thing in the world, Outlaw couldn't help but see a bit of himself in the arrogance of one of the few men he allowed to escape from his city with a life that should have been taken.

Truthfully, he knew that January being shot was never Legend's fault; however, it didn't matter. He'd still been too close to the situation. Too close for comfort. And in Outlaw's opinion, when it came to the safety of his family, anything that made him uncomfortable was worth taking a life.

"I know it," Legend replied with a slight tilt of his head. "But I thought given the circumstances—"

"Given what circumstances?" Outlaw interrupted, leaning back in his chair. Propping his hands behind his head, he leaned back into the palms of his hands, appearing relaxed only in posture. The deadly stare in his eyes was still fully intact.

"You think just because you secured the safety of my daughter, you're owed a pass? You've done me no favor. You owe her your life until the day you die. You do know that, right?"

Lips pulled tightly in a straight line, Legend nodded his head. "I do," he replied. "But, even if that wasn't the case, I would still do whatever was necessary to spare her life in exchange for mine."

To some, it may have been a statement of valor, but Outlaw still wasn't impressed. He would expect any member of Black Bag Mafia, former or not, to give up their life for January. That was a necessary vow to make before even being welcomed into the fold.

"The only reason I'm even allowing this," Outlaw began, his patience already wearing thin with the small talk. "Is because you were like a son to me. My right hand outside of my brothers and one of the closest men on my team. If you had been anyone else—"

"I know," Legend cut in. "If I had been anyone else, I would be dead right now."

"You would have been dead *back then*," Outlaw corrected him. "You would've never made it to right now."

"Noted," Legend replied.

Neither spoke a word, allowing for several moments of dense silence in which each retreated in his own thoughts, wondering what to make of the man who sat before him. Interestingly enough, Outlaw had been considering asking Legend if he would be open to considering returning to the fold for a while. Of all the men he'd brought into Black Bag Mafia, Legend had not only been one of the best, but he'd also been one of the most loyal, a fact that was further solidified even once he'd left.

Not once in all the years that followed, even with a price on his head, had he ever spoken a word against the BBM or any member of the team. He'd never worked for an enemy or taken a job that would interfere with any of the territories. His loyalty was present even when he'd been stripped of everything and made to look like a traitor to a cause that he'd pledged his life to.

Many men had turned their backs on Outlaw for much less, but Legend never did. Not to mention, he'd taken a mission that he didn't have to. One that put him at odds with people he was still tied to, simply because Outlaw needed it. To be honest, he couldn't afford to not have a man like him in his circle. Legend was too golden of a character to lose. He was too solid to not bring back in. However, the fact that he had defied a command that he'd so vehemently obeyed up until this point made Outlaw curious about the reason Legend requested this meeting so unexpectedly today.

What could he possibly want to speak on that was worth risking his life for?

"So, what is the reason you've come here today?" Outlaw asked, lying back in his chair. "What is it that's so important to you it's worth risking your life?"

"January," was the single thing that Legend said.

Her name came right out of his mouth without a moment's hesitation. His eyes were piercing, his spine straight and tall. There wasn't a shred of fear within him—a remarkable feat for any man approaching Outlaw to speak to him about his daughter.

"Motherfucka, you better be referring to the fuckin' month," Outlaw said, curling his brow as he stared down at Legend. "I know damn well you ain't walk your ass up in here to talk to me about my motherfuckin' daughter."

Standing tall like the soldier he was trained to be, Legend showed absolutely no changes in response to Outlaw's aggression. He wasn't afraid of him. He wasn't afraid of any man. He respected him, but he wasn't afraid. There was a clear difference and both men knew it.

"I did," Legend told him with a slight nod. "I want your permission to date her, if she accepts. And I also would like reinstatement in BBM."

"You got some fuckin' nerve," Outlaw replied, his voice dangerously calm. "You ain't even supposed to be here. You protected her for me and brought her home because you owed me a favor. How the fuck you walk in here acting like the shit's flipped and you get a fuckin' prize?"

Outlaw was playing hard because he had to. Legend was a man who was showing interest in his daughter. And, for that reason, he had to put up a challenge to allow Legend to show that he was worthy. January wasn't easy and she wasn't simple. She was royalty and when it came to value, she was priceless. Outlaw would only be supportive of her entertaining a man who saw her the same way. She was one of two of the most important people in his life.

"It's not about winning a prize." Legend paused, thinking about what he was about to say next. He was about to make a confession that he hadn't made to anyone yet, but he knew it was time to come clean and admit what he knew to be true.

"I love her," he said, looking Outlaw square in the eyes. "I love her more than I've ever thought I'd love anyone. I love her more than I love myself."

Holding his hardened gaze, Outlaw thought for a moment about what he was hearing. Then, suddenly, his mind went down memory lane to his experience when it had come to Janelle. Her father hadn't wanted him with her. He didn't think Outlaw was good enough. But Outlaw knew that no man on Earth could possibly ever love her the way he could. When he looked at Legend, he could see the same conviction in his eyes. The same boldness and fearlessness. The same stubborn qualities that he saw in himself.

"I hear what you're saying, but there is one thing that's missing. You might love January, but that doesn't mean a damn thing if she doesn't love you."

Legend nodded his head. "I know," he replied. "I've made some mistakes and it's my goal to right my wrongs. To tell her how I feel. To tell her the truth about everything. I messed up and I just want to spend the rest of my life making it right. If she will have me."

Leaning forward, Outlaw finally relaxed the hardened look on his face and allowed his lips to spread into a smile.

"All bullshit aside, it'll be my honor to have you back," he said, holding his hand out to Legend's. "You've always been like a son to me and you're one of the best I've ever had on the team."

Delivering a small smile of his own, Legend nodded his head and reached forward to shake hands with Outlaw.

"But the decision isn't mine to make," Outlaw continued, settling back into a straight expression, staring at Legend with piercing eyes. "It's January's. If she says you can stay, you stay. If she wants you to go, you gotta get the fuck outta here."

With a nod of his head, Legend sat back once Outlaw released his firm grip on his hand.

"I understand," he said. "And I wouldn't have it any other way."

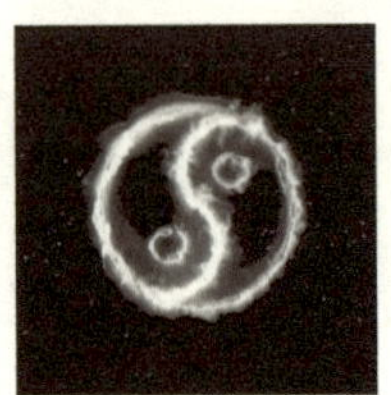

YOU'VE DONE GOOD, OUTLAW.

Standing in front of the door of her studio, she hesitated briefly before sucking in a breath and pushing the door on. Once again, tears came to her eyes. For the second time that day she was in her emotions, and it wasn't even noon yet.

A burst of energy came forth from somewhere deep within her and she suddenly felt like a new person. A renewed person. One who didn't have any of the fault, insecurities or fears that she wore like a badge before. She took one step forward, placing one silk shoe onto the studio floor and, instantly, it felt like she was transported in time.

All of a sudden, she wasn't twenty-something January anymore. She was back to the January she was from before the gunshot. Before the moment in time that had nearly ended her life. She'd wanted to go back to that January for so long, but she'd been at a complete block on how to get there. Now she knew how and she knew why. She understood the answer lay in the problem. But she hadn't realized that until now. She hadn't seen that the problem was that she couldn't dance and the solution was to *dance anyway.* The only powerlessness she felt was in reveling in the moment of when her power had been taken away. As long as she allowed herself to become a victim of that moment, to continue to sell herself short on the dreams that she believed had been taken away, the longer she would live a life unfulfilled. Now she had the clarity she needed. She could see it clearly.

The key to changing my life all this time was to fight for what I wanted. To stop being a victim of circumstances. To get knocked down and get right back up and fight anyways.

She had been fighting all this time, but January had been fighting the wrong things. She had been fighting against herself instead of fighting for herself. It wasn't until she hit rock bottom that she realized that she was her only resistance. Just like Legend, she was also a fighter battling it out in the ring. The difference was that she was fighting herself. And she was tired as hell of fighting her own damn self.

"Ah!" she gasped, feeling a weakness in her ankle. Pausing mid-pirouette, she placed her hands on her hips and lifted her right leg up, wiggling her ankle to shake out the discomfort.

"Don't stop," she heard a voice say.

When she looked up, she found herself looking into the eyes of her father.

"Don't stop," he repeated again. "Shake that shit off, breathe, and then get back to it. You can do this."

Swallowing hard, January dipped her head to look once more at her ankle, feeling fear creeping up on her from the baseline of her neck. A sudden heat made additional drops of sweat bead over her forehead. Deep down, she knew she could do this. She knew she could trust her body. But her fear was still there.

Looking back up at her father, she found comfort, security, and support in his eyes. But the strongest emotion she saw there was his love. And it was his love that seemed to be everything she needed.

Lifting her arms back in the air, January started to dance again, her mind and all of her focus intent on nailing the pirouette. She danced and twirled up to that moment, building up in confidence, warming up her body in preparation for the moment when she would test it again.

Adrenaline rushed through her and her nervous energy began to rise. She took a deep breath and closed her eyes, mentally telling herself that she was going to be alright. She'd done this many times before. And the body's memory was the most perfect memory of all. Nothing stored information, feelings, and movement quite the same as a body did.

Hands in the air, January launched her body forward, falling into a perfect transition to complete not one but three pirouettes in a row. It was a movement that she hadn't done in nearly a decade but she nailed it, finishing her impromptu performance with a perfect landing.

A smile spread across her face at her victory, but the second that her eyes hit her father's and she saw the tears in his eyes, she became daddy's little girl again. Collapsing onto the floor, she cried harder than she could ever remember doing in life, wailing as loudly as she felt she wanted to, releasing everything and holding back nothing.

This was the breakdown I was waiting for, Outlaw thought as he watched his daughter.

Strong as ever, January was doubly as stubborn as both of her parents put together. She was a force to be reckoned with, and would be a challenge for any man who had the mental fortitude and guts to date her. She wasn't easy. She came with some shit. Most Black women did. They were the women who had the longest legacy of trauma when it came to love. It would be dumb to think that it would ever be 'easy' to sincerely love one. However, for those who were man enough to stick around, it was always worth it.

The fact that January had lived in the comfort and luxury that came with the life of a mafia princess had nothing to do with it. Response to trauma was something that was built into DNA. It was a real thing. Outlaw's way of coping with his own trauma was to pass his trauma on to another, either through fighting, shooting, or robbing. It wasn't until he met his match in Janelle that she forced him to release his anger in another way. Janelle was the woman who showed him that resolving his pain by inflicting pain was killing him and he had to change. Fortunately, he loved her enough to rise to the occasion.

"This is what I was trying to teach you, January," Outlaw said, walking over to her once she stopped crying. "No matter what dumb ass motherfuckas you gotta deal with out there, you can always come in here to release the negative shit. Why you think I was so supportive of your dancing? It was because I knew you would need to use it as an outlet one day. Everyone needs a way to release. You know what I mean?"

Sitting up, January nodded her head, wiping the tears from her face. Outlaw took one look at her and pulled the Gucci shirt off his back and held it out to her.

"Wipe your tears. Don't use your hands to clean your face. And blow your nose," he said.

She crooked a brow. "You want me to blow my nose… on your brand-new Gucci shirt?" Fanning his hand at her, Outlaw sat down on the floor next to her and frowned. "You wasn't concerned the one time you peed on my shit."

"I was a child," she said, rolling her eyes. "A baby to be exact."

"Yeah, those were the days," Outlaw replied, smiling even harder than he had when he walked in and saw her back in the studio. "My baby girl. Those were the days."

Leaning back on her father's legs, she felt comforted by his embrace as she allowed her mind to retreat into her thoughts.

"So, what you want me to tell this knucklehead boy?" Outlaw asked suddenly, finally bringing up the real reason he had come home looking for January in the first place.

He knew how he felt about Legend. He'd always seen him as the son he'd never had the chance to have. God's offering to him after the devastation he'd suffered was how he felt about it, in a way. For that reason, Legend would always have a special place in his heart, but the shit was different when it came to his daughter. He knew the type of misfortune that came to a woman when she fucked with a nigga who wasn't ready. He knew it because he was it.

It haunted him to this day to think about the things he'd taken her mother through before he finally surrendered his player card and decided to put in work to become the man he needed to be for her. He almost lost her in the process—not once but twice—to other men who wanted to put in work to give her better. They would never be him but they were promising not to bring the chaos he brought to their situation. And if Janelle hadn't loved him as much as she did, she would have let him go and went for that. And he couldn't even blame her if she had made that decision to give up on him. Any *normal* woman would have. But their love wasn't normal. From the beginning, it was extraordinary. Which meant he had to be extraordinary for her.

January was the same way. She demanded a man who would rise to the occasion to do some extraordinary things in order to be worthy of her. Could Outlaw see Legend doing that? He wasn't totally sure, which was why he had to run it by January.

"What is he asking you for?" she asked, wanting to make no assumptions. She'd had her heart broken already by assuming things. She didn't want to play that game anymore. If Legend wanted to be here and wanted to be in her life, she had to know the truth, the whole truth, and nothing but. She didn't want to play 'he loves me or he loves me not' games with her heart.

"He wants to be allowed back as a member of BBM."

January crinkled her nose. "That's it?"

It hardly seemed like something worth coming to her and having a discussion for.

"That, and..." Outlaw took a deep breath and let it out in a sigh. "He wants to know if he had my blessing to ask you out on a date... should you decide you want to date his ugly ass."

In spite of the fact that she was hearing the most unexpected thing she'd heard in a while, January couldn't help but laugh. A memory came to her mind of the one time she'd called Legend 'ugly' to his face in his apartment.

A nigga been a lot of things, but I ain't never been ugly, he'd said.

"I think you should allow him back into BBM. At heart, Legend is a good man. He's just trying to find his way."

Nodding, Outlaw smiled. It was comforting to know that his daughter saw in Legend the same thing that he did. To him, Legend had always been a good kid. He reminded him so much of himself in so many ways. He would have hated to have to kill him if he'd done some fucked up shit to January. He'd have hated it... but he would do it anyways.

"And should I give my blessing?" Outlaw asked.

Sighing, January took a minute to think the question through, piecing together what she truly wanted when it came to that situation.

"You can give your blessing if you choose," she said, moving around to stand to her feet. Outlaw jumped to his to help her up, giving her a quick hug and a kiss on the forehead before letting her go.

"However," she quickly began to add. "Whether or not I decide that he's someone I would grace with my presence on a date... is yet to be decided. A date with me has to be earned. A mafia princess can only date and be surrounded by people who demonstrate that they are worthy of being trusted. And I'm not sure he's done that yet."

With that said, January did a fancy twirl on her heels, channeling all the grace that a professional dancer of her possibly could, and sashayed away as her father watched in awe.

"Ain't have no sons but I still raised a motherfuckin' boss," he said, patting himself on the back. "Outlaw, you've done well."

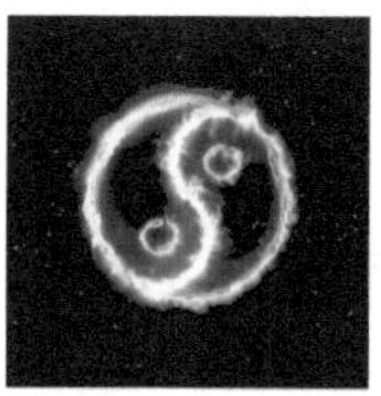

ENDLESS LOVE.

In the end, it's not winning that matters. What matters is the love.

PORSCHA STERLING

LEGEND SAT WAITING OUTSIDE OF JANUARY'S FINAL CLASS OF THE DAY, his mind playing tug of war between what he wanted to say and what he knew he should. Deep down, he couldn't help feeling like he should cut things off with her and leave her alone. He couldn't help feeling like he wasn't good enough. Not because he didn't have the capacity to be, but because he didn't want to be. He was at the beginning of reaching his dreams—ones he hadn't even dared to dream yet. No matter what January felt about his mafia affiliation, he couldn't shake the deep inner knowing that it was part of his life plan.

With Outlaw accepting him back into Black Bag Mafia and elevating him to a position that ensured he would one day take over the throne, Outlaw was molding him to be his predecessor, the next in command of something that had the potential to be huge, utterly world changing. The amount of influence that Legend would have once he was able to fulfill the vision he had in his mind was limitless. Unfortunately, as with all things, the bad came along with the good. All of his actions and decisions wouldn't be up to par with January's standards and morals in regards to how she wanted to live her life and what she wanted to be joined together with. He knew that she would have her reservations about what he was choosing to be a part of, but Legend felt like she wasn't seeing the bigger picture. In the end, as much as he loved her, he had to be true to himself and what he knew deeply that he had to do.

The only thing he could hope for was that she would understand.

The bell rang, signaling the end of class, and he felt his heart skip a beat in his chest. Frowning, he almost chuckled to himself at the knee-jerk emotion. The more time he spent around January, opening up to her, he was beginning to notice these small bursts of emotion even more. It was odd to him, foreign even. Especially in comparison to how he'd gone through life before: completely void of all things except the dull aching somewhat-bliss that came from inflicting pain. Now he realized that it wasn't joy he had been feeling at all. It was curiosity and obsession—he had been obsessed with seeing the reaction to pain he wouldn't allow himself to feel being expressed in others. In some twisted way of living, he'd made this his emotional outlet through years of training himself on how to turn his feelings off. The entrance of January into his life shined a light on all that he'd kept hidden, everything that he'd pushed into the dark recesses of his subconscious mind. He finally realized that she brought out the best parts of him.

"Legend! What are you doing here?" January's voice interrupted his thoughts.

He looked up, unsure of what to expect, but relaxed completely when he saw her smiling up at him as he stood. The unexpected but pleasant emotion sent him into a daze and, for a brief moment, he seemed to lose his thoughts, wanting nothing more than to stare into her eyes. The effect she had on him was intoxicating… but in a way that he would never push away. Not again. Throughout his life, he'd subjected himself to many forms of torture, but love was the sweetest kind.

"I came to see you," he replied with a shrug.

Both of January's brows lifted and then slowly one dropped, leaving the other lifted as she stared at him with a question in her eyes. Feeling his muscles suddenly grow taunt, Legend looked away. He knew what was coming next by her expression. She wanted to know what he'd chosen to do. If he'd taken Outlaw's offer. He would have to answer her, but he wasn't ready yet. He didn't know what would come of them in the moments after, and he wanted to enjoy what could possibly be his final moments in her presence.

"Shouldn't you be…enjoying your first day of work?" she asked, mincing her words carefully.

And there it was. As usual, January wasn't beating around the bush, she got straight to the point, asking the question that had been weighing heavily on her mind. She barely had been able to pay attention in class because she'd been wondering so much about what would happen with Legend. Not that she worried he wouldn't make a decision that benefitted her, but that he wouldn't make a decision that benefitted *him.* Somehow, in between her confusion of fighting the war between loving him and loving herself, she realized that it wasn't a war at all. There was no either or. She wasn't damned to love one at the expense of the other. *Both* of them could love each other wholly and completely while living the life they wanted to live. *Both* of them could be free.

There was no need to control anything. There was no need to expect any particular outcome. The only thing she had control over was herself and her decisions for her life and what she wanted to be involved in. And she would love him with her whole heart in the moments they spent together. Whatever he chose to do when he was separate from her was his decision, and she had to trust that he was making the best choices based on how he wanted to spend his life. That was the only way that he would truly be satisfied with her place in it. No one wanted to be with someone by way of control and ultimatums. That didn't breed love. That only bred resentment.

Legend lifted his head to look at her and January could easily pick up on his apprehension and fear. It wasn't visible; he made sure of that. But though he tried to keep his expression stoic and did a great job of masking his emotions, there was no way to hide true emotion that was felt. And January was an empath; she absorbed his feelings as if they were her own. She didn't have to see his unease. She could *feel* it for herself.

Curling her lips into a playful smile, she turned her body to face his, looking at him eye-to-eye. She sent him love from her heart, wanting to put him at ease. To be his peace. Wanting him to know that there was no judgment in her and no reason for him to fear. Whatever he felt was the best thing for him was the best thing. And she wanted him to know that.

"I did… I mean, I was," Legend began, pausing to lick his lips.

Damn, nigga, are you nervous?

He almost couldn't believe it.

"I left so that I could see you here and…"

He paused again. Frowning, he tried to figure out what the hell was wrong with his mouth. Why was it that he had all the words in his head but now, somehow, couldn't speak? In the back of his mind, he knew what it was, but he didn't want to admit it. There was a lot of new shit going on, but this one emotion was one that he was uncomfortable admitting that he felt.

Fear. A young gangsta's kryptonite. It was the first thing he'd buried when he decided to live life on the streets. It was the one thing that he'd been taught had to go when it came to being a man. But here he was, standing in front of the most beautiful woman, 5'5 with brown eyes and thick thighs, who couldn't throw a punch worth shit, and he was afraid. He knew what he needed to say to January, but he couldn't. He was truly afraid of what she would do once he did. He was afraid of what it would do to him if she exercised her right of free will and chose to leave.

"Legend, I'm here for you either way. I want you to live your life and be happy. And I want to live my life and be happy. But I also know that I'll only be happy with you in it. Whatever happens, I'm here to stay. I'm clear on that. You're not dispensable to me. I trust you enough to know that you won't make any decision that you think would hurt me."

He stared at her, unable to say anything in that moment. No words came to mind, but her love was definitely felt. He reveled in it as he watched her radiant glow, seeing that she wasn't playing him or being fake. She was completely genuine. It was such a foreign concept to him for someone to love him without expectations, without control and without defenses. He'd never known anyone, woman or man, to trust him this completely. It was new territory; a new type of experience. Which made perfect sense as to why every day he was feeling new emotions to go along with it. He'd thought that he loved January before, but it had nothing on the love that he felt for her now. There was something special, almost unfathomable, about truly being loved by a person to the point that they could do nothing at all to make you want to leave. To love them enough to trust that whatever they said they needed was what you believed they needed and you let them have it without the threat of taking your love away.

His fate was sealed. He was going to be a mafia king, that was a definite. If January agreed to be with him, it would be as his wife. He was young but his mind was at an age where he was over playing games. He knew who he wanted and how he wanted to have her.

But being with him would make January a mafia wife, something that she'd always said she never wanted to be. It would require her to turn a blind eye to the dark side of things she knew he would have to be involved in. It would subject her to a life of merging duality. In Legend's role, he would consistently blur the line between good and bad, the way that her father had done. She would have to allow him to live freely during the day and then lay her head next to his at night with a clear conscience, believing that everything he did, both bad and good, was necessary. She would have to trust in his ability to lead them correctly even if not everything he did was something she would have agreed to.

Making her his would be asking a lot. It required more than he was sure January was prepared to give. But God, he prayed every day that she would.

"I can't make you be someone you're not, just because it benefits me," he continued, taking the leap of faith to explain his position and hope that the outcome would be in his favor. "You know how I feel about you and it's real on every level. I promise if you accept me how I am, if you agree to be with me how I am, I'll spend every day of my life making you happy that you chose to take a chance on me."

If ever in his life there had been a time when Legend was nervous, the time was now. He wasn't a man of many words and he wasn't a man who dove deeply into his feelings. Up until the point of meeting January, he wasn't even sure that he had any feelings to begin with. He'd thought that when the Creator was mixing up his recipe of life, blending up all the ingredients that came together to make whatever a hood nigga like him would be, that he'd given him a generous portion of anger and hate in order to settle his emotional detachment. Experiencing real emotions and real vulnerability wasn't something he was used to.

January could see the discomfort in his eyes, she read everything about him in her heart as if it were a book that she'd written herself. She knew where his worry was coming from. She could see the fear in him clearly because it was the same fear that had been coursing through her, fucking with her mind on the daily, in those days when she thought she might lose him again. She had been fearful because she didn't understand a concept that she now fully understood.

Legend was her soul and she was his. And nothing came from separating from your soul but misery.

"I love you enough to accept you as you are, how you are, and to not change anything about that. But my love for you is unconditional. Which means that no matter where you go and what you choose, I will always be there for you. I will never stop loving you. Of all the things you have to worry about… that one isn't it."

It was like a weight lifted off his shoulders. January said the words that he hadn't even dared to believe could be said. In his life, he'd learned that disappointment came from expectation, so he chose not to accept anything when it came to her. He gave her the freedom to make her own choices but, in this moment, he was happy as hell that she chose to be with him.

Lifting his head, Legend stared into January's eyes and grabbed both of her hands in his. With his heart beating wildly in his chest, he lifted her hands to his lips and gave them each a kiss. It was almost as if he could feel his love grow.

"I love you, January," Legend said, speaking the only words that came to his mind. "Forever. Always. In this lifetime and the next."

In a house divided, those still dwelling inside will become each other's enemies.

January couldn't help but think on the words her mother had said to her one day. She hadn't understood it at the time, but she did now. Now she realized how it applied so well when it came to her and Legend.

Nothing good came out of division, especially in matters of the heart. She could never unlove Legend. The blueprint to loving him was written in her soul. It was a piece of her that she would never be able to rip away. Forcing herself to pretend that she didn't would be like agreeing to a life of killing herself slowly. Every single moment she would think of the love that could've been, waiting for this life to be complete so that she could rush into the next and have a chance to right her wrongs. A chance to truly love him again.

"I love you too, Legend," she replied, staring in his eyes. "Always have and always will. In this lifetime and the next."

Leaning into her, he grabbed her by the hand, and they sealed their love with a kiss. Neither one of them knew what would happen in the future. Neither one cared about what happened in the past. All they had was the present moment and, in this moment, he was hers and she was his. And if Legend had it his way, there would be many more present moments, like this one, to come.

Even

After

All this time

The Sun never says to the Earth

"You owe me."

Look

What happens

With a love like that.

It lights the whole sky.

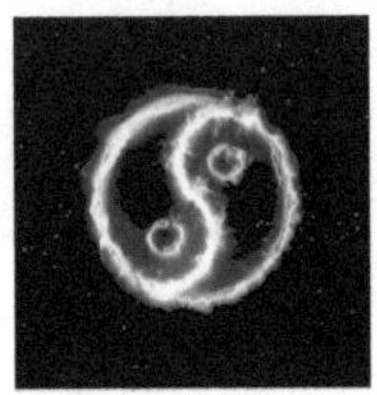

EPILOGUE.

She is a beautiful piece of broken pottery, put back together by her own hands. And a critical world judges her cracks while missing the beauty of how she made herself whole again.

JMSTORM

Nervous jitters swirled around in January's stomach as she practiced some light steps of her routine, visually working through the entirety of it in her mind.

This was the day that she'd been waiting for. The one she'd always dreamed of from the time that she was a little girl. She was officially a member of Alvin Ailey's Dance Company, as well as a senior student at Julliard, and she was about to perform the lead for *The Black Swan.*

Although this was such a happy moment for her, a monumental one, she hadn't told anyone about it. Keeping it close to the heart seemed to be the only way that she could manage her nerves. She didn't want any pressure. She knew that she could do it; she'd completed the steps perfectly from the beginning, which was how she'd won the part. She knew the routine by heart and she won the lead off her own merit. Yet another reason she didn't want her family knowing. If her father knew how to do anything, it was intervene. It was important to her that she did this right. And completely alone. It was important that she proved to herself that she had the power to commit to and fulfill her dreams.

The curtains opened and the next thing January knew she was dancing in front of a sold-out theater. As if none of that mattered and it was just her alone in there private studio, she completed each routine perfectly. It all felt like a dance that she was doing for herself. There was so much passion in her every move, every step, every twist and pirouette. Everything she did had personal meaning.

The *Black Swan* is about the dual nature of personality, the good and bad nature that everyone has inside of them. It was so personal to January and it meant so much to okay the part. She felt like she was both. She had the innocent and graceful aspects of the White Swan and also the guile and sensuality of the Black Swan. She was a complex woman, not an easy woman to love. But if you could get through all of her walls to see the love that she so protected deep down inside, you would know that she was well worth the fight.

Landing the last step with precision, grace and power, January lifted her head in the air, embodying her full role as the queen of the dance as the curtains closed. Tears swarmed her eyes. Opening night had ended and she had fuckin' nailed it.

In the next second the curtain opened again and she relaxed, smiling hard as she waved at the crowd who were all on their feet giving her a standing ovation. This was all her. This was her stage. No one knew her as the infamous Outlaw and The Honorable Janelle Pinckney-Murray's daughter. She was just her. A dancer—an excellent one at that. She was making a name for herself that was hers alone. No one knew her as the mafia king's daughter.

Or at least not yet.

"That's my motherfuckin' baby!" she heard someone yell suddenly.

Instantly, she recognized the voice and peered through the crowd.

"Daddy?" She said, although she knew there was no way anyone could have heard her through all the applause and laughing.

Lifting her eyes to the balcony, January's heart warmed instantly when she saw not only her father, but her mother, Brooke, and Onyx. Tears came to her eyes. She had no idea how they'd known. Although it was a big show, she'd tried as hard as she could to keep the news from them. She figured they would find out once the showing started—word of mouth was a motherfucka and *everybody* knew her parents—but she had thought they would find out after opening night was done and gone. But here they were.

Seeing her family was a welcome surprised that brought tears to her eyes. But somehow, she couldn't stop her mind from instantly going to Legend. It had been a year since she'd seen him. And that had only really been for a couple of days. He never stayed around for long. While she dove into her studies, he dove headfirst into his own things. Being the leader of BBM wasn't no small task, but he took it on like he did everything. Like a boss.

Bending low into a curtsy, January bid farewell to the crowd and turned around to go backstage and undress. She had a show every night for the next couple weeks. It was a lot on the body. She had to get her beauty rest.

Grabbing her phone from her locker, she unlocked it, somewhat hoping that she would see a text from Legend. For some reason, in this moment, he was super heavy on her mind. Much more than ever before. With the connection they had, it seemed like whenever it happened like that, she would look at her phone to find that he'd texted randomly, and it would put her mind to ease. It was always a text, never a call. And she only received those text once or twice a month.

January didn't complain because she knew why. In these moments, their journeys had taken them away from each other and the only way to get through it was with distance. The more they interacted, the harder it was to go through the days without each other. But they both had their own personal goals and missions to complete in this life. And for whatever reason, right now, they had to do them separately. She had to be okay with that. So she didn't press or complain about not seeing his face or hearing his voice. The distance made the separation hurt less.

"We're going to go on home. But we are so proud of you!"

January smiled, looking at the video her parents made after the show. They appeared to be standing right in front of the theater, walking down the street.

"Janelle, stop being all proper in front of these white folks. Let them hear how you talk at home," her father cut in, jumping in front of the camera. "Baby girl, what your mama really wanna say is 'we are so motherfuckin' proud of you! You did that shit! You did amazing baby girl. You did it. That's your talent. That's the gift God gave you to share with the world. Don't ever let any motherfucka on this Earth take that away from you. It's yours. Do your work, baby girl. I love you."

"I love you too, daddy," January said, wiping a tear from her cheeks.

"And what about me? I want some camera time!" Brooke yelled.

"And me too, bitch!" Onyx snapped at her, shoving her over so that she could share the camera space.

"We love you, January! You did the damn thing. Mama Nelle told us that you gotta stay focused so you can't turn up with us tonight. So, in that case, we promise to turn up extra hard to take up for what you cannot do."

"Yaaaaaasssss," Onyx added, throwing her hands in the air.

"We will come back when all the shows are over so we can party with you properly. We love you so much." Brooke gave her a kissy face. "Oh, and before I

forget—look!" She threw up her hand showing off a beautiful princess cut diamond on her left hand, ring finger.

"What?! Oh my God—"

"Calm down, calm down, girl, because I know you in there screaming. It's not an engagement ring, it's a promise ring. You know Nico still on that high school shit." She rolled her eyes. "But that's my boo though. Officially. He decided to go ahead and break me off with that commitment."

Wiping tears of joy from her eyes, January finished the rest of the video and then got dressed before saying her goodbyes to the other girls for the night. She was tired, but she felt accomplished in a way that she never had before. Life was really, really good.

"I know you ain't think you was going to go home tonight without hearing from me," a voice behind her said, the second she'd started down the sidewalk.

She felt a leap in her chest. Her heart literally felt like it jumped. She knew the voice. She loved the voice. And she loved the man behind the voice. More than any man she'd ever loved before. Or ever would.

Turning around, January dropped her duffle bag and ran straight at Legend, doing a graceful ballet leap into his arms. Releasing the tears that she had been slowing allowing to fall, she buried her face in his neck and wrapped her legs around his waist. The streets of New York were always busy but she didn't give a damn. The President, Dalai Llama, Oprah and her fantasy-boo Kendrick Lamar could have been around and January's response wouldn't have been any different.

"You act like you missed a nigga," Legend laughed after they'd finished their embrace. With absolute care, he took his time lowering her down to her feet.

"I miss you every day," January admitted, speaking from the heart. "Every minute of every day. Every second of every minute. Always."

"Damn, that's some deep shit," Legend said with a shrug, acting as if it was nothing. He was playing with her, putting on an act, and January was able to see right through it. She bore into the side of his face until his expression cracked into a smile.

"Princess, you know I'm just playing with you," he said. Pulling her in under his arm, he kissed the top of her head as they walked together down the sidewalk. "You know I missed the hell out of you, too."

Stopped for a moment to grab her duffle bag, Legend then remembered the bouquet of flowers he'd had in his hands.

"I bought these for you." He held them out to her and then frowned as he looked at them. "They are a little smooshed now from how you rushed a nigga, but—"

"They are perfect," January said, grabbing them. She stuck her nose inside and took a deep smell of the roses.

Absolutely perfect.

"How long are you here?" January asked, once they started back walking down the sidewalk. Lucky for her, her apartment was only a block away. Her father, true to his nature, had purchased the entire condo unit, renovated it to his liking—which basically meant he had outrageous requirements that probably would be considered too much to an Arab king—and cleared it out of all residents that weren't 'up to par' for living close to his daughter. Legend took the lead in walking her to her apartment and she didn't even bother asking how he knew where she stayed. One thing she'd leaned about Legend was, when it came to her, Legend knew *everything.*

"How long am I back," he repeated, running his hand over his chin. "That's a good question. It's actually something I should be asking you. How long you want me to be back?"

January giggled. "Legend, that was never my decision to make. You left when you had to go."

He shook his head. "Love, that was *always* your decision to make."

January gave him a sideways look and he smiled. He knew she didn't understand what he meant. She didn't know that from the beginning, she was the one with all the power. He moved when she moved. That was how their relationship would always go.

"You told me you weren't ready for anything solid yet. You have things you want to accomplish. And a lot of that contrasted with the way I live my life. I respect that. I honor your choice, January. I left so that I could give you your space. You know shit always goes sideways when we're together, but our paths are meant to merge in some way. When the time is right, it'll happen. Until then, I want to make sure you're ready for whatever bullshit destiny throws at us this time around. Because whatever the hell it is, we gon' have to ride that shit out together. Full trust, no take-backsies."

She snorted out a giggle. "No take-backsies?" You know what the fuck I'm talking about," Legend chuckled, grabbing her hand. Holding it to his lips, he kissed it softly. Gently. Fully enjoying her sweetness.

"When I come back, I'm coming back with a plan. And the only thing on that bitch is for us to be together. That's it. So, like I said, it's on you, love."

Nodding, January fully caught his drift. And hearing him explain everything that way to her only made her love him even more. It was an insane love. A love that the world would call so toxic, but it was actually exactly the type of love the world was looking for. They *were* trauma bonded. But while the world would put the emphasis on the trauma, January and Legend choose to focus on the bond. It was a perfect bond. A bond that wasn't jealous, wasn't possessive, wasn't needed or obsessive. It was pure unconditional love where two people who had met in the worst of times had learned to love each other in the best—regardless of if how they defined that 'best moment' for themselves to mean that they would be apart, separate or with another. They just wanted each other to be happy.

"I think…" January began squeezing her eyes nearly closed as if she were thinking hard as she could. "I think… I'm ready for you to come back."

Legend grinned. Not smiled… grinned. His lips spread further East and West than they'd ever did.

"Word?" He asked, looking at her.

"Word," she nodded her head.

Tugging at her hand, he stopped her from walking and pulled her so that she faced him. They were nearly to her building, standing in the middle of the sidewalk, making people cut around them, but they weren't aware of anything else but each other.

"Well, since you said that, I got something for you that I've been carrying around."

Legend reached into his pocket and January's entire mind, body and soul lifted when she saw him pull out a small black box.

"Oh my God!" She exclaimed as she looked at it. But then, being reminded of something, she stopped and calmed herself.

Calm down, bitch!

It was like she could hear Brooke yelling in the back of her mind.

"Wait a minute," she said, cocking her head to the side. "Is this a promise ring?"

"The fuck?" Legend said, so confused that he almost choked. "A promise ring? What kind of high school shit is that?" Then, as if a light switch had been cut on, it dawned on him. "Oh, hell nah. That's that shit Nico scary ass be on. Ain't no promise ring in here."

Chuckling a little to himself, Legend ran his hand over his mouth and took a deep breath to reset his mind. January was funny as hell. She had to know him better than that. Wasn't no need for a promise ring because from day-one, his heart had always been committed. It just took a while for his mind to catch up to what everything else about him already knew.

He was hers from the day they'd first laid eyes on each other. Real shit, he was hers from the beginning—lifetimes before.

He would never tell her but since they'd been apart, he's started reading up on some of the spiritual shit she believed in. The same stuff he used to tease her about. Crazy enough, a lot of it made a lot of sense. There was just too much evidence. Too many coincidences. Too many instances of unexplained serendipity to say that they weren't supposed to be together. He believed the love they had was brought about because it was destined to be that way. It was his fate. And there was no reason to play with that. It made no sense to delay the inevitable. What was the point of dating your wife just to prolong making her your wife? Legend just wanted to marry her now. They had the rest of forever to go on dates.

"Now I know you don't like the traditional shit, so we can make this as traditional or untraditional as you want it to be," Legend said, starting to bend to one knee. "But the outcome of whatever we make it is still the same…"

"Oh my God!" January shrieked into her hand, nearly about to jump up and down. She never thought in her life she would want a man to give her a traditional proposal. She'd thought it was cheesy. But now that Legend was doing it, there was no way on Earth she was about to stop it.

"January Lukeisha Murray, will you do me the absolute honor of riding with me through this life, through whatever comes next whether good or bad, until the day I die?"

A non-traditional proposal for a non-traditional man. January wouldn't have expected anything else.

"Yes," she replied, wiping her tears from her eyes. "Of course, Legend. I will be more than happy to spend the rest of my life loving you."

Grinning, Legend stood to his feet and pulled January into his arms as the people around them, side-swiped by them, carrying on with their own business, in true New York fashion.

"Well, my nigga, welcome to the fuckin' family," a voice said from their side.

January pulled away and saw her father and mother standing to their right, holding hands. Janelle had tears streaming down her face. She was so happy that it was beyond words. Outlaw, being the asshole she married, hadn't even warned her in advance about what they were about to witness. Instead, he waited until Brooke and Onyx left to fake chest pains, acting like he was about to have a heart attack and told her that he wanted to take a breather on the bench next to January's apartment. When Janelle saw January walking up with Legend, he covered her mouth and told her, in true selfish ass Outlaw fashion, "Don't say a word or you might ruin this moment for me." He was older and had matured. But he was still the same ole Outlaw nonetheless.

"Real shit, I always knew it was gonna be you, man." Outlaw said, speaking to Legend. "Something told me from the first time I set eyes on you that you were my son. Another nigga may be your father biologically, but it didn't mean shit to me. You've got me in, Legend. My ways, my beliefs, my thoughts. I saw you and was like, 'this nigga a fuckin imposter. He even kinda look like me'."

Everybody has to laugh at that. Even January and Janelle as they wiped away their tears.

"They say history repeats itself and it did with you. But you're a better version of me. The kind of man I wish I could've been from the very beginning. Welcome back, son. It's an honor to hand my daughter over to a man like you."

Bowing his head in respect, Legend felt his heart swell even more than it had already. His emotion didn't show on his face but what Outlaw had told him hit deep. So many times, Legend had wondered if the decisions he was making were wrong. If he needed to do things differently. He was so intent on doing things right that he was always feeling like he was fucking up. To get this compliment from Outlaw on the same day that January solidified her place in his life, meant everything.

"And I'm honored to be the one who will be marrying you," Janelle chimed in. "As a Federal judge of my caliber, I know you would have it no other way."

"The fuck, Nelle?" Outlaw snapped frowning. "What you mean? I already did the online thing to get approved for it. I'm the one gonna be proctoring this shit!"

"Outlaw, it's not a test. It's a wedding. You don't 'proctor' it. You officiate." Janelle rolled her eyes.

"Oh, you just think you so damn smart. Well, officiate this, your honor. I got my papers off the internet yesterday so you can be up there if you want but I'm gonna be standing right next to you, as your accomplice," Outlaw winked, grabbing his wife's hand, they started to walk in the opposite direction after saying goodbye to January and Legend with a simple wave.

"Accomplice?" Janelle groaned as they headed away. "Now we back to robbing banks. Jesus."

"Ride or die, Nelle. That's what you promised me, remember?" Outlaw replied. "But you know that don't apply to robbing banks when it come to you. The last time we had issues. Don't wanna go down that road again."

"Ugh," Janelle groaned and placed her hand to her forehead. "Don't remind me."

NOTE FROM PORSCHA STERLING

Thank you so much for reading! I hope you've enjoyed reading about January & Legend. It's been a long time of riding with the bad boys crew, but it's time to say 'goodbye' to the original characters… for now. Maybe I should say 'see you later' instead because something tells me they'll find their way back in my head one day.

Now on to Gunna, Capone, Supreme and the other men who make up the families of the *Black Bag Mafia*. I'm so excited for the next book!

If you haven't already, join my reading group now. If you're not in there, you've been missing out on some great things!

Please make sure to leave a review! I love reading them!

I would love it if you reach out to me on Facebook, Instagram or Twitter! Also, join my reading group!

I love to interact with my readers because **I appreciate all of**

you. Hit me up anytime and tell me what you think about the book 😊

Peace, love & blessings to everyone.
I love you all. 👑

Porscha Sterling

ABOUT THE AUTHOR

Porscha Sterling is an African-American Romance author and publisher of Royalty Publishing House, Inc.

Join Porscha's Mailing List. Text PORSCHA to 25827
To find out more about her, visit her website

www.ingramcontent.com/pod-product-compliance
Lightning Source LLC
LaVergne TN
LVHW091112080826
845145LV00008B/1889